UNWANTED WORLD

THE EMP SURVIVOR SERIES – BOOK 4

BY CHRIS PIKE

Dedication

To my readers: Thank you. This story would not have been possible without you and your encouragement. Y'all are the best! And to my family who has put up with all my crazy ideas and work-shopping sessions, y'all are the best too.
- *Chris*

"Never, never, never, give up."
—Winston Churchill

AUTHOR'S NOTE

Unwanted World takes a turn back in time to the day the EMP struck, instead of sequentially following real time after the catastrophe. It was necessary to do this to tell the story of the two main characters—Nico Bell and Kate Chandler. In Book 5, which will be the final book of the EMP Survivor Series, Nico will play a pivotal role, so I decided he needed his own book. He's an interesting character who will form an alliance with Kate Chandler, who is part of the sharpshooting Chandler clan. I like to think of the Chandler family as modern day Sacketts of Louis L'Amour fame. They are honest, determined, and they do what is necessary to survive.

This is also a complete book with a beginning and a logical plot leading to an ending without a cliffhanger.

There's no rough language, vulgarities, excessively gory or graphic details, or adult situations, so this book is appropriate for all ages, although it doesn't mean there won't be casualties or things blowing up, because, you know, that happens in the apocalypse.

Also, this book is the longest of the series, but doesn't contain boring descriptive minutiae leading to an inflated word count. It's the story that matters.

As one of my readers said: Read, enjoy, learn, and save some more food.

If you've read the series then you know the recurring theme appearing in all the books is: Faith, Family, and Firearms...

Forever!

The Travis Letter

Commandancy of The Alamo
Bejar, Feby. 24th 1836

To the People of Texas & All Americans in the World –
Fellow Citizens & compatriots –

I am besieged, by a thousand or more of the Mexicans under
Santa Anna – I have sustained a continual Bombardment &
cannonade for 24 hours & have not lost a man – The enemy has
demanded a surrender at discretion otherwise, the garrison are to be
put to the sword, if the fort is taken – I have answered the demand
with a cannon shot, & our flag still waves proudly from the walls –
I shall never surrender or retreat. Then I call on you in the name of
Liberty, of patriotism & everything dear to the American character,
to come to our aid, with all dispatch – The enemy is receiving
reinforcements daily & will no doubt increase to four thousand in
four or five days. If this call is neglected, I am determined to sustain
myself as long as possible & die like a soldier who never forgets
what is due to his own honor & that of his country – Victory or
Death.

William Barrett Travis
Lt. Col. comdt.

--As transcribed by The Texas Heritage Society

PROLOGUE

Current Day
Rio Grande River
Border between the United States and Mexico

Waiting was the hard part for Nico Bell, but he used it to his advantage. While hiding in the South Texas woods adjacent to the Rio Grande, he focused his ever-active mind, giving him opportunity to go over every possible approaching contingency, yet there was one possibility he hadn't planned on, prepared for, or even remotely thought about.

Three simple letters which would change his world.

EMP.

Nikolai Belyahov, aka Nico Bell, was a tall man, standing at six feet and one half inches with the scales tipping at one hundred eighty-five lean pounds of pure determination and resolve. Whatever task he needed to complete, he did so without hesitation or indecision, and when he walked into a room both men and women gave him an appraising onceover. The men would give him a challenging look, and he'd toss it right back at them. Not a challenge, rather a promise.

They looked away first.

They always did.

The women would meet the challenge, only to be discouraged when they didn't hold his interest.

He checked his watch and glanced at the sky. High above, a white jet contrail arced in the crystalline blue. For a brief second he thought it was too high, and it didn't look like the normal contrails he was used to seeing. These fluffy puffs were misshapen and had an odd color to them, like they were struggling to form in the thin air. Maybe the jet had surpassed the standard cruising altitude, a fact he had learned in school. A thick contrail indicated high altitude humidity and could be an indicator of a storm, while a thin contrail formed in low humidity signified fair weather.

If science was right, they were in for a massive storm.

Later he'd realize how right he had been.

A brief thought crossed his mind that the jet was out of control and had suffered some sort of catastrophic failure. Malaysia Airlines Flight 370, which vanished in the expansive Indian Ocean, came to mind. If such was the case, there was nothing he could do, so he concentrated on his mission.

He waited.

Patience was definitely a virtue in his line of work.

He thought he heard something other than the rustling leaves of the stately mesquite where he had taken cover. If they weren't here soon, the plan would fall through, and Nikolai Belyahov didn't like to fail.

The October sun in South Texas beat down on the grassy banks of the Rio Grande River. A hot breeze stippled the muddy water.

A fish jumped upstream and his eyes gravitated toward the movement.

A cicada buzzed, then another, the sound reaching a crescendo until it faded away along the languid river.

A mosquito buzzed his cheek and he slapped it away. He lay hidden in a tall clump of grass under the dappled shade of the mesquite tree. Peeking through the canopy, his eyes swept over the murky river, across to the other side, then beyond into Mexico, looking for them.

Them being Jose and Emiliano. Or those were the names he had been given. He didn't know their last names. It was just as well because no doubt they were using aliases. Drug runners tended to do the same.

He ought to know since he was using an alias too. Running with the same crowd tended to make a person nervous and paranoid, unwilling to divulge real identities. They knew him as Carlos Garcia. He passed for being of Hispanic heritage with his dark hair and eyes, tanned skin, and passable Spanish. He had a knack for languages, speaking three, though only two fluently.

Nikolai Belyahov had changed his Russian name to a more American sounding name when he came of age. He was American by birth, but also had deep ties to Russia. His father had been a Russian oil executive working for one of the world's largest oil and gas companies, and had married an American woman during one of his overseas assignments in the States. She was a striking woman with American Indian and Spanish heritage, dark hair and soulful eyes, some might even say sad eyes, having descended from a survivor of the Trail of Tears.

Nico had inherited his mother's mocha complexion and dark hair, traits some mistook for Hispanic. He had also inherited the DNA of her ancestors which gave him the resolve to survive. It had served him well.

Nico had learned to speak English and Russian without an accent due to his father being transferred back and forth between Russia and America. His mother spoke to him in Spanish and a few phrases of Cherokee, wanting him to continue her heritage.

Toss in Russian school on Saturdays while Nico's family was in the States, and Nico had also learned to read his father's native language.

As he was getting settled into whatever school he was attending, his father uprooted the family once again. Maintaining friends and long term relationships became a casualty of his early lifestyle. Except for one. And lately, he had been thinking a lot about her.

Nico wondered briefly how he had gotten himself into this profession. He was miles away from where he really belonged, a place rooted deep in Texas culture, a place where famous Texans had taken a stand against an overwhelming Mexican army. He was at ease there, standing amongst the historic site with century old oak trees, a spiritual place where one of the first Spanish missions in

Texas had been established.

Brave men had died there, and when Nico first learned about the battle he made it his life's mission to live in the same city where warriors had fought.

The Alamo. San Antonio, Texas.

He had to go back there for more reasons than one.

He was a warrior, and it's where he had met *her*.

However, he had other things on his mind right now so he concentrated on controlled breathing to lower his heart rate. He had worked long and hard to finalize this meeting, and if everything went okay, he'd get what he was after.

If he could deliver, he'd be able to land a meeting with the big boss, which would lead to bigger and better things. On the other hand, it could mean him landing a meeting with the biggest boss, the upstairs boss, the last boss on the chain of bosses.

He lowered his head and said a silent prayer to the Almighty to keep him safe, to steel his jumpy nerves, to return him to what he needed to do, and to return him to her.

A bead of sweat trickled down the side of his forehead. He wiped it away with the back of his hand. He was thirsty. He unscrewed the lid of the thermos and took a long, cold drink of water.

The untraceable burner cell phone in his back pocket vibrated, indicating he had received a text.

He looked at it. Excellent. It was from them.

The text read: *Are you ready to trade?*

Nico replied: *Yes. Do you have the package Santiago wants?* He waited a moment.

The response: *Yes. Meet in middle of river*

Nico thought a moment, then tapped as fast as he could, which wasn't all that fast. He had big hands meant for chopping wood or carrying a heavy weapon, not for fast texting on tiny buttons.

Nico: *No can do. Raft no good. Has a hole in the side. You come to me. Bring the package.* Nico waited for a response. A slew of Spanish profanity escaped the thick tangle of cattails.

He stared at the screen, waiting. Nothing, not even the blinking dots indicating a response was being typed.

It was hot and his back was itchy. Earlier, he had sprayed a copious amount of mosquito repellant on his back, legs, arms, and neck, but the sly little devils always found the one spot the spray missed. He curled his arm around and reached for the itchy spot out of his reach. He scratched his back anyway. What he wanted to do was to get up and scratch his back against the hard bark of the mesquite tree where he had taken cover, although that would have to wait.

Tomorrow he'd be paying the price of hiding in the grass. Red bugs. Invisible to the naked eye, they always found the tender skin around his belt line. Merely thinking about the inevitable red welts made him itchy. He scratched his lower back.

Finally, a reply: *We come now*

Lying flat on his stomach on the grass, which come to think of it was itchy too, Nico propped his elbows on the ground, lifting himself up. He peered through the wispy leaves of the mesquite, sweeping the ground from a low branch. The six foot tall cattails on the Mexican side of the river parted, revealing two men sliding into the river.

They each wore a hardened expression and tanned skin, darkened and lined by the South Texas sun. They put their AKs in the raft and, holding onto the side of the camouflage colored raft, the men lowered their bodies into the murky, sediment-laden water until only their heads bobbed on top. They paddled across the water, each nervously glancing around.

The men reached the invisible line dividing the United States from Mexico.

Nico thought he saw hesitation in one of the men. When they reached American waters, Nico let out a long held breath. He checked his watch and looked skyward. It was a clear day and puffy white clouds floated on a hot, silent draft. A buzzard lazily glided high overhead.

Time was running out.

Deciding to take a chance, Nico stood and emerged from his hiding place. His boots tamped down the high grass as he pushed through the tangled brush. Emerging into the open, he waved the men over.

Then he heard the sound.

A Black Hawk UH-60 chopper, flying low and fast, swooped in and hovered over its prey.

Nico muttered an obscenity.

All hell was about to break loose.

CHAPTER 1

A week earlier, Nico Bell had been at the Minor Hotel, located across the street from the Alamo in San Antonio, Texas. He had checked in using the name Carlos Garcia, a common enough name which he thought fit him well. Although the hotel was a hotspot for tourists, Nico was not there for pleasure, and he surely wasn't a tourist.

He was there for three reasons.

The first reason had to do with the fact the Alamo was his favorite place in San Antonio, so whenever he had the chance to visit it he did. Standing on the sacred ground where brave men had fought brought peace to Nico. He could tune out the noise of the city and the crowds waiting in line, knowing he would have fought to the death if he had been there. He was that kind of man with deep national pride, rooted in his American Indian ancestry.

He had listened with fascination when his grandfather told him stories passed down from generation to generation about his people. Strong people who lived by their own code of bravery, a code with which Nico identified.

UNWANTED WORLD

On Sundays, before the horde of tourists invaded the place like a swarm of locusts descending on a crop, he often walked inside the chapel, a quiet and spiritual place cooled by the thick walls. Visitors from all over the world recognized the sanctity of the place and the historic value it had in shaping Texas culture.

This afternoon Nico was at the hotel bar where he nursed a longneck bottle. He was taking a break from being cooped up in a second floor room where he could hear every honk, whistle, and the clomping hooves of horses carting sightseers gawking at the Alamo. He had been given instructions to wait at the hotel where his contact would find him. That was the first reason.

The second reason had to do with the pretty hotel bartender, whose name he learned after much haranguing was Kate Chandler. She was from Austin, hadn't been home in a long while, and had two brothers who would "beat the crap" out of him if he didn't leave her alone, or so she'd said. Her oldest brother was due back any day now after a stint overseas serving his country, while Kate explained the middle brother was also threatening.

They sounded like his kind of guys, and he hoped they'd show up so he could meet them. Not deterred by the threat of getting beaten up, Nico asked her out, but she only looked at her large dog who then took one look at him. A long, piercing look like the dog thought Nico was a competitor. Like the dog was thinking *Don't even try it again.* For a moment, Nico thought he detected the dog's lips curling into a snarl. When Kate spoke to the dog, he had gazed upon her with a longing Nico didn't know could have existed between human and dog.

Nico spied the dog with speculation, noting the camo colored vest the dog wore. He wondered if he was a service dog, but thought those dogs wore brightly colored vests, and had the disposition of a friendly yellow lab. He also thought those dogs were the big friendly types, waiting for a pat, not this kind of dog looking like he might tear off the hand offering him a pat. Nico unconsciously rubbed his hands together making sure he still had both of them.

On the other hand, the dog *had* to be a service dog, otherwise it wouldn't be allowed in a restaurant or bar. Kate sure must have the respect and admiration of the manager to continue working, especially if she had some type of problem serious enough to warrant a service dog.

8

Nico also noted the pouches secured by Velcro which contained unknown items big enough to pique the imagination. The pouches might contain dog biscuits or other treats for rewards.

Nah. No way.

On several occasions, he had noticed Kate reach behind the bar then give a treat to the dog. So what exactly was big enough and heavy enough to weigh down the pack causing it to tip to one side? He'd like to know the answer to the question. Now that he thought about it, there were a lot of questions he would like to have answered, like what had happened to her to require a constant companion.

Curiosity finally got the best of him. "Is he a service dog?"

When Kate didn't reply, he said, "There's no shame if he is. Have you been in the military?"

Kate replied tersely, "It's none of your business."

Okay, so she was a private person, one who probably had a good reason for having a service dog. Nico understood that. In his line of business he dealt with all sorts of problems people had. He had found it was the guy or gal who looked like they had the world in the palm of their hands who had the most problems. Everybody he saw had problems nobody knew about, which was why he tried to give people the benefit of the doubt.

Kate might be one of those people who appeared to have it all. Young, confident, had her entire life in front of her, to make it whatever she wanted. He noticed she had an exemplary work ethic being at the bar starting early afternoon until closing time, standing on her feet the entire time, and in perpetual motion wiping down the bar, mixing drinks, dusting, washing, and checking stock. During the week he had been here, he never saw her goof off, always staying busy with some sort of bartending duty. During her lunch break she tended to her dog by taking him outside for a walk.

When she sat on a bench located on the tree shaded plaza in front of the Alamo, he caught her looking pensive while staring off into the distance, as if she was missing someone, or longing for something. She'd stroke her dog between the eyes, over the flat part of his head, then to the ruff on his back. He'd paw her occasionally when she was deep in thought. Perhaps she was thinking about an old boyfriend. Maybe she did have a boyfriend, which would account for her brushing him off. Or it might have been a bad breakup. Regardless, neither her surliness nor the dog's deterred Nico. When he asked again if she'd go out with him, the answer had been an unequivocal *no*.

Getting her to say yes to his invitation had become a challenge, and Nico liked challenges.

So not only did Nico have to win over Kate, he'd also have to win over the dog. Some big mutt Kate said she found in the alley behind the hotel two years prior. Named him Reload.

The dog had been hanging around the hotel's garbage bin, and after weeks of feeding him, he finally let Kate pet him. He appeared to be a mix of Labrador, Belgium Malinois, German Shepherd, and a smattering of other indistinguishable large and threatening looking breeds.

The third reason Nico was in San Antonio, and specifically at the Minor, was the free room and board he'd been offered where he'd meet his contact. Someone by the name of Santiago.

Word on the street indicated the elusive Santiago was becoming the next dominant drug lord and had connections Nico needed.

Nico had been given a general description of an overweight, average height, balding man of Spanish origin which could describe about half the tourist population in San Antonio. Nico thought the appearance was a good thing since his contact would blend right in. Throw in a Hawaiian shirt, a ticket stub to the Wax Museum across the street where tourists took pictures with movie stars and historical figures, and there you go. He looked like the locals.

Between watching the door for his contact and the clock on the wall which ticked torturously slow, Nico had been trying to make nice with Kate. She was in her mid-twenties, possibly a runner, model worthy hair, and flaming eyes challenging him like no other woman had. For the past week she hadn't given him the time of the day. She only took his money, scowled, and didn't even say thanks.

He wasn't used to that. Not the thanks part, because he had a thankless job, but the part about being challenged.

It had become his mission to get a smile, a nod, or some other indication she might be interested in him. However, after a week of being given the cold shoulder by the bartender, Nico thought it was time to throw in the towel.

Movement at the entrance to the hotel caught his eye.

Nico turned.

The doors embossed in gaudy gold toned trim swung open. He had expected his contact to walk in because after a week of waiting, Nico had decided to blow this place and the claustrophobic crowds amassing at the Alamo.

What he wanted was to get out to the wide-open plains of South Texas and to the salty breeze hinting at the gulf waters close by. Yeah, after this was over, he'd take off for South Padre where the sand was white, the surf high, and where the women were friendly. The pretty bartender surely wasn't the poster child for the Texas motto of being the friendly state.

Yeah, the waiting was getting old.

Instead of his contact walking in, a woman wearing sunglasses, Dallas sized hair, tight white pants, a low-cut silk shirt, bangly bracelets, high heels, and carrying an expensive oversized purse on her shoulder breezed in. She stopped out of reach of the doors, and immediately locked eyes with Nico.

She must have been forty something and a good ten years older than Nico. She didn't interest him in the slightest, not because Nico didn't appreciate a mature woman and the confidence this woman obviously had, but she was way out of his league. Like World Series homerun out of his league.

If she was looking for a sugar daddy, she had picked the wrong guy. He wouldn't even be able to afford the pair of shoes adorning her manicured toes.

Nico swiveled the barstool a quarter rotation back to what did pique his interest: Kate, who had pretended not to notice the woman walking in.

The moment Nico swiveled back to face the bar, Kate raised an eyebrow and gave him *that* look. *That* look being: *This is going to be funny.* She turned her back on him and resumed cleaning a tumbler with a white towel. The problem was either Kate was bored or absentminded, because she had been cleaning the same glass for five minutes.

It was so clean and sparkly it now squeaked when she turned it.

Nico noticed things like that. He also noticed Kate throw him a look of warning, but of what? Nico could handle himself in dangerous situations, including the woman who walked in who obviously had eyes for him.

Nico took a long pull of the beer and was about to set the bottle on the counter when the woman came over to him and asked, "Is this seat taken?"

He swallowed the gulp of beer, wiped his hand across his mouth, and before he could answer, she slid into the seat.

Nico set the bottle on the counter. A river of condensation melted down along the slender bottle then to his fingers. He idly twirled the longneck, as if it was the most interesting bottle of beer he had ever seen. Come to think of it, the condensation had morphed into interesting shapes, probably something an artist would appreciate, but since Nico was no artist, he smudged the condensation with his finger.

"I'm guessing the seat isn't taken." Her voice was sultry and had a rich Spanish inflection to it.

"You guessed right," Nico said without inflection.

Without missing a beat, the woman said, "I'd like a Bailey's, and," she paused, looked at Nico then to the bartender, "he'd like another one of whatever he's having."

It had been a long time since a woman had bought Nico a beer, so what the heck?

Scowling, Kate retrieved a beer and set it down hard on the bar. Her eyes pierced right through Nico, as if saying, *Really? Her?* Kate shook her head in disgust. "Unbelievable," she muttered.

Nico returned an expression of *What I'd do? You had your chance.*

"Be a doll and pop the top for him," the woman said.

Kate angrily snatched the beer off the bar and popped the top then set the beer on the counter. If looks were daggers, Kate sent the woman a complete case of WWII Fairbairn-Sykes commando knives.

"If your sharp wit matched your intellect you wouldn't be working behind that bar," the woman said, making direct eye contact with Kate.

Kate stood straighter, shoulders back. "I do an honest day's work. I doubt you do."

The women only returned an icy stare as she brushed a strand of hair out of her face.

Kate's gaze went to the woman's nails, freshly painted with a pale French manicure. Kate was keenly aware of her own hands, rough from washing and cleaning around the bar. She dropped them to her sides.

Nico took several big gulps then set the beer on the bar. "If you ladies don't mind, I'm going to leave you two to whatever it is you're talking about." He pulled out a ten and slapped it down. He looked at the woman. "Thanks for the beer. I can't be bought."

Nico slid off his seat, took two long strides to the front door, and was about to exit the hotel when the woman with the Latin accent said, "Does the name Santiago mean anything to you?"

Game on.

CHAPTER 2

Nico stopped in mid-stride, turned around, and made direct eye contact with the woman. "You know Santiago?"

"I thought it was you," she said. "Carlos Garcia, correct?"

"I am."

"I thought you'd come back."

"Santiago sent you?"

"Yes."

Hmm, this was getting interesting.

Nico strolled back to where the woman was sitting at the bar. He sat back down in his seat, leaned into the woman, and said, "Your name is…"

"Marisa Sanchez."

An alias, no doubt.

"Meaning…that's not your real name?" Nico asked.

"Marisa Sanchez will do. What about you? Need I ask?"

"Carlos Garcia will do." His tone was mocking as if they needed to confirm each were using aliases. "Your relation to Santiago? Sister or wife?" Nico asked. He casually picked up the beer and took

15

a swallow.

"None of those. For the record, my relation to Santiago is none of your concern." Marisa stood up and faced Nico. "Stand up, please."

"What for?"

"Do you have to ask?"

"I'm clean."

"I'd like to check for myself."

Nico slid off the stool and faced Marisa. He towered over her in a commanding and challenging way, not so much threatening but the way a man stands when he knows he's in the right. He held his arms away from his body, and Marisa patted him down, checking under his arms, then sweeping around his back and chest. She patted the outside of his thighs then right before she moved inward, asking, "You mind?"

"I do mind, but I don't think it matters to you. Like I said, I'm clean."

She gave him a quick pat in the soft flesh of his groin and returned to her seat.

"Why isn't Santiago here?"

"Couldn't make it, which is why I'm here." Marisa eyed the bartender, deciding she was in earshot. "Let's go someplace private where we won't be overheard. Perhaps your room?"

"No way," Nico replied. "I'm not going anywhere with you alone."

"Why? Are you afraid of me?" She smiled coyly.

"Not in the slightest. Rather him." Nico jerked his head in the direction where the mean-looking hombre had been standing during their conversation. The big guy had on a pair of sunglasses and a suit which probably concealed his weapons of choice.

"Thought you hadn't noticed him," Marisa said.

"I notice everything."

Marisa gave a slight, unimpressed nod.

"We can sit over there," Nico said. He flicked his eyes in the direction of a seating area. He took her by the elbow and guided her to a chair and sofa in the foyer, motioning for her to sit.

"I want to get paid first," he said, taking a seat.

"No so fast," Marisa said. "Let's talk about specifics first. I'm a woman of many talents and I don't like being told what to do.

16

Santiago hired you for a reason to trade for a very valuable commodity, so when you fulfill your part. I fulfill my part."

"What will I be bringing back?"

"That is none of your business. It's an exchange. That's all. If you're successful, I'm sure Santiago will want to meet you. Word is you do what is asked of you, and have never failed. We have lost couriers before. You're the best."

"I am the best," Nico said. He meant it. "Like I said before, I want to get paid first. So unless you hand it over, I'm outta here."

The woman didn't bat an eyelash.

"Your loss," Nico said. He stood, squeezed between the lounge chair and the sofa, and took a step to the door.

"Wait," Marisa said. "I'll pay half now, and half when you deliver the package to me."

"I want to know what I'm delivering to you."

"That's none of your concern," she said. "As long as it's intact and hasn't been tampered with, you'll be highly compensated. I can tell you it's not dangerous and no explosives are involved. If you do this, I'll guarantee a meeting with Santiago."

Nico returned to the sofa. "I can work with that."

Marisa opened her large purse and retrieved a thick envelope, bulging to the point the flap on the envelope wouldn't close. Holding onto the envelope, she handed it to Nico. He grasped it, but Marisa wouldn't let go. "Instructions are inside where you'll meet with Jose and Emiliano. Don't even think about double crossing Santiago, or think about skipping out with the package and the money. Santiago will hunt you down and kill you."

"No doubt about it," he said. "I personally guarantee I'll be back with the package."

"In a few days from now, you'll meet your contacts at the Rio Grande border at a pre-arranged place. Once they have the duffle bag you will be delivering, and you have Santiago's package, report back here at the Minor Hotel. Santiago will get in touch with you."

Marisa motioned for the big man to come over. He handed her a large duffle bag then she dismissed him. She handed the duffle bag to Nico. "Give this to Jose and Emiliano. In turn, they will give you the package for Santiago."

"Why don't you go down there and get it?"

"I can't. I have my reasons and I don't need to explain them to

17

you."

"Fair enough."

Marisa stood, wobbled for a moment, then hastily sat down. She pulled a Kleenex from her purse and coughed into it.

"Are you okay?" Nico asked. "You don't look well."

"I'm fine," she said icily.

Marisa reached into her purse and pulled out two pills. She popped them in her mouth, downing them with the Bailey's. She set the glass on the coffee table, put her sunglasses on, and unsteadily stood up. The big man, worthy of being a sumo wrestler, took a step forward. Marisa waved him off. He melted back into the wall.

"One more thing," Marisa said. "Be back here in a week or I'll put a bullet right through your bartender girlfriend's pretty little head."

"She's not my girlfriend," Nico said coldly.

"But you want her to be."

Nico said nothing.

"I thought so. Now, if you don't mind, our meeting's over."

Marisa brushed past Nico. She left the hotel, followed by the big man. They disappeared, mingling into the crowd of tourists who drifted along the street, past the stores, the Alamo, the ice cream shop, and into the labyrinth of sidewalks and narrow walkways above the Riverwalk level.

Nico wondered what was so all important about the item he needed to deliver back to Marisa, requiring the exchange of who knew how much money for whatever the duffle bag contained.

Whatever it was, it had to be of life and death importance, but more importantly was the promised meeting with Santiago.

Months of dangerous work would finally pay off.

CHAPTER 3

"You disappoint me," Kate said. She was standing behind the bar. Her hands were finally still and calm, having set the tumbler down. She flipped a white towel across her shoulder.

She also had Nico's full attention.

"How so?" Nico asked. He walked back to the same seat he had been previously sitting in.

"I never pegged you for running drugs," Kate said. She took the hand towel from her shoulder, folded it, and placed it on the counter. "I'm a good judge of character and you had me fooled. I can pretty much guess what a person does by how they are dressed, and how they treat me."

"And how have I treated you?"

"Not the way a drug runner would have, which makes you a conundrum, Carlos Garcia." She studied him, noting the dark eyes and the expression of a man who knew what he wanted. "*If* that's your real name."

Nico took a swallow of the beer. "You remembered my name.

For a while I didn't think you did." Nico put a hand on the bar and leaned closer to Kate. He raised an eyebrow and with a mischievous tone he said, "It might even lead to you agreeing to go out with me."

"Never. I don't go out with drug dealers."

"You just said you didn't peg me for a drug runner."

"If you're doing business with the woman who obviously is running some sort of drug operation, well, a person can tell a lot about someone by the company they keep."

"Who? Marisa?" Nico huffed and glanced away. "She ordered some tile from Mexico and wants me to go down to the border to pick it up. It's specially made and quite expensive, and she doesn't want it going AWOL. I did work at her house recently, so she knows she can trust me. That's all there is to it." He didn't exactly like lying, but Kate was on a need to know basis, and she didn't need to know all the particulars.

Kate narrowed her eyes. "I didn't know house remodeling required the use of a bodyguard."

"You noticed him?"

"How could I not? It's hot, he had on a full suit, sunglasses, and his face was frozen in a perpetual frown. If he wasn't overweight, he might pass for Secret Service detail. Plus he left right after she did."

"She's a rich lady," Nico countered. "She needs a bodyguard."

"You're working for her alright," Kate said, "but I doubt you know how to use caulk or a nail gun." She leaned into Nico, challenging his space. He didn't budge. "And who's Santiago?"

Nico thought fast. "A contractor who skipped out on her after she paid him."

"Oh really?" Kate didn't believe that for a second. "Tell me, are you blackmailing her? I won't tell anybody."

Nico let out a belly laugh. "I've been accused of a lot of things, but being a blackmailer is a first." He took the last swallow of his beer and set the bottle on the counter. "It's been nice talking to you. Maybe some other time. I'm leaving now. See ya later." He slid off the bar stool and headed to the front door.

"When will you be back?" Kate asked.

There was a slight hesitation and a hint of anxiety in her voice which Nico picked up on, and he stopped. That wasn't something he expected to hear.

"I don't do windows," Kate said. "I'm a lousy cook, and I'm not fond of doing dishes."

"I'm okay with that. I grill a mean steak and I don't mind doing dishes," Nico said.

"I'm not a movie and a dinner kind of girl."

"What kind of girl are you?"

"The kind you'll like."

"I think you're already the kind I like. Don't go anywhere."

"Don't plan to."

"I'll be back in a week."

"It's a date then," Kate said.

Nico winked. "You betcha it is. I'll make you the best steak you've ever had."

"There's only one caveat, though."

"Hmm. Lawyer speak. I like lawyer speak."

"First, you'll need to tell me your real name."

A slight smile spread across Nico's face. "There are things I want you to answer too."

"Like what?"

"I'll save the game of twenty-one questions for later." With that declaration, he dipped his chin, looked her square in the eyes, and said, "I'll be back in a week."

"I'll be waiting."

"My name's Nico Bell. Nice to meet you."

* * *

After Nico left, Kate picked up the tumbler and polished it. The repetitive movement calmed her in times like these. The actual bar had become a barrier, both mental and physical, which Kate used to keep her distance from her customers. It had become a real crutch for her to stay isolated.

She had told herself it was better that way, so she wouldn't get hurt again.

She rotated the glass a quarter of the way, twirled the towel, then repeated the procedure, counting slowly. One, two, three, turn. One, two, three, turn. Until she had reached a count of one hundred. Keeping both sides of her brain busy didn't allow her to think, or remember.

When it was quiet and when she was idle, her thoughts took her back to that time she prayed to forget, willed herself to forget, would do anything God wanted her to do, if only she could erase it from her memory.

Reload sensed her rising anxiety. He padded over to her and nudged her hand until she responded.

"I'm okay, boy."

The after five crowd had not yet breezed into the bar, offering them a brief escape from their mundane eight to five jobs, corporate red tape, and everything else preventing them from achieving their dreams. They'd come in and loosen their ties, kick back, eat bar food, and watch the sports channel.

Kate had heard it all—mortgages, problem children, bosses, paychecks, lousy economy, wives, ex-wives, husbands, girlfriends, bankruptcy, you name it. She needed to hear it, to listen to her customers' problems, but when she was asked a question, she'd laugh and deflect it by asking a question. It was a strategy that served her well, one she had learned a long time ago.

Don't get too close to anyone.

Memories she wanted to forget would creep into her everyday life at the most unexpected moment. The rattling of change, the peculiar leathery smell of paper money, a door clanging shut, a loud noise...

Customers had asked her if she was alright, noticing her rapid breathing and the pained expression on her paling face. If there was no response, they'd politely ask again then glance around for help or instructions on what to do next. Some would excuse themselves, citing an important errand, pretend to be looking at their phone, or take a phone call on an otherwise quiet phone.

Reload had been sitting patiently at her side, never far from where she was, waiting, watching, and studying his mistress until he could predict her moves. He'd sense the changes while they happened, before she could react, before she could hurt herself. Reload would become aware of the minute changes in her body chemistry, her shallow breaths, and stiff posture.

The large dog swung his snout from side to side, taking in her essence, worrying over her reactions. She was sweating, not from the heat, or from talking to the man who had left. She was sweating from an internal struggle. He had observed the reaction on multiple occasions, but normally when she was by herself. Sometimes she'd curl into a little ball, others times she'd freeze, unaware of her surroundings. While Reload didn't understand the causes of her behavior, he was keenly aware of her reactions.

The large dog went to her and nudged her leg with his large muzzle until she snapped out of the dark place her thoughts had taken her to.

Kate bent down and took a handful of fur, her hand acting as a lightning rod to conduct her emotions. Reload's worried expression and floppy ears confirmed Kate's sadness. So much sadness in a young person and in the people who frequented the bar. Reload much preferred to be outside, but since his place was by her side that's where he would stay. It was what he was meant to do. She had saved him, and now he was saving her.

"You're a good dog, Reload. I don't know what I'd do without you. I'm okay now." She spoke to him as if he could understand her. In his own way, Reload did understand her. Kate smiled ruefully. Her sweating had stopped so Reload padded back to the corner of the bar where he would not be underfoot. He lowered himself to the floor, put his front legs straight out, then with a sigh he rested his chin on his paws.

Kate swiped a hand towel across the length of the shiny mahogany bar to remove any condensation left from Nico's beer. She folded the towel then took a moment to polish the brassy knobs.

Her eyes swept over the bar looking for another task, any task to keep her busy. She straightened the glasses behind her for the second time, then turned her attention to the liquor stacked behind her. A bottle of bourbon sat askew so she picked it up, dusted it off, and set it back so the label was straight with the other bottles.

Five minutes later she was back polishing the same glass, back to counting: one, two, three, turn and polish, repeating it until the glass squeaked. Nobody was keeping time on how long Kate cleaned the glass. It was more to keep her busy or appear to be distracted. To undiscerning eyes, she was busy and just another good-looking bartender who played by the rules.

Although in reality, Kate only played by *her* rules. Not the rules society tried to constrain her with or the rules which kept people in line where *no cuts allowed* was the standard.

She had been what people called "a willful child." She was

headstrong and formed her own opinions of people through their actions, not through what someone else had told her. She would decide for herself.

She was self-motivated and inner directed, and impervious to peer pressure. She had been a challenge to her parents from an early age, fought with her brothers, challenged her parents and teachers through her use of logic. She rebelled against rules and regulations, hated when the little guy got picked on, and had been expelled from school for knocking a classmate who had been bullying a smaller classmate, to the ground.

When she became old enough, she left home.

What was it her mother had said? She lived her life at *full throttle.* Until that fateful day.

She had her back to a raucous group of four seedy looking men smoking and drinking at a table. Every few seconds she glanced up in the mirror to keep an eye on them, mostly so they wouldn't skip out on the tab, though also because she had a bad feeling. The kind of feeling deep in her gut which made her stomach do flip flops; the kind of feeling she had when Nico walked into the bar.

The Minor Hotel was built in 1859, only nineteen years after the fall of the Alamo, to accommodate the guests of a brewery a German businessman had built. The original fifty room, two-story hotel had survived into modern times and now boasted five stories, doubling the number of available rooms.

The Minor hosted prominent guests including U.S. presidents, and titans of oil, commerce, and politics. It was where Theodore Roosevelt recruited his famous Rough Riders cavalry brigade. Oil deals and cattle sales were sealed over handshakes and shots of whiskey at the bar where Kate Chandler now worked.

The hotel was situated a stone's throw away from the Alamo, and while historic charm survived the ravages of times, the area around it had been paved over and was now littered with tourists, a large mall, a wax museum, a cowboy museum, vendors, restaurants, and more hotels, all to lure in the acclaimed tourist dollar.

With tourists came the people needed to work in the industry: hotel managers, busboys, maids, waiters, bartenders, and now Kate Chandler, the bartender known to have the disposition of a rattlesnake.

"Hey!" one of the card-playing men yelled.

Kate ignored him.

The man leaned back in his chair and raised his empty glass. "Get me another one, will ya, Honeypot?" He laughed.

If there was one thing Kate hated, it was the synonyms guys used when trying to get her attention. Honeypot. Sugar Plum, Sweetie Pie, Buttercup.

With a thud, Kate put down the glass she had been cleaning onto the wooden top of the bar. She looped the hand towel over her shoulder, put a smile on her face, and did what she did best. She poured another round.

* * *

At her sprawling estate in a trendy part of San Antonio, Marisa Sanchez nervously paced the marble floors of the expansive foyer. Every minute or so, she peeked out the window expecting her visitor at any moment. She sipped on the last of a homemade foul-tasting, gray looking concoction, one that had been promised to help her.

Thirty minutes had passed, and as Marisa was about to make a phone call, a low riding, beat-up Honda Civic with tinted windows slowly drove up the half-circle driveway, smoke trailing out of the exhaust pipe.

A man wearing baggy pants emerged from the vehicle. Hunched over, he warily glanced around then put a hoodie over his head to hide his face not only from strangers and the law, but also because of the jagged scar. Although it was supposed to have faded with time, it only became more prominent, more wicked looking, which garnered unwanted attention of stares and whispers.

With a cocky swagger of a much older and experienced man, he jogged up the sidewalk.

Marisa smirked at him having to hold up his baggy pants so they wouldn't fall down. She reluctantly opened the door and invited him in.

"Quickly, Pablo. Come in." She glanced left and right, shut the door, and closed the curtains. Like a mother, she admonished his choice of clothes and car. "You should dress better. Those pants, or what you call pants, draw attention. In our line of work, we need to blend in."

"You're one to lecture me," Pablo said.

"Stop," Marisa said. She waved him off. "I've paid you well and have taken care of you all these years. What I have is yours. It's always been that way. Please, get yourself a better car."

"I'll think about it."

"Do you have it?" Her voice was laced with the desperation of a junkie.

Pablo reached into his jacket and withdrew a package about the size of a paperback. He handed it to her, and she snatched it away, ripping it open. "You will be pleased with what the *bruja blanca* has made for you."

She looked at him, waiting. "I don't believe in hocus pocus."

"You should. This one has special powers. I don't think you have much choice now, especially after what the doctors—"

"That's enough of your insolence. I don't even know why I bother with you."

"Because we are *familia*, my sister. Because I'm your only blood relative, and I expect to be treated with respect." He leaned closer to Marisa. "Because I know your secret."

"You'd better deliver on your promise, Pablo. You better make sure the package is ready."

"I will. I always do."

"Good, now get back to the Alamo Plaza. Stay out of sight and don't cause any trouble. Try not to get noticed."

Pablo laughed. He thrust back the hoodie to reveal the jagged scar. "Kinda hard not to with this."

Marisa turned away. "Just do it, and keep your eyes open for any opportunity. You need to be ready."

CHAPTER 4

Current Day
Rio Grande River
Border between the United States and Mexico

Whump, whump, whump.

The blades on the Black Hawk UH-60 spun in perfect tandem, whipping the air and creating a downward blast of spiraling air, lashing the water, sending shockwaves of water outward.

The men in the river looked skyward, saw the helicopter with **Border Patrol** embossed on the side in big, bold letters. They pumped their fists in Nico's direction, yelling something in Spanish, probably a profanity, and they scrambled back into the raft. Using the oars, they swiveled the raft around, and once it faced the Mexico side, they plunged the oars deep into the water, trying to gain speed. Water sloshed in all directions and the raft wobbled unsteadily from side to side.

The Black Hawk swooped in low, hovering on the American side of the Rio Grande.

A burst of semi-automatic fire came from the brushy Mexican side of the river, and the helicopter took evasive action.

Nico ducked into the tangle of reeds and thorny bushes then scrambled to the mesquite tree to take cover. Peeking around the hardened bark of the mesquite, he brought up his Glock, sighted the cattails, and sent his own volley of semi-automatic fire.

The men in the raft ducked.

A round blasted the tree sending splintered bark in every direction.

Nico fell to the ground and covered his head. He glanced skyward trying to find the helicopter. He could hear it, but couldn't distinguish which way the sound was coming from.

More Spanish profanity garnered Nico's attention.

The two Mexican men had stopped paddling and were jouncing up and down in the raft. If Nico didn't know better, he'd think they were dancing. On closer inspection, the raft had been hit by a round and was taking on water.

The helicopter came in low downriver, peppering the river and hiding places with a volley of good old American firepower.

Nico kept his head down.

The drug runners reached the Mexican side of the river, jumped out of the now-sinking raft, and splashed awkwardly to the bank. They scrambled into the cover of the thick cattails where they disappeared.

Nico couldn't hear above the roar of the helicopter, so it was unclear if they were still under fire. He peeked around the tree and looked across the river. A trail of dust appeared over the tops of the marshy area, then vanished, no doubt from a truck the drug runners had stashed for a quick getaway.

The helicopter was now directly above the river, perhaps forty feet or so. The rotor wash whipped the trees and brush, and Nico held onto the cap on his head so he wouldn't lose it.

A brilliant white flash high in the atmosphere sparkled over the otherwise ordinary landscape, brightening it intensely. Nico closed his eyes and tucked his face into the crook of his arm, concerned his eyes could be burned.

An odd sensation overcame him, followed by a rumble and some type of intense pressure rolling over the land. It clamped down on him, as if he was in a vise, compressing his chest. His ears popped and he fell to the ground. He grabbed the front part of his shirt and gasped for air.

Maybe he blacked out a second or two. Maybe not. He wasn't sure.

When he came to his senses, he stood, checking the surroundings.

The helicopter banked toward the American side, the engine sputtered, the chopper lurched, and the whumping of the blades ground to a slow, sickening halt.

The chopper listed to the side and the pilot frantically worked the controls trying to regain lift.

Nico watched from the sidelines, a mere spectator, unable to stop the inevitable.

The Black Hawk listed to the side, the still spinning blades groaned, fighting for power, then the chopper tumbled into the Rio Grande and hit the water with a thud.

The blades rotated once, slicing through the river bottom, pitching mud into the air. Foamy brown water splashed into the air. Waves of murky water rippled across the river and rushed to the shore.

The chopper bobbed on the water for a minute until an odd sucking sound followed, like liquid was being slurped through a gigantic straw.

The pilot appeared to have been knocked unconscious.

The chopper floated for a moment, then with a gurgling whoosh and a sputter, the river washed over it, gobbling it.

Nico jumped out of his hiding place and barreled through a bramble of thorny cactus and huisache, a native Texas tree armed with two inch spines. He raced to the river, mesquite branches slapping his face.

Coming to the edge, he tore off his shirt and body armor, unlaced his boots, threw them aside, and high-stepped into the river. It was colder than he thought it would be on this October day even though the sun was hot and high in the sky.

He waded into the water until it lapped his thighs. He stretched his body out, put his arms straight over his head, and dove into the water. He swam with the ease of an Olympic swimmer, reaching for a handful of water, pulling it back, barely causing a ripple.

With his adrenaline racing, the shock of the cold water abated.

His focus was on what he needed to do.

Nico swam to the middle of the river, treaded water for a moment, then ducked his head under. Of all the places for the chopper to go down, it had to be in one of the deepest parts of the river. He opened his eyes to visibility of about an inch. Coming up for a breath, he shook the water out of his eyes. The current was stronger than he had anticipated and it had already pushed him a few feet downstream of where he thought the chopper had gone down.

He stretched his legs down into the water and used his toes to search for the helicopter. He found nothing so he swam a few feet and tried again.

Still nothing.

Time was running out.

He glanced at his hiding place behind the stately mesquite tree, recognizing the chopper would have fallen into the river a few yards upstream. Swimming like he was in a race, he went to the spot he estimated the chopper was, took a deep breath and submerged, feet first. His toes came into contact with the smooth metal of the chopper's underbelly. It must have flipped over in the water.

Nico shot up to the surface, inhaled several deep breaths, and expanded his lungs to the fullest to saturate his blood with oxygen. With one last big breath, he closed his mouth tightly and submerged, diving face down into the water. He struggled to remain submerged and his heart beat hard against his chest. He exhaled a few bubbles to decrease the buoyancy his expanded lungs had caused.

His hands searched the remains of the chopper. He palpated it like a doctor would a patient's abdomen looking for an internal injury. His hands swept over the metal, touching various parts of the chopper, and when he found the door handle, he clicked it open.

Nothing happened. The water pressure was too great.

Rocketing to the surface, Nico gulped air. He shoved his hand in his pocket, searching for his knife. Taking a big breath, he submerged again and quickly found the door. He used the knife blade as a pry bar until he levered his way in.

Reaching in, his arms swept the cockpit for body of the pilot. His hand brushed against an arm floating in the water. Using both hands, Nico tugged on the pilot to free him.

He was stuck.

The seatbelt!

He unbuckled the pilot from the seatbelt, looped his arm around the pilot's waist, and tugged him out of the chopper. Nico kicked his legs and tore to the surface. He treaded water, gulping several breaths of air. He flipped the pilot on his back so his face was out of the water.

For a moment he was disoriented, unsure which was the American side of the river.

There, he saw it. The mesquite tree again.

Swimming toward it, Nico slugged the unconscious pilot through the water. When his feet touched the muddy bottom of the river, Nico stood and looped his hands under the pilot's armpits. He dragged the unconscious pilot out of the water then heaved him onto muddy ground. Using his index and middle finger, Nico checked for a pulse.

It was weak, but still there.

He began CPR, cycling several times until the pilot gasped a breath.

Sitting back, Nico waited.

The pilot sputtered water, looked at Nico and said, "Next time you get to fly the bird."

CHAPTER 5

"I thought you were a goner," Nico said. He was leaning over his partner, Tony Garza, studying him for any injuries.

"Me too," Tony replied.

"Are you hurt?"

"Don't think so." Tony flexed his fingers, wiggled his toes, and tested the use of both arms and legs. He sat up. "Everything seems to be working."

Nico stood and looked around. The drug runners across the border were nowhere in sight. That was a good thing. With the situation temporarily secured, Nico decided he'd better clean his wet Glock best he could.

A gun that jammed during a gunfight wouldn't do him any good and could cost lives. Nico unholstered his Glock, ejected the magazine, then locked the slide back, which jacked the extra round out. He peered into the chamber looking for sand or mud the river water could have churned up. He spotted a clear puddle so he decided to rinse his Glock. He submerged the gun, swished it a few times, then shook it out. Next he emptied the magazine, pocketed the bullets, and rinsed the magazine in the water. It wasn't the best solution to clean a sandy gun, but it would have to do for now. Once he got back to his truck he'd replace the loaded magazine with a clean one.

"What happened up there?" Nico asked. He took the bullets out of his pocket and inserted them back into the magazine.

"I don't know." Tony rubbed his temples. "I remember a bright flash. Was I hit by a ground to air missile?"

"There was no missile," Nico said.

"That's so strange. Both engines simultaneously quit on me, and the next thing I knew the bird hit the water. I don't remember anything after that," Tony said.

"Just as well," Nico said.

"I don't think I want to remember drowning."

"I wouldn't either. How do your lungs feel? Think you got any water in them?"

Tony took a deep breath and let it out, testing his lungs. "I don't hear anything gurgling. I'm good."

"Glad to hear," Nico said. "I thought you had the chopper inspected not long ago." He stepped over to where he had thrown off his boots and socks. Picking them up, he went back over to where Tony sat.

"I did. It was in perfect working order and everything checked out. You know how Kent is a stickler for safety, always hammering us to be careful."

"I guess Kent won't be too happy about it when he finds out the department's one and only Black Hawk chopper is in the middle of the Rio Grande," Nico said. He sat down, brushed off the sand from his feet, and put his socks on. "Department cutbacks and everything."

"Yeah, the boss has been ridin' my ass about turning in expense reports for the past six months. Wait 'till he sees this one." Tony laughed at the thought.

"There may not be enough spaces on the expense report for it. Kent gives me grief when I expense a cup of coffee. A multi-million dollar expense? Let me know when you tell Kent and I'll make sure to be long gone," Nico said.

"There goes my raise," Tony added.

"Mine too." Nico tied his boot laces and straightened his back.

He removed his Glock and racked the slide back, checking to make sure a round was in the chamber.

"Did you get the package?" Tony asked.

"After you showed up early our friends hightailed it back to their side. Next time we need to make sure our timing is perfect."

Tony sat up, squinted at the river, and pointed. "Hey, would ya look at that?"

"What?"

"I don't think you'll go back empty handed after all."

Nico looked in the direction Tony pointed. There, bobbing on the river surface, was a package wrapped in cellophane. "I'll get it. I sure don't want to go back to San Antonio empty handed."

"Is that the package you're after?" Tony asked.

"I hope so. If it's not, I won't get to meet Santiago."

"Where's the money you were supposed to have traded?"

"It's in a duffle bag at the truck."

"Good idea. If anything went wrong, the money might have ended up in the wrong hands, and we need the money as evidence, otherwise Kent would've thrown a fit."

"What do you mean?" Nico asked.

"You're forgetting one minor thing."

"What's that?"

"The chopper."

Nico grimaced. "You have a point there. We'll have to break the news nice and easy to the boss. On second thought, since you were the pilot today, you get the honors."

"Thanks," Tony said sarcastically. "At least we know where it is."

"I suppose." Nico waded into the river to retrieve the floating package. Bringing it ashore, he put it in his backpack. "Can you stand?"

"Think so." Tony stood on wobbly legs, teetered for a moment, then sat back down.

Nico looked at him in worried consternation. "Let's get you out of the sun and into the shade."

Tony put his hand to his forehead, cradling it. "I thought I was going to pass out."

"Considering what you've been through, it's not a surprise." Nico looped his arms around his partner and helped him up.

UNWANTED WORLD

The October sun was high in the sky and with his adrenaline dump waning, Nico was keenly aware of his thirst. His truck was hidden about half a mile away in a thicket of mesquite and huisache. When Tony got his wits about him, they'd head on over to the truck then back into town.

* * *

Del Rio, Texas. A border town on the Rio Grande River. The city is on the northwestern edge of the South Texas brush country, a place where everything stings or bites among the mix of desert shrub, hardy vegetation, and stunted trees.

It's also home to Laughlin Air Force Base, the busiest United States Air Force training complex where pilot training is conducted for the United States Air Force, Air Force Reserve, Air National Guard, and allied nation air forces. Pilots train on T-6 Texan, T-38 Talon, and T-1A Jayhawk jet trainers. After an intensive 52 week course, some four hundred new military pilots earn their silver wings.

* * *

Partners for several years, Tony and Nico had worked undercover fighting the flow of drugs funneled into the United States along the border rife with lonely spots to enter the country undetected. Nico and Tony made it their mission to secure a swath of the twelve hundred and fifty mile long border Texas shared with Mexico.

After Nico put the package in his backpack, he told Tony it was time to go.

Hobbling through the brush while Nico supported some of his weight, Tony asked, "One package? What's so important about one package?"

Nico stepped around the cactus. "I don't know. I only get to meet Santiago if the package's seal is unbroken. Considering how it was taped and sealed with wax, it would be difficult to open it undetected."

"What about your contacts on the other side of the river?" Nico laughed. "You should have seen the look on their faces. It was

36

priceless."

"What did they do?"

"Hightailed it back to their side. I lost track of them when the chopper went down."

"Thanks for saving me," Tony said.

"No big deal. You would have done it for me."

That was right. Tony would have done it for Nico. As partners, they had worked hard to gain the trust of the drug runners, working in dangerous places and being out in the wee hours of the morning. Tony spoke fluent Spanish, and while Nico could understand the language, he had trouble speaking it. His proficiency in Russian didn't exactly come in handy on the Mexican border.

"You doing okay?" Nico asked. He had noticed Tony breathing hard.

"Good enough," Tony lied.

His right side hurt like the devil. Each time he took a breath, a sharp stab of pain pierced his chest. If he breathed shallow his lungs didn't hurt, but knowing it was bad to breathe like that, he breathed deeply and tried not to let Nico see him wince.

Five minutes later they were at the truck, a beat-up tan Ford Bronco that had been confiscated in a drug raid.

Nico helped Tony to the side of the truck where he told him to lean against it. Nico dug around in his pockets where he had dropped the keys earlier. Finding them, he was thankful he hadn't lost them in the river. He pointed the key fob at the truck. Nothing happened. He got closer and clicked the key fob again. Still nothing.

"Maybe water got into the battery," Tony suggested, "shorting it out."

"Probably."

"Unlock it manually."

Nico inserted the key and unlocked the truck. He clicked open the door locks then helped Tony into the passenger seat.

"I think we need to get you to the hospital," Nico said.

"I think that would be a good idea." Tony awkwardly repositioned himself, grimacing at the shooting pain in his side.

Nico noticed the face his partner made. "Hang in there. We'll get you fixed up in no time." Nico looped around to the driver's side. With one hand on the steering wheel, the other on the key, he inserted the key and turned it. Nothing happened.

He tried again. Still nothing.

"The battery might be dead," Tony said.

"Can't be. I had a new battery put in a couple of months ago."

"You're kidding. Kent approved a battery?"

Nico shook his head. "I paid for it."

Tony looked around. They were in the middle of the South Texas brush country, were miles away from the nearest gas station, and the highway was about a mile north of where they were. Trying to convince a local to go off road to jump the battery wasn't looking too good.

"Better call it in," Tony said. "Have Kent send someone out to get us."

"If the battery is dead, the radio is dead."

"Of course," Tony said. "My head isn't too clear. Got a cell phone?" He patted his pockets. "I must have lost mine in the river."

Nico pulled out his burner phone and looked at it, thinking he hadn't turned it off. He tried clicking it on. Nothing happened.

An expression of disbelief came over him. "The phone doesn't work either. What are the chances of all the batteries dying at the same time?"

"You'd probably have better chances winning the lottery."

"What the heck is going on?" Nico asked.

"No idea," Tony said. He squinted and looked at the sky, and an expression of disbelief spread across his face.

"What is it?" Nico asked.

"The military jet. It looks like it's about to crash!"

CHAPTER 6

Nico swung open the door and scrambled into the bed of the truck where he stood to get a better view of the jet, now spiraling out of control to the ground.

The jet hit the hard-packed ground and shards of jagged red-hot metal erupted from the crater, splintering out in all directions. A cloud of black smoke and flames burst into the air like a geyser full of boiling dust.

Jet fuel instantaneously vaporized the nearby foliage of trees and grass, sending a mix of incinerated fuel and powdered vegetation skyward.

Trees weakened from the year-long drought that hadn't been vaporized in the initial crash caught fire.

Sparks sizzled in the windstorm of debris and jet fuel.

Embers glowing red floated on silent air drafts, searching for another victim which would succumb to the fiery flames.

Thick smoke crawled along the ground in waves, obscuring escape by anyone or anything unlucky enough caught unprepared.

Seconds later, the shockwave from the massive explosion

rumbled along the ground at breakneck speed like an out of control locomotive.

Nico instinctively ducked and hunched over.

Simultaneously, an immense fireball, black and orange and angry, exploded in all directions, searing the ground and sucking oxygen out of the air. Towers of black smoke billowed upwards in the sky.

A nearby flock of white-winged doves scattered through the air, away from the carnage.

Nico estimated the impact was about a mile away from where they were.

"Jesus Christ Almighty!" Tony exclaimed. He hobbled out of the truck. "I've never seen anything like that happen in all my life. And I've lived here all my life. We're so used to the training missions happening 24-7 and all the flyovers that we don't pay any attention to them anymore."

Nico squinted and scanned the sky in all directions.

"What are you looking for?" Tony asked.

"The pilot. He could've ejected."

"Hopefully so."

"Yeah, there he is," Nico said, pointing in a northeasterly direction where there was a break in the smoke.

A moment later the pilot, secured into a parachute, floated down to the ground.

"Stay here," Nico said. "I'll go check if he's okay. It looks like he landed not too far away. I'll be right back."

Nico dashed through the high grass and brush, jogging the half mile or so to where he estimated the pilot had landed. He came upon the shell-shocked pilot who was lying on the ground still strapped into the harness, the parachute billowing behind him. He had cuts and burns on his face due to the canopy jettison and fragmented plastic. His eyes were bloodshot.

"You okay?" Nico asked.

"Whatd'ya say?" the pilot asked. "I can't hear."

"Are you okay?" Nico yelled.

"I don't know," the man replied, trying to blink his eyes into focus. He shook his head trying to clear his fuzzy brain. "I'm having a hard time hearing!" he yelled. "I think I lost consciousness. Those G-forces are a killer."

"You don't have to yell, I can hear you."

The pilot nodded.

"G-forces can do some real damage. Can you move your arms and legs? You need to check if anything is broken."

The pilot made a fist to test his fingers then flexed both arms. He wiggled his feet and bent his legs at the knees. "Guess I'm okay. I've heard about other pilots not being so lucky."

"Yeah," Nico said. "I had flight simulator testing when I was a cadet at the Air Force Academy, but I never got to fly a jet."

"When were you there? I went there too."

"Several years ago, probably before your time. I had to leave after my sophomore year...family problems."

"Oh. Too bad you had to leave. Flying is the boss, until you have to eject."

"I know." Nico helped the pilot out of the harness, hooking his arms under the pilot's to steady him until he stopped wobbling.

"Thanks, I think I'm okay."

"You sure?" Nico asked. He was skeptical the guy could stand on his own.

The pilot's legs buckled and Nico caught him before he fell over. "You need to sit back down."

"Okay."

"I'm Nico Bell. I'm with Border Patrol."

"Nice to meet you," the man said. He held up a hand to shake. "I'm Josh Lopez. I'm stationed at Laughlin Air Force Base."

"I figured. If you don't mind me asking, what happened?"

"I was about to bank to the left and head back to base when I saw a bright flash in the sky. Then the alarm bells and whistles went off. I've trained for most everything, but not an instantaneous total lack of power. I lost radio contact, and I had no choice but to eject. Fortunately the ejection system was still working."

"A miracle for you it did," Nico said. "Hitting the canopy inside the cockpit would not have ended well."

Josh agreed.

"So all systems stopped working at the same time?"

"They did," Josh confirmed.

"Hmm." Nico ran a hand over the stubble on his chin, thinking. "That's the strangest thing. Same thing happened to my partner. We were about to make a drug bust at the Rio Grande when the chopper lost power. You're describing exactly what happened to my partner."

"Is your partner okay, or did he…?"

"He's okay. The chopper isn't. It went down in the middle of the Rio Grande. I was able to get him out before he drowned. He's with my truck. I think he's got broken ribs."

"Do you mind giving me a ride back to the base?" Josh asked.

"I would if I could, but the truck won't start."

Another explosion ripped the countryside, and the men ducked. The frown lines on their faces deepened with anxiety.

"We'd better get out of here," Nico said, coughing. "If the smoke doesn't get us, the fire will. It looks like it's gaining on us. We need to head to the truck where my partner is. I can't leave him there." He pointed in the direction where the truck was. "Let's go."

Nico helped Josh up and steadied him for a moment. When it became clear he was still lightheaded, Nico instructed Josh to put an arm around his shoulder. Nico looped an arm around Josh's waist and let him lean into him. They clumsily jogged through the flat land of dry brush, dodging fire ant mounds, deadwood, cactus, mesquite and huisache trees.

They coughed at times, and the odor of burning jet fuel and blackened brush filled the air with a putrid smell, a cross between burning chemicals and a brushfire.

The roar of the fire came closer.

The wind changed directions, blowing embers high in the air like a sparkler from a fourth of July celebration had exploded. During a lull in the wind, embers floated to the ground, igniting clumps of dry grass.

Nico stopped, leaned over, and put his hands on his thighs, breathing hard and fast. "I'm not exactly sure I'm going in the right direction."

Josh ran a hand across his forehead, thinking. "I'm disoriented. I'm not sure which way to go either."

A faint yell came from somewhere in the distance. "Hey! Over here!" It was Tony. He sounded like he was in a tunnel.

When they were within yards of the truck, Tony waved them closer. He looked curiously at Josh, noticing his flight suit.

"Come on, let's get out of here!" Josh yelled. He opened the truck door and got in.

"I told you it won't start!" Nico yelled.

"We can't stay here," Josh said. "We'll die."

"Grab anything you can from the truck, and let's head to the river. Hurry!"

Nico reached into the truck and heaved his backpack over his back. Josh retrieved a satchel and the thermos of water, along with a holstered Glock. Tony slung a light, low-hanging pack across his chest. He winced in pain.

"Nico, you go on," Tony said. "I'll be right behind you."

"I'm not leaving you here. I'll help you."

"I'll only slow you down."

Josh stepped on the other side of Tony. "I'll help too."

Pinioned between Nico and Josh, Tony hooked his arms around their necks for support.

Nico and Josh held Tony by the waist, and the three hobbled toward the river, ducking under branches and weaving around impenetrable thorny brush.

The fire hissed and crackled, crimson tentacles of flames reaching out, devouring anything in its path, leaving scorched earth. It moved like a living, breathing thing intent on winning the race to the river.

Sweat beaded Nico's forehead and dripped to his eyebrows, then to his eyes reddened from the smoke. He wiped it away and blinked his stinging eyes. The heat became palpable. His heart beat fast and he coughed.

"We're almost there!"

Stumbling toward the river, the three men fell into the water, the coolness a stark contrast to the searing heat and smothering smoke. They waded in until the water reached their waists, then they crouched down on their knees until only their heads were above water.

"Take your shirt and hold it to your nose," Nico instructed.

The fire roared and lashed waves of flames at the sandy bank, searching and struggling to breach the barrier. Flames whipped the trees into submission until the limbs and leaves succumbed to the power of the fire.

For hours, the three men stayed in the river, bobbing and swaying. There were no words, only the realization they had lived, for now. Without any more fuel to satiate the fire's appetite, it slowly withered, shrinking until only feeble smoking embers were left of the once powerful force.

CHAPTER 7

"I think it's safe to get out now," Nico said. He waded out of the river and onto the bank. He let the water drain from his clothes, briskly rubbing his arms trying to warm them. Tony and Josh followed his lead.

The warm October sun had slid beyond the horizon, letting the cold of the night creep in, causing misery. Nico shivered in the waning light, letting his eyes roam over the scorched earth. Smoldering trees lay in dying ruin, stretched across the landscape. The stately mesquite tree he had hidden behind had become a blackened skeleton. The fern-like leaves of the mesquite had curled inward in a desperate attempt to survive the inferno.

"I know this sounds dumb, but we need to get a fire going, otherwise we're all going to get hypothermic," Nico said.

"Do you have any coats in your truck?" Josh asked. "Most of my survival kit was lost." He showed Nico a wide tear in his flight suit.

"I had one coat, but I'm guessing the fire probably destroyed everything. You can check if you want to. Feel free to volunteer any of the survival gear you have left."

"You're right," Josh said, "Everything's probably gone. I'll try to find some wood for a fire."

"I'll look for embers, and there's some grass over there," Nico said, jerking his head in the direction, "we can use to start the fire. Tony, you stay here. You okay?"

Tony nodded. "I'm not good for anything right now." His teeth clattered and he was shaking. "I need to sit down." Tony sat down on the riverbank, pulled his knees to his chest, and wrapped his arms around them, shivering uncontrollably.

Nico had become alarmed at the way Tony was acting. His mental state was no longer sharp, and Nico had to restrain him from getting out of the river while the wildfire raged. While they were in the river, Tony had mumbled something about putting milk in the refrigerator otherwise his wife would get mad. Nico and Josh had to keep him talking, afraid he might pass out. They took turns holding his head above the water.

"You sit here," Nico instructed. "Don't go anywhere, okay?"

Tony nodded. "I'm going to lie down if you don't mind. I'm not feeling well."

"That's fine. Just stay here." Nico noted Tony's pale skin and labored breathing. He needed to get him to a hospital, but without transportation or communication, they'd have to wait out the night.

Minutes later Nico and Josh returned with usable wood and grass. Tony had curled into a little ball and fallen asleep, snoring lightly. Nico carefully set some embers he found into a hollow of a piece of bark.

Working together, Nico and Josh placed the dry grass on the ground then topped it with varying sizes of twigs. Nico placed the embers on the grass and blew on them until they glowed orange and the grass caught fire, then Josh placed larger branches he had broken off from dead trees.

After a while, the campfire roared.

"Let's move Tony closer to the fire so he can stay warm," Nico said.

Nico held his arms, while Josh had his feet, moving him like he was a sack of potatoes. Even though he was being jostled, Tony did not stir.

In the waning light, Nico walked a hundred yards up and down the river searching for errant flotsam deposited by thunderstorms of months past. He found two shirts tangled in a tree, a Styrofoam cooler washed up on the banks, a metal pan, fishing line, one tennis shoe, and several pieces of driftwood. When he dug the Styrofoam cooler out of the mud, he removed the lid and found two beers in it, figuring it had fallen off a fishing boat. He took his bounty back to the meager campsite and asked Josh if he'd like a beer.

"Need you ask?" he replied.

Josh pulled out an orange foil-covered block from a zipped pocket. "It's an apple cinnamon emergency food ration bar. Not exactly the best pairing with beer, but better than nothing. We'll save some for Tony to eat when he wakes up."

Nico placed the shirts over Tony to cover his arms and chest. Tony had rolled over onto his back while Nico had been away. Even in the low light, he looked pale.

"How's he doing?" Nico asked.

"Not good," Josh said. "I can't tell if he's sleeping or unconscious. Were his injuries bad?"

"I'm no doctor so I don't know for sure. His chopper went down in the river but I was able to pull him out and get him breathing again. When he woke up he said his side hurt."

"There's not much we can do for him at the moment. Let's keep him warm during the night."

The night and the chill it brought descended upon the land. The wind moaned through the reeds and cattails on the opposite side of the river and somewhere a fish jumped, and eastward the river ran a race to the mighty Gulf of Mexico. An owl hooted, then another answered from far away. Nikolai Belyakov lay awake contemplating his life, his parents, and those before him. He was a descendent of a survivor of the Trail of Tears, where Native American Indians were forced to walk from their homeland of Georgia, Alabama, Tennessee, and other southern states to Oklahoma. The Indian Removal Act, it had been called.

Nico's grandfather had told him stories passed down through the generations, and one day Nico would tell his children so the story would not be forgotten or relegated to a downward blip on the line graph of history.

He felt no anger over what had befallen his ancestors, or regret. It was a part of him, a legacy he would pass down. Something to be proud of because of his ancestors' resolve to survive.

It was hardwired in his DNA.

He also thought about the woman who would become his wife, but had he even met her? There had been those who had wanted to tame him or mold him into living a life society said he should. A two-car garage in the suburbs which came with a substantial mortgage; two children; a dog, a cat; PTA meetings; soccer, baseball, football, dance, ballet practice and recitals; carpools.

Then Tony came to mind, and the home where his wife waited for him. Where she had kept his dinner warm for him, kept a bed warm. At times Nico envied the family Tony had built, a son who would go to college, a daughter, smart and at the top of her class.

The nine to five life wasn't for him. Nico needed to be outside, he needed to fight bad guys, and he had hoped to do it from an Air Force fighter jet, but his dream had been waylaid due to family obligations and the unexpected death of his father. A heart attack the doctors had said. A healthy man who ran three times a week, watched his diet, and didn't have a clue his heart was failing.

Nico had gone home to be with his mother, who had spent her life by her husband's side and to wherever he had been transferred, making new friends, establishing a new home, a vagabond lifestyle, never staying in one place to settle down.

His mother never recovered and died of a broken heart within a year of burying her husband. She said it was a love that only comes once in a lifetime. If only Nico could be so lucky to find a soul mate as his parents had.

It may never happen and the lifestyle would kill him as sure as it killed his dad.

No, it wasn't for him.

He couldn't be tamed and he thought it was the Indian who lived on in him, the proud American Indian who conquered the land, who fought there, who died there.

He'd never be tamed.

Nico had excelled in school and sports, which led to a scholarship at the Air Force Academy, but the greatest of life's lessons he had learned in the woods near one of his childhood homes.

He welcomed the solitary life and the peace it brought when he camped in the woods where he learned to make a fire and to eat the game he caught. He had learned to make a shelter when a sudden rainstorm appeared. He had learned which berries and plants were edible.

Yet his solitary life was missing something, and when it was quiet, his thoughts went to Kate Chandler and what she had said. *"When will you be back?"* When Nico met her eyes he saw a flicker of hope and hurt, a lost love, and a love she was looking for again.

He recalled what she said. *"I don't do windows. I'm a lousy cook, and I'm not fond of doing dishes."* Nico was fine with that, because when he asked what kind of girl she was, she had replied, *"The kind you'll like."*

She wouldn't be tamed either.

Was it her heritage, or something in her past, molding her into what she had become? He needed answers to those questions, and when he got back to San Antonio, he'd keep his promise about grilling the steak.

Nico stretched out on the hard ground and clasped his hands behind his head.

Shifting embers of the fire crackled, sending sparks in the night air. Something in the darkness stirred, something unconcerning, and Nico drifted off to sleep.

He woke during the night and stoked the gray ashes of the fire to life. He added more driftwood and waited for the flames to wake. It was chilly and he cupped his hands to his mouth, blowing in them to warm them.

CHAPTER 8

Morning came, raw and new, the scent of charred earth permeating the air. The sun peeked over the horizon and Nico's eyes roamed over a broad swath of land. Pockets of smoke wafted in the air from hot spots, trees blackened, grass withered to the nub, but the waters of the Rio Grande flowed uninterrupted.

Josh yawned, stretched, and rose. He still had on his flight suit and boots, and had stayed somewhat warm during the night. Whenever he had gotten cold, he flipped over so the campfire could warm him.

Josh got Nico's attention and pointed to Tony. He whispered, "You think he'll be able to walk?"

"I hope so," Nico replied. "If not, we'll have to make a stretcher for him. I found some heavy duty fishing line yesterday we could use to tie sticks together. The sooner we get going, the sooner we'll get him help."

Tony was on his side, his legs bent at the knees, his back to the fire, facing away from Nico. He was so quiet and still.

"It's time to wake up, Tony." Nico knelt next to him. "Tony,

51

wake up. We need to get going."

There was no answer.

"Tony, we need to go. Can you hear me?" When there was no response, Nico put a hand on Tony's shoulder to wake him. He was cold, too cold.

Josh asked, "Is he okay?"

Nico didn't answer. He said more urgently, "Tony, wake up." Nico took him by the shoulder and turned him over. A breath escaped his lips at the sight of the mottled skin and unseeing eyes. Nico fell back and sat down. He dropped his chin and put his hand to his forehead, kneading the space between his eyebrows. "Oh, God, no. Tony."

The river water lapped at the shore, a flock of sparrows flew in the distance, unaware of the tragedy unfolding. The man who lived his life to protect his fellow Americans, the man who helped Nico find his way, the man whose wife waited at home with their children, lay dead on the banks of the Rio Grande.

Josh dug the toe of his boot in the sand. "I'm sorry about your partner. His injuries must have been more serious than we thought."

"This isn't fair," Nico said. "I should have been the one flying the chopper. We changed places at the last moment because his wife didn't want him on the ground. She thought it was more dangerous facing the drug dealers than being in the air." Nico sighed long and heavy. "What am I going to tell her? His kids are so little."

Josh wasn't sure what to say about telling his wife. Instead he said, "What do you want to do with him?"

"I can't leave him here for the buzzards and wild animals to tear apart."

"We'll bury him, and I'll help you," Josh said. "We'll place a marker at his grave so someone can come back to get him for a proper burial."

Nico thrust his hands into the soft earth and scooped handfuls of sand, flinging it away. He dug faster, angrier, taking his frustration out on the ground. When he reached the top of the water table, he grabbed handfuls of mud and hurled it far away.

Josh stood to the side and let Nico dig only until he thought enough time had elapsed for Nico to expend his anger.

Josh came up to Nico and put a hand on him. He said softly, "Enough. You need to stop. We can't bury him here, you know that."

Nico sat back on his knees and hung his head.

"I have a solution, so please listen to me for a moment," Josh said. "Let's take him back to the truck and bury him next to it. The truck can be his marker for now, and it will be easy to find at a later date. If we bury him here this close to the river, it will be next to impossible to find him. There aren't any landmarks, especially since the fire burned the trees. And if a flood comes this way, he'll be washed away and never found."

"You're right," Nico said, trying to keep his emotions at bay.

"Let's get going before it gets too hot. I'll take his hands, and you take his feet," Josh said.

Nico slung the thermos over his shoulder then the two men worked together to take Tony's body away from the river and onto dry, higher ground. Fortunately the land sloped away from the river at a gradual slope, and while Tony's weight was considerable and his body had stiffened, taking him to the truck was a feasible solution. The truck had been stashed about half a mile north of the river in a thicket of mesquite, so by the time Nico and Josh reached their destination, their muscles told them they needed to rest.

They gently placed Tony's body on the ground, and Nico covered Tony's face with one of the shirts he had found the previous day. He needed to protect his partner's face from flies buzzing around trying to alight on it. He figured it was the least he could do.

The truck had succumbed to the fire as suspected. Tires had been flattened, windows busted, and the interior gutted. Josh peeked in, making a quick check if anything of value was left. A plastic water bottle had melted into the seat which showed the spring coils poking through the charred upholstery. The plastic floorboard mats had disintegrated and the hardened dashboard had warped. Whatever food or water might have been in there was now burned rubbish.

"I'll check the back for the shovel," Nico said. Using his index finger, he tapped the truck handle testing it for latent heat. It was still too hot for his bare hands, so he removed his vest to use it as a potholder. Wrapping the vest around his hand, he opened the trunk, spied the shovel, and removed it.

Nico drank thirstily from the thermos then handed it to Josh. When he finished, he placed it on the ground.

While Nico dug, Josh scouted the surrounding countryside

looking for rocks to place atop the grave to prevent wild animals from digging up Tony's body.

Josh made several trips out into the charred land to collect stones, one time returning with a jagged piece of his crashed training jet.

The rising sun unleashed hot and miserable agony, and with the humidity increasing, rivers of sweat soaked Nico's shirt. After an hour of digging, the shovel hit a hard root of a mesquite tree and progress ground to a halt. Nico sat down to take a breather.

Josh came back with a handful of stones and emptied them onto the ground next to the grave. He dusted his hands on his flight suit and surveyed the grave. "I think that's deep enough for the time being."

Tony's body had become stiff with rigor mortis. His legs had frozen in place, bent at the knees, with his arms close to his body. Josh and Nico lifted Tony's body and placed him in the grave, face up. Nico repositioned the shirt over Tony's face, an act of reverence for his partner.

He hated thinking his last memory of Tony would be his ashen face. He cleared his throat, picked up the shovel, and started tossing dirt into the grave.

After only shoveling a bucketful of dirt into the grave, Nico stepped back. He thrust the shovel into the ground blade first. "He still has on his wedding ring. I think his wife would like to have it." Nico tentatively stepped into the grave, slid Tony's wedding ring off his finger, and dropped it into his pocket. He bent over and searched Tony's pockets. First the shirt then the pants. He removed Tony's wallet and slipped it into the same pocket which held the ring.

Nico stood there a moment straddling Tony. An odd expression spread across his face and his shoulders dropped. He realized the predicament.

"What's wrong?" Josh asked.

"His legs," Nico said, motioning to them with a wave of his hand. "They're bent and the grave isn't deep enough to cover his knees."

"You're right." Josh scratched his itchy neck. "Step out and I'll try to straighten them."

"I'll try," Nico added.

"No, you've done enough. I'll do it."

Unwilling to argue and thankful Josh had volunteered for the gruesome task, Nico stepped out of the grave and stood to the side.

Kneeling at the side of the grave, Josh used his hands to push down on Tony's right knee. Nothing happened. Josh tried again. Still no luck.

Nico said, "Hold his leg in place and I'll step on his knee. I think my body weight will loosen it." Nico stepped over to Tony's body, and said, "Forgive me, Tony." Nico put a hand on Josh's shoulder for balance then stood on Tony's knee, letting his weight push the leg straight.

With a crack, the leg straightened.

"It worked," Josh said. "Try the other side."

With Tony's legs now straightened, Nico shoveled dirt over his partner's body. When he finished, Josh worked quickly to place stones and the piece of his crashed jet on the grave. He methodically placed stones onto the grave, picking through the pile for the right size and shape as if he was searching for a piece of a jigsaw puzzle.

Afterwards, Nico and Josh stood to the side and observed a minute of silence in honor of Tony.

"Well, I guess we need to head our separate ways," Nico said.

"What are you planning to do?" Josh asked.

"I'm going to head over to Tony's house. His wife is probably out of her mind with worry about now."

"Where's the house?"

Nico gave the approximate location and mileage to where Tony's house was. "From here, the main highway is about three miles to the north. When we get there, I'll flag down a car and ask if I can use their cell phone. There'll be someone at the station who can pick me up." Nico paused. "Come with me, and I'll get someone to take you back to the base."

"Sounds like a plan."

CHAPTER 9

After an hour of walking through the charred, flat land, Nico and Josh came up to the barbed wire fence set back from the road.

"What the...?" Nico exclaimed, trailing off.

All along the long stretch of country road, cars and trucks sat idle. Fortunately, the grass fire that had incinerated the grass and half-grown trees on the east side of the road had not been able to jump the pavement.

"What do you think is going on?" Nico asked.

"I don't know. It's the weirdest thing I've ever seen," Josh replied.

Nico pinched down the top rung of the barbed wire, and gingerly stepped over it, then held it down for Josh. Choosing a careful path, they maneuvered the sloping sides of the ditch then stepped onto the road. A woman who was about a hundred yards down the road waved frantically to them. She yelled, but the wind and distance carried her voice away.

"Let's see what she needs," Josh said.

Jogging to her, they stopped when they approached her car. "Do you need help?" Josh asked.

The woman looked at them quizzically, glanced at the car, then slowly stepped away.

The car door swung open and a man brandishing a semi-automatic pistol jumped out and waved the gun.

"Give me your money and credit cards," the man ordered. His eyes were bloodshot, he looked like he hadn't slept in days, and smelled about the same.

Nico shot a quick glance at Josh, who returned a wide-eyed scared-as-crap expression.

"Did you not hear me?" the man asked. "Give me your money!"

"We don't have any money," Nico said. His Glock was concealed under his vest, but he had no time to draw it. The man didn't know he was armed, allowing Nico to use it to his advantage.

"Don't lie to me." The man waved his pistol threateningly. "I'll shoot you if you lie to me."

"We're not lying," Josh said. He shot a quick glance at Nico. "His truck burned up in the fire and I had to eject when my plane went dead. We don't have anything."

"I'll empty my pockets for you," Nico said. He put his hands out to show there wasn't anything in them. "I'm going to reach into my pockets now. Okay?"

"Yeah, I guess so. Don't make any quick moves."

Nico kept his eyes on the man as he reached into his pockets. He slowly pulled the white cotton liner out for the man to see. "I told you we don't have—"

Josh lunged for the man. The man flinched and swiveled the pistol to Josh. He pulled the trigger but nothing happened.

The pistol had jammed.

In the second the man tried to unjam the pistol, Josh rushed the man and grabbed his gun hand.

Nico lunged forward and using both hands, he wrestled the pistol from the man.

Josh grabbed the man in a headlock and threw him to the ground face down. He shoved a knee into the man's back while twisting his right arm up to his neck.

Nico stepped back, peered into the chamber, and unjammed the pistol. He ejected the rounds and pocketed them, then tossed the pistol into the high grass on the other side of the road.

The man kicked his legs and flailed his unrestrained arm. He screamed, "Stop! Stop it. You're going to break my arm!"

"Stop struggling or I will!" Josh shouted.

The man continued to struggle.

Nico unholstered his Glock and fired a round into the air then aimed the pistol at the man. Finally the man stopped struggling. "Good. I've got your attention. You make one move and I'll blow a hole in you. Understand?"

The man turned his head and looked at Nico. "Yeah."

"Josh, you can let him go. I've got him covered."

When the man pushed up on his hands, Nico said, "Stay on the ground. Don't move until I tell you to. Got it?"

The man nodded.

"Josh, search the car for any more weapons."

"Don't you steal anything of mine!" the man yelled. "I swear I'll get you if you do."

Josh opened the front door and checked the console and glove compartment then swung his hands under each seat.

"You," Nico said, pointing to the woman who had flagged him down. You sit next to your boyfriend. "Got any weapons on you?"

The woman shook her head. Her eyes were wide and she looked like a deer in the headlights. "What are you going to do?"

"Nothing, if you do as I say. Now sit down."

The woman did as she was told and sat down next to the man. "Do you know what's going on?" she asked. "We tried calling for help after our car stopped, but our cell phones aren't working."

"Mine isn't working either," Nico confirmed.

After Josh shut the back door, he yelled, "All good."

"Alright," Nico said. "We'll be going on our way."

"What?" the man exclaimed. "I want my gun back."

"So you can try to shoot me? No way," Nico said.

"You can't leave us here without any protection. Suppose somebody else comes by? How am I supposed to protect myself?"

"You should have thought about that before you tried to shoot me."

The man scowled. "You can't leave us here. Aren't you the law or something?"

"I am, and I should arrest you, but I'm not going to. If I ever see you again, I will, so you'd better stay low. Understand?"

"Yeah. But I still want my gun back."

"You saw where I tossed it. You can get it when we leave."

"I want the bullets back too. A gun without bullets is no good," the man said.

Nico retrieved the bullets from his pocket, jiggled them in his palm, then tossed the bullets over the fence and into the pasture. "You have your bullets now."

* * *

Once Nico and Josh were further down the road, Nico glanced back at where the man and woman were. They were in the pasture, their heads lowered, and looking for the pistol and the bullets.

"Think they'll find them?" Josh asked.

Nico shrugged. "By the time they do, we'll be long gone."

The South Texas sun rose high in the sky and the men plodded on, one tired step after another. Nico uncapped the thermos and took a swallow of water, then handed it to Josh. "You can finish it. There's only a little left."

Cars had haphazardly stopped on the road, and each time they passed a car, they peeked inside, looking for water.

A cloud floated high in the brassy sky casting an island of shade upon the weary travelers.

Yards ahead, an old Suburban appeared to hold the most promise. Nico had observed several traffic stops of SUVs, noticing the amount of stuff people kept in them, so as he approached the vehicle, his apprehension grew. He peered in the back and spied an entire case of bottled water still wrapped in plastic, the kind bought at Costco.

"There's water," Nico said. He tried opening the door. "It's locked. Check if it's locked on the other side."

They wiggled each door handle, only to find the car locked.

Josh stood to the side. Sweat beaded his forehead and he wiped it away. They had not seen anyone else since the couple who had tried to rob them. "I don't know about you, but I'm really thirsty."

"Me too," Nico said.

"Think it would be okay for us to bust a window out?"

"Considering this is an emergency, I would say it's okay. Got anything we could use?"

60

"I'm all out of rocks," Josh said. "I'll check the culvert over there. There's probably a loose piece of concrete. Or better yet, you could shoot out the window."

"Let's try to break it first. I need to conserve ammo."

"Gotcha. Be back in a moment," Josh said, sprinting to the culvert.

While Nico stood guard at the car on the outside chance another wayward traveler would want the water, Josh dug around the culvert looking for a piece of useable concrete. He pushed tall grass out of the way, stepped over a puddle of water, and brushed aside some loose gravel. Spying a crack in the concrete drainage pipe, he tugged at it with both hands. Using all his weight, he planted his feet, and pushed and pulled the cracked piece. It only wiggled a bit.

He stood back and thoughtfully assessed the pipe. From the looks of it, the pipe had been here for years and was slowly succumbing to the rain and wind, freezing temperatures, and blistering sun compromising the integrity of the structure.

Getting an idea, he clambered up the side of the ditch, stood atop the pipe, and put all his weight on the edge.

It moved.

He stepped back and planted his left foot to the side then pushed down on the pipe with his other foot.

"Any luck?" Nico shouted.

"I'm just about there!" Josh yelled. "Give me a moment."

After several tries, a chuck of jagged concrete broke loose and fell with a splash into the mud puddle.

Coming back to the SUV, Josh showed Nico his prize. "Think this'll work?"

"Go for it," Nico said.

Josh put his left arm over his eyes to protect them, then with the power of a major league pitcher, he hurled the concrete block at the front passenger side window. It shattered on the first try, leaving tiny cubes of safety glass to decorate the seat and floorboard. Reaching in, Josh manually unlocked the SUV.

Nico looped around the SUV and opened the trunk lid. He retrieved several bottles of water, handed a couple to Josh, then kept two for himself. Tired from the walk and the stressful events of the previous day, the two men sat on the back, taking advantage of the shade the raised trunk lid provided.

Nico downed the water in several gulps then placed the empty container in the trunk. He started on the next one, this time drinking slowly. Josh drank thirstily and when finished, he wiped the back of his hand across his mouth.

The sun beat down on the land, making the scorched earth hotter and drier. A meadowlark landed on a fence post, tweeted a melody, preened its feathers, then flew to a more suitable spot on the opposite side of the road to hunt for insects where the land and livestock had been spared from the wildfire.

A prickly pear cactus decorated the otherwise dull land in a welcome hue of green pads that looked like large, thick leaves. Ripened purplish fruit begged to be picked.

Mesquite trees dotted the flat land. In the pasture, several cows idly chewed cud and glanced curiously at the travelers.

"I could use something to eat," Josh said.

"I'll check if there is anything in the console," Nico replied.

Digging around the console, he pushed aside a plastic wrapped traveler sized Kleenex package. At first he was uninterested in it, then thought what the heck, he might need those for later use so he pocketed it. There were several packets of mayo and ketchup, napkins from Shipley's donuts, then digging further, he found two peanut butter and oats nutrition bars. Satisfied there was nothing else of use, he opened the glove compartment and found several individual packages of Fig Newtons.

"Look what I found," Nico said. He proudly held up the bounty he had found. "Lunch is ready." He handed Josh a nutrition bar and Fig Newtons.

"I'm so hungry, I could eat anything," Josh said. He tore open the nutrition bar, broke off a piece, and ate it. He let out a satisfied sigh. "It's almost as good as pancakes and crispy bacon."

"Almost," Nico said.

For a while the two men ate the meager rations and drank another bottle of water. Nico was the first to speak. "So, Josh, where are you headed?"

"I guess into town with you. The base is too far from here to walk. I'll try to catch a ride in town somewhere or find a phone to call in."

"How many jets do you think were in the air when you were?" Nico asked.

"I'm trying not to think about it. Considering we're the busiest Air Force training base…" Josh dropped his head. "I had several good buddies flying at the same time I was."

"Maybe they were able to eject like you."

"Possibly." Josh wasn't too confident about his reply, and didn't want to think about what had happened to his buddies. Changing the subject, he said, "You got a girl?"

Although he didn't answer immediately, Nico's thoughts went to Kate, reflecting on their brief conversation. He wanted to say *Yeah, I do*, yet he didn't. She would never belong to anyone. She was too spirited.

If Nico was lucky, he'd earn her respect, so he could be *her* partner.

CHAPTER 10

Kate was behind the bar at the Minor Hotel, inventorying the spirits, making sure glasses were clean, and ensuring no dust had accumulated on the shelves. She wiped down the counter for the third time that afternoon in anticipation of the after five crowd arriving.

Dan Gonzales, the hotel manager, walked into the bar and took a seat on one of the stools. He had been managing the Minor for five years and knew all his employees, by name, including the wait staff of the restaurant and housekeeping employees. Kate had walked into the hotel a couple of years prior, asked for a job, and he had given it to her on the spot. She later went to bartending school at night to learn how to be a bartender, and to also receive her Texas Alcohol Beverage Commission certificate. It paid better than working the front desk. Her personality was better suited for being a bartender than placating unhappy guests. He'd seen her put a drunk or two in their places when they had gotten out of hand.

"How's it going, Kate?" Dan asked.

"The usual," she said. "Just getting ready for the five o'clock

65

rush."

"Business has been good, hasn't it?"

"We've been very busy."

"If I wasn't still on the clock, I'd have a drink."

"I won't tell anybody if you want a shot."

"We're on camera," Dan said, motioning to the unobtrusive closed circuit camera in the corner.

"Right. Big Brother is always watching."

"Only if there is trouble. Have you had any troublesome customers lately?"

Kate replied in a long, drawn out, "No." She briefly considered telling her boss about the well-dressed Hispanic woman and her bodyguard, ultimately deciding against it. Then the memory of Nico flashed in her mind. She had to admit, she hadn't ever met anyone like him, but her hurt was still lurking under the surface of the brave veneer she put on for customers. While Nico had promised he'd be back, she didn't keep her hopes up. But hadn't he been sincere? She recalled what she had said to him, hoping he'd be turned off by it. Rather, the opposite had happened. Maybe it was time to move on, to let go of the past, but it was too difficult. It was easier to live in the past. He had probably meant well. Oh well. No harm, no foul, Kate's dad used to say. She'd forget about him soon enough. Life goes on, at least for most people.

"Earth to Kate," Dan said. He waved a hand to get her attention.

"Hmm?"

"You looked like you were a million miles away."

"Sorry. I'm tired." Kate took a hand towel and folded it lengthwise then slung it over her shoulder.

"You work too much, Kate. You're young, you don't have kids, and aren't tied down with a mortgage. Go out and have fun. Take a trip. Find somebody while you're at it. Don't you think it's time you let go of the past? I know it was hard losing—"

Kate cut him off, unwilling to go down that path. "I'm fine. Really I am. I'm doing better. Reload helps me before I get a full blown panic attack."

Hearing his name, Reload lifted his head and cocked his ears. The big dog lifted up off his dog bed and padded to Kate. He sensed her sudden uneasiness and saw her furrowed brow. He was a master of body language and Kate was sending strong signals she was experiencing duress.

Her heart rate had increased and Reload had been trained to go to her, to calm her. She reached to him unconsciously, and when she petted him, her tension evaporated.

It was his duty to calm her, to protect her, like she had done when she found him starving in the alley. She had saved him in the same sense he was saving her now, and he would never leave her. She said something to him, words he didn't understand, but Reload didn't need to understand words. One look at Kate and he would understand what she was feeling. He nudged Kate with his snout and leaned into her. She offered him a hand and he licked it.

"I appreciate you letting Reload stay with me while I work," Kate added. "And letting me live here. I can't bear to live at the apartment by myself." Kate's mind wandered to the life she had planned. She still grieved for the life she'd never have, and hadn't even told her parents about what happened.

"It's the least I can do after what you went through." Dan paused, recalling how Kate had called him when she was in the hospital's waiting room, anxious to hear from the surgeon. "How are you doing, Kate? How are you *really* doing?"

Kate shrugged. "Some days are harder than others."

"People handle grief in different ways, but working twelve hours a day won't let you deal with your grief."

"I don't want to deal with it. I want it to go away." She swallowed the lump in her throat and breathed stunted breaths, trying to stifle emotions she worked so hard to suppress. A pained expression washed over her face. Kate blinked fast and turned away.

Reload nudged Kate, and when she didn't respond, he huffed. Her eyes went to her dog. "I know," she said. "I'm trying."

Dan's gaze swiveled from Kate to Reload. "Does he understand you?"

"More than you'd know."

"My wife is making a chicken casserole tonight. Why don't you come over for dinner?"

Kate cleared her throat. "Trying to fix me up again?"

"Sorry about the last time." Dan shifted on the barstool. "My wife was responsible, not me. Cross my heart and hope to die. I knew absolutely nothing about her inviting her cousin for dinner."

"She should never admit to being a blood relative to that guy."

Dan broke out laughing.

"It's forgiven," Kate said.

"Great. Then come over and have dinner with us."

"I can't. I'm working until closing."

"You have my permission to take the evening off. I'll get another bartender to fill in for you."

"They've got other jobs they're at. I need to stay."

"You work too much. Come over on Saturday and have leftovers. It would do you good to eat a home cooked meal for once. The same old hotel food we serve must be getting old."

"Then you haven't eaten brunch here lately. The fruit is fresh, omelets cooked any way you like them, and they have the best bacon and sausage anywhere around here."

"You didn't answer my question."

"Thanks for the offer, but I can't. I'm scheduled to work tomorrow, so I need to get some sleep after my shift is over."

"You're working seven days a week now?" Dan was perplexed.

"I'm a hard worker. What can I say?"

"You can say you'll take a day off, and that's a direct order."

"I'll think about it."

"Alright," Dan sighed. "That's better than nothing. I've been meaning to ask you about something. Are the bikers we have staying here causing any trouble?"

"Those guys? Nah, they're good. They tip well, and say yes ma'am and no ma'am, although I don't think I'm old enough to be called ma'am."

Dan laughed. "I thought the same thing the first time I was called sir. Get used to it."

The lights flickered and the TV went dark.

Dan groaned. "Not another power outage." He put a hand to his face and massaged the space between his eyes, hoping to thwart a headache that was sure to follow. "These power outages are causing havoc on the AC system. Customers don't like it when the AC and cable goes out. Guess we'll have to discount the room cost." He paused then with emphasis he said, "Again. It always costs us money when this happens."

Dan kept his eyes on the still flickering lights, praying the electricity would stay on. No luck. The lights went dark, followed by the low groan of the inner workings of the hotel grinding to a halt.

"You might want to get the AC upgraded," Kate suggested.

"That will cost millions," Dan said.

"Let's hope the electricity won't be off for long. Don't worry," Kate said.

"Gotta go," Dan said. "Break's over. I need to make sure the generator is running so the food in the kitchen won't go bad. Next thing you know, I'll have a city inspector telling me the food hasn't been kept at a proper temperature, requiring it to be all thrown out."

CHAPTER 11

After Dan made a hasty exit, Kate was alone at the bar. Light filtered in through the door opening to the street next to where the Alamo was located. She stepped over to the door and peered out through the glass. A horse-drawn carriage with a driver and two tourists passed by. Normal enough.

The street was busy with tourists coming and going from the Alamo or Riverwalk back to the plethora of nearby hotels. Several vehicles appeared stalled and the drivers were standing by their cars. One had the hood open and a man was peering into the engine, fiddling with something.

The door to the street opened and a man walked in. "Can I borrow your phone? My cell phone battery must have died and I need to call a wrecker."

"Sure," Kate said. "The phone is at the end of the bar. I'll get it for you."

Kate placed the old black rotary dial phone on the bar. The man picked up the receiver and looked at Kate. "Do you know a wrecker I can call? All my contacts are in my phone."

"Check the bulletin board behind you. I saw a card for one the other day."

"Good idea." A minute later, the man found a card and returned to the phone. Picking up the receiver, he put it to his ear. "That's odd. There's no dial tone."

"Let me try," Kate said. She picked up the receiver and confirmed it was dead. She pushed the plunger down several times and listened again. No luck. "I'll check to make sure it's plugged in. Sometimes it comes loose from the wall." Kate followed the telephone line to the outlet in the wall, bent down, and wiggled the connection to make sure it was solid. She stood back. "It should work. Try it now."

"No, it's still dead. Is there another phone I can try?"

"Absolutely. Go out this other door," she said, pointing to the door leading to the main part of the hotel. "Turn right, and you'll see the front desk on the right. I'm sure they can help you."

"Thanks."

After the man left, Kate wiped down the tables and scooted the chairs closer together. A picture hung askew on the wall so she straightened it, and righted a table lamp knocked over the previous night. She stood back and examined the table placement, chairs, and the overall tidiness of the bar. Satisfied everything was okay, she thought to inventory the amount of bourbon they had, then decided the task could wait until electricity came back on.

Dan pushed open the door and burst into the room. "Kate, have you seen what's going on outside?"

"What do you mean? I looked outside earlier. There are a few stalled cars on East Crockett."

"You won't believe this. Let's step outside."

"Sure. Let me get Reload. He probably needs to do his business."

Dan ushered Kate and Reload outside where they stood on the sidewalk. Kate loosely held Reload's long leash, letting the dog sniff the nooks and crannies of the sidewalk.

The south side rock wall of the Alamo grounds prevented a view northward, while the tall hotels and winding streets to the east merging into a V obscured a view of the nearby interstate.

Dan said, "Step over here and look at the street in front of the Alamo."

Kate peered in that direction, flabbergasted at the amount of stalled cars and trucks. Even the buses weren't working. Tourists and office workers, cabbies, and people on the street stood around dumbstruck. Several people were looking at their cell phones curiously. A horse-drawn carriage clopped along as if nothing had happened. A red trolley car sat idle.

"What's going on?" Kate asked.

"I don't know. Not only are hotel phones not working, cell phones aren't working either."

"Impossible," Kate said. "Unless the battery died, cell phones should work."

"If you don't believe me, check your phone," Dan said.

Kate slipped her cell phone out of her back pocket and pressed the home button. Nothing happened. She tried turning it off and on, and waited a moment. She scratched the side of her head. "That's odd. I charged it this morning. Why isn't it working?"

"Look," Dan said. He pointed to the tree-shaded plaza in front of the Alamo. "There's a crowd gathering around Frank."

"Frank?"

"The policeman stationed inside the Alamo to make sure cameras aren't used. I know him."

"Right. Frank Ybarra. He's been there a long time."

"Let's see what he has to say."

Kate gave a tug on Reload's leash. "Come." Reload trotted in step, keeping to Kate's right side. He was used to the throngs of tourists and their different smells and voices. He lifted his snout, tasting the molecules of the world drifting along air currents. Car exhaust, cooking odors, sticky kids with ice-cream covered hands, perfume, sweat, a full diaper, birds, possum scat, food vendors. The odors formed a picture in his brain of the outside world.

None of it interested him.

However, the anxiety laced sweat of Dan did interest him. Reload recognized the man as one who was used to being in charge and who made decisions and gave orders. Normally cool, this unusual release of sweat interested Reload. He needed to stay aware, not only for Kate, but for Dan. Unknown to Kate, Dan slipped him tidbits of hamburger or sausage from the kitchen. Reload appreciated the special food so this man had earned his protection.

Dan and Kate crossed the street and hurriedly walked along the sidewalk a few paces until they reached the canopy of oak trees shading the lawn in front of the Alamo. A policeman was standing on the brick boundary of the plaza where a crowed had congregated, waiting for instruction.

Reload tugged backwards to keep Kate from getting too close to the group, knowing from experience she became anxious among crowds.

Taking her faithful pet's cue, Kate held back. "Dan, stop," she said.

"What's wrong?"

"I don't know. Reload is trying to prevent me from getting any closer, so something must not be right."

The crowd surged toward the policeman.

"When will the electricity come back on?" someone demanded.

"Why did all our cars die?"

"And what about our phones?" chimed in another person.

Frank Ybarra put his hands in front of him and motioned for people to quiet down. "I don't know what's going on. Stay calm and I'm sure everything will be okay."

"*Yo no entiendo!*" an elderly Hispanic woman cried out, deep worry lines etching her bronzed face.

Frank repeated in Spanish what he had said so she would understand.

"What does police headquarters have to say?" a tourist asked. "I'd call, but my phone doesn't work. I've got a plane to catch this afternoon."

Mumbled voices in the crowd confirmed there were no working cell phones.

"All communication appears to be down. As soon as I know something, I'll let you know," Frank said. "In the meantime, stay in the shade, or visit the Alamo. If anyone wants to visit the gift shop, it's still open. If anyone is thirsty—"

The loud report of a shot sliced the air, followed by another one.

The crowd ducked, and someone screamed.

Frank Ybarra stumbled back and clutched his shoulder. Another shot rang out, hitting him in the leg. He crumpled to the ground. Frank tried to draw his service weapon but his right arm dangled uselessly to his side.

A man with baggy pants and a hoodie ran up to Frank. He pointed a 38 Special at the longtime policeman. "I hate pigs."

Dan and Kate watched in horror as one shot after another rang out, jerking Frank's body with each round.

The tourists stood frozen in disbelief.

The man whipped around. "Don't anyone move! Give me your money!" he ordered, pointing the gun at a mother holding a child.

The teen swiveled the gun at another tourist. "You! Give me your jewelry. Now! Hurry!"

As he was unable to control the entire crowd, men and women scattered in all directions.

"Kate!" Dan whispered through tight lips. "Let's go."

Kate didn't hear him. Her mind raced at warp speed, trying to understand what she had witnessed. Emotions and memories she had tried hard to suppress came flooding back. She fixated on the man taking in his posture, clothes, mannerisms, his face.

Especially his face.

That face.

That scar.

The scar she could never forget. A burst of adrenaline flooded her body, and she trembled.

Reload's gaze swiveled from Kate to the man, then back to Kate and he recognized it was the man in the hoodie causing Kate's reaction. Her stance, her eyes, her unresponsiveness propelled Reload into action. His ruff bristled and he growled low in his throat. A look of laser sharp determination captured his dark eyes, and with all his might he lunged forward.

The leash flew out of Kate's hands, snapping her out of her trance, and before she could command Reload to stop, he bolted to the crowd's direction. He ran low to the ground, legs stretching out and gobbling distance.

"Noooo!" Kate yelled. "Reload, come back!"

A woman in the crowd screamed.

The man swiveled and his eyes went wide at the beast of a dog barreling toward him.

In the moment it became clear what the dog was doing, the man brought up his gun and fired.

The shot went high.

Undeterred, Reload stepped on a tourist who was face down on the ground, leapt up to the curb, stretched his legs out, and all seventy pounds of snarling dog launched through the air and landed on the man, knocking him down.

The gun flew out of the man's hand and clanged on the concrete pavement, only inches away from his hand.

Reload lunged and the man flinched, defensively putting up his left arm to ward off the attack. Reload sunk his teeth into the thick sweatshirt, shaking the man's forearm.

The man screamed and kicked at Reload.

Dan sprang forward. He yelled, "Stop!"

Reload refused to obey.

"Stop!"

"Get him off me!" the man screamed.

Dan grabbed Reload by the tail and pulled him off. He pointed an angry finger and said, "Stay!"

Reload hesitated then acquiesced to the command. Panting heavily, the dog sat on his haunches.

As the man pushed himself up, Dan grabbed him by the wrists. They struggled and Dan was surprised at the man's strength.

With weight and height on his side, Dan threw the man to the ground and struggled with him.

Determined not to be cast aside, Reload latched onto the man's ankle and bit with wild abandon. The man yelped and kicked Reload.

Dan continued to struggle to pin down the man. In the melee, the man freed an arm, reached into his pocket, and pulled a knife. He slashed Dan across his left arm, then with lightning fast speed drew it back against his right arm. Dan instinctively fell backward, grabbed Reload by the collar, and jerked him back.

The man with the scarred face scrambled to his feet, picked up his gun, aimed it at Dan and pulled the trigger.

Nothing happened.

In the charged atmosphere, he hadn't noticed the pistol was empty. His eyes jumped around from the crowd, to Dan, to the dead policeman, then to the pistol still clutched in his hand.

Recognizing the opportunity, the man ran to the dead policeman and pried the service pistol out of his hands. He stopped for a moment and cast an angry expression at Dan. He brought up the pistol, aimed, and—

"Stop! Police!"

Two policemen ran toward him.

The man flipped the middle finger at them, bolted across the plaza to the landing, and then to the steps leading to the Riverwalk. Like a Westminster show dog maneuvering an obstacle course, he easily navigated the concrete benches and metal poles meant to keep cars out. He took the steps two at a time, pushed people out of the way, and disappeared into the labyrinth of stores and shops lining the Riverwalk.

The two policemen ran after him.

Stunned, Dan sat there for a moment to gather his wits. With his adrenaline dump waning, Dan stood and looked around. The plaza was empty, even the snow cone vendor had left her stand unattended. The Chihuahua the vendor kept to entice tourists to stop was gone too.

A few feet away, Frank lay dead.

Reload went to Frank and sniffed him. This was the man who Reload recognized from his time patrolling the Alamo Plaza. He was the man who spoke softly to him, offered him a treat, and said kind words to Kate. Reload had witnessed death before and sensed there was nothing else to be done.

With the excitement over, Reload waited for Kate to instruct him. She stood alone on the sidewalk, vulnerable, confused, overwhelmed.

She was sweating and something was incredibly wrong with her.

Understanding she needed him, Reload dashed to her. When he came to within a few feet of her, he stopped and with great trepidation slowly padded to her, always keeping his eyes on hers, attuned to her needs.

She was in the full throes of a panic attack.

With his large muzzle, Reload nudged Kate. He lifted her hand expecting a response but she only stood there, catatonic. Her heart beat fast and he sensed the increase in blood pressure. Her eyes were glassy. He licked her hand like he had done before and when she did not respond, he huffed a loud and throaty bark, jerking her out of whatever she was experiencing.

Kate put a hand to her mouth and she let out a gasp at the memories she had suppressed. The face, the scar.

Before Kate could fully remember the man, Dan called to her. Without regard for her own safety, she ran to Dan. Reload was close behind. "Are you okay, Dan? Are you hurt?"

"I don't think so."

"Are you sure?"

"I don't know."

"Look at your sleeves."

"Huh?"

"That guy pulled a knife on you."

Dan looked at his suit. Sleeve material had been sliced open on both arms. His white shirt had been ripped open too. An insignificant amount of blood stained the shirt. Dan gingerly inspected his arms feeling for injuries. "I'm okay," he said. "It's a little nick. I guess my suit saved me."

Kate glanced at Frank. She put a hand to her mouth. "Is he…?"

"I believe he's beyond help."

"What are we going to do?"

Dan thought a moment about what to do. "There's nothing we can do. One of the police officers will stay with him. I'm not sure the police will want us to move him. We really should leave him here. It's a crime scene. They won't want it disturbed."

"Oh," Kate said. "Are you going to stay with him?"

"I can't. I need to be at the hotel. I'll see if someone in our security detail can stay with him until those two policemen come back." Dan stood and dusted off his pants. "What happened back there, Kate? Were you having an episode?"

"I, uh, I don't remember. My mind went blank for a moment and I started remembering…" Kate looked pointedly at Dan, recalling the jagged scar of the man who had caused her pain. "It was him."

"Are you sure?"

"I'm positive."

"Kate, we need to get you out of here."

"No," Kate said with a newfound determination. "I'm not leaving."

"I know not to argue with you once your mind is made up. Why would he hang around so close to where the bank robbery was? It would be stupid."

"I don't know. His home turf maybe? Wounded animals always go back to where they feel safe."

"Possibly," Dan said. "I've heard about the gang called the Hyatts named after the hotel on the Riverwalk having been seen around here. Maybe he's one of them. Let's get you back to the hotel. It's not safe out here. You should take the afternoon off."

"I'd rather stay busy. If our guests don't have anything to do, they'll be coming to the bar for a drink."

"You sure are stubborn."

"My mom used to say the same thing."

"Kate," Dan said, "you should tell your parents what happened to you."

"I can't. They wouldn't understand."

"Have you tried telling them?"

"I don't need to."

"It's okay to lean on someone, Kate. We all do."

Kate didn't immediately reply. Her thoughts went to the conversation she had the previous week regarding what Nico had said. "I'll be back in a week." She had replied, "I'll be waiting."

CHAPTER 12

"You never answered my question," Josh said. He stepped away from the SUV and stretched. "You got a girl?"

Nico wasn't sure how to answer. He knew so little about Kate, but the mystery was what made her so interesting. He mentally went over what he knew about her: she was from Austin and had been working at the Minor as a bartender, had a service dog, and was suffering from some sort of trauma. She still had a spark though, not completely darkened by whatever she was enduring, and it showed in the way she challenged him. She challenged him like no other woman had, and Nico had met the challenge head on. Walking away from her, she had asked him, "When will you be back?"

He'd be back alright, if he had to fight his way back to her, because she was worth fighting for.

What had transpired between them other than a few lines of conversation? Had she alluded to something more? Or promised anything? He knew the answers to those questions because it had been in the way she had looked at him. She had wanted to say more to him, but held back. Was she afraid of him? What could he offer her other than a week's worth of an unshaven beard and the promise of a lousy salary? He called no place home, a vagabond living in hotels wherever it suited the government's need. He had not divulged anything personal about himself other than his real name.

Yet, he trusted her enough to tell her his real name. A rule he said he'd never break in his line of work, but he did.

Kate was a rule breaker too, and he admired her for that quality. Sitting pretty and nice never got anyone anywhere, other than high priced clothes or a house coveted by the neighbors.

America was built by rule breakers, and by those who stayed strong and didn't conform to outside pressures. Yeah, he admired her.

Nico finally said, "I got a girl. Her name is Kate."

"Hmm, okay," Josh said.

"Why do you ask?"

"No reason. Only making conversation."

Nico accepted the plausible explanation.

"So," Josh said, "what kind of work do you do?"

"I'm with Border Patrol and have been working undercover," Nico explained. "Local authorities asked for my help since the guy they had blew his cover. I've been trying for a year to infiltrate a gang of drug suppliers. I had finally gained the trust of someone I think is connected to the guy I'm after. I was required to make a special run to the border to pick up a package, and if I delivered it back on time, I'd get a meeting with Santiago. Word on the street says Santiago is making the Riverwalk area his new turf."

"Interesting," Josh said. "What's in the package?"

"No clue."

"So does your girl know what kind of work you do?"

"She doesn't. She will though. I promised her I'd be back in a week."

"If you're going to make your deadline, we better get going."

Nico patted his shirt pocket, making sure Tony's wedding band was still there. He absolutely dreaded telling Tony's widow what had happened.

"I feel bad about what happened to Tony," Nico said. "His wife is so young. Two kids. She's about your age."

Josh didn't say anything, deciding it would help Nico to verbalize his anguish.

"It should have been me flying, not Tony." Nico hung his head. "I don't know how I'm going to tell her."

"I'll help you."

"Thanks. I appreciate it."

* * *

The walk was long and boring across Highway 90. Without a map or GPS, Nico and Josh were concerned about getting lost if they took a shortcut on the winding back roads of the flat and dry land of South Texas.

They trudged past cars sitting idly on the road. A biting fly kept buzzing Nico's head and he swooshed it away. The sun rose higher in the sky, beating hot and hard on the two men. Scrubby brush and stunted trees dotted the landscape along with livestock in pastures.

To pass the time, Nico and Josh talked about their childhood and families, with Josh doing most of the talking.

"I didn't know you were from Del Rio," Nico said.

"I'm the first American born citizen in my family."

"I was too."

"If you don't mind me saying, your first name doesn't exactly sound Spanish."

"It was Juan, but I decided to change it to Josh."

"I did the same thing with my Russian name. I changed it from Nikolai Belyakov to Nico Bell. It's much easier to say and spell."

"Russian, huh? I would have never figured you for Russian. Hispanic maybe. I thought all Russians were blonde and blue eyed."

"My mom had Cherokee blood in her."

"That explains it," Josh said.

"You went to high school here, right?" Nico asked.

"I did. I even managed to get a scholarship to the Air Force Academy. I couldn't wait to get out of small town America." Josh bent over and picked up a pebble on the road. He hurled it into the pasture and watched it disappear into the beige landscape. "Funny thing though, I had to leave in order to appreciate this town and my family. Now that I'm back, all I want to do is stay. I won't be able to." A long sigh escaped his lips. "Then it was flight school, so here I am, walking instead of flying."

"You're lucky to be even walking," Nico said.

"I suppose so."

"Is your family still here?"

"They are. Whenever I can, I have Sunday dinner with them. My mom makes the best tamales. They'll be surprised to see me. Hey, you should come over and have dinner with us."

"I can't. I don't have time. I really have to get back to San Antonio."

"Maybe another time."

"Maybe," Nico replied wistfully.

Nico and Josh steadily walked on, the sounds of the country accompanying them on their journey. The wind whistled through the trees, brushing the grass. A grasshopper skittered across the road, and a field sparrow chirped a melody.

Nico's thoughts took him to his own time at the Air Force Academy and his acceptance into flight school. He was on the fast track to be a fighter pilot, training on flight simulators and real-time experience flying helicopters until family problems intervened and put the kibosh on his plans. His dad had become ill first, then a few months later his mother was diagnosed with terminal cancer. Nico had gone home to be their caretaker and to get their finances in order. After his parents died, he didn't have the will or drive to finish flight school so he had been released from his commitment.

He sold his parents' house and put the money into real estate in East Texas where he bought land in the country. He had paid extra to buy out the property owner's mineral rights which someday he thought would pay out. If not during his lifetime, then he could pass it down to his offspring. The ranch had a three bedroom wood frame house, probably built in the 1950s, and the heirs to the house left the furniture and other belongings. Without someone to share the place with, it didn't feel much like a home where he could hang his hat after a long day.

Nico envied big families where the kids had built-in playmates, and from what he learned when he got older, the kids grew into adults and had become friends. When his parents died, he had felt like an orphan without ties to anyone or anyplace. He closed the house and hired a local cleaning lady to go to the house once a week to turn on the AC or heater, check the faucets, run the shower and tub, and sweep out the front porch and make sure a raccoon or other animal hadn't made it their home.

For a while he considered selling it and had briefly entertained accepting a good offer, yet he held back. For what, he wasn't sure. His thoughts took him to what his mother had said. *"Find somebody to share your life with, Nikolai. Before it's too late. Before you're too old."*

Here he was, early thirties, and he had not yet found the woman he wanted to share his life with. Or had he? It was possibly the reason driving him these past few days. When he had asked Kate, "What kind of woman are you?" she had replied, "The kind you'll like."

After he shuttered his parents' house, he wandered around taking odd jobs here and there, but it left him unfulfilled, a life with no purpose until he landed in San Antonio. He immediately took to the culture and people, and the history behind the Alamo. His flying experience won him a job working with Border Patrol, and he found if he couldn't take down bad guys from the sky, he'd do it on the ground.

He'd thrived in San Antonio, a bustling historic city, which hailed as the seventh largest city in the United States, and had a population of 1.4 million people. It was located on the southwestern corner of an urban megaregion known as the Texas Triangle, anchored by three main cities of Houston, Dallas, and San Antonio, home to 70% of all Texans.

San Antonio was home to five 18th century Spanish frontier missions including the Alamo, whose architecture was known around the world and was synonymous with perseverance, dedication, and bravery among the men who faced overwhelming odds. The motto had been "Liberty or Death."

Located on the Balcones Escarpment, geology's most prominent mark on Texas, San Antonio was the land of cactus and cows, stunted trees, and cracked rock extending in a prominent arc from Waco to the north, and to Del Rio due west near the Mexican border. It was where the Hill Country was with upthrust hills, spring-fed rivers, and millennia of limestone erosion from turbulent thunderstorms, leaving rich topsoil and fertile land for crops.

Once a natural dividing line between east and western migration, the line was now blurred with cities and agriculture sustained by underground aquifers.

* * *

An hour later, a humming, churning, mechanical sound crept closer to Nico and Josh as they walked along the blacktop road.

"You hear that?" Nico asked. He couldn't quite place where the sound was coming from.

"Yeah," Josh replied. "What is it?"

"Don't know."

Nico's eyes swept over the land, searching for the sound akin to the whirling of a distant helicopter. But it wasn't a helicopter. It was a sound of a simple engine. He visually checked the abandoned cars and trucks on the blacktop road in case one of them worked. Nope. All still. He spied an abandoned UPS truck in the middle of the road. Packages had been scattered around, probably the work of a looter Nico surmised. Nothing moved except for the shimmering heat. Nico looked behind them. Squinting, the approaching vehicle came into focus, crawling along at a snail's pace.

Josh turned around, curious what Nico was looking at. Squinting from the sun-glare, Josh scanned the horizon.

"A tractor," Nico said.

"No kidding?"

Way in the distance, past the shimmering heat bouncing off the blacktop, past the pastures and abandoned vehicles and where the road curved in their direction, the shape of a tractor came into view, slowly rising like the mast of an approaching ship on an ocean.

Nico and Josh stepped to the side as the tractor inched closer. The rancher driving the tractor waved. Nico returned it.

"Do you know him?" Nico asked.

"No," Josh said.

With difficulty, the rancher pushed the brake to the floorboard and the ancient piece of rusted farm equipment groaned and lurched to a stop, bouncing as it idled.

"Where y'all headed?" the rancher asked. He stepped off the tractor and offered a hand to Nico.

Above the roar of the engine Nico yelled, "Into town!"

"Hop on," he said. "I'm Emmett Jackson. I've been ferrying people who have been stuck on the roads back to their homes."

"I'm Nico Bell, and this is Josh Lopez."

Emmett spied Josh's flight uniform. "You from the base?"

"Yes, sir. I had to eject when my jet lost power."

Emmett took off his cap and ran his fingers through his hair. "Yup. I heard about several planes nose-diving to the ground. You're lucky you got out."

"Have you heard of any other pilots ejecting?"

"Sorry, son, I haven't." Emmett noticed Josh's shoulders drop. "Don't worry," he said, "it's a big area they fly over. They could've ejected a hundred miles from here."

"I hope so. We were all taking our first solo flight." Josh kicked the toe of his boot on the road. "What an initiation."

"There's nothing we can do for the moment," Emmett said. "Hop on and I'll take you into town."

The tractor only managed a few more miles per hour than Nico and Josh could walk, but considering how tired they were, they welcomed the offer of a ride into town and a chance to rest their aching feet.

The rancher explained his wife sent him to town to get milk and bread the previous day. "Then all these people came running up to me begging for a ride. It's the oddest thing with electricity not working and the cars not starting. I thought it was bad luck or coincidence out at the ranch. Considering it's happened across a wide area, it can't be a coincidence or multiple blown transformers as some people have surmised. What do you think is going on?"

"Don't know," Nico said.

"Josh," Emmett said, "you're in the military. What do you think?"

"If I told you, you probably wouldn't believe me."

"Try me," Emmett said.

"Do you know what an EMP is?"

"Nope."

"It's an electromagnetic pulse, caused by the sun or even worse, a nuclear bomb detonated high in the atmosphere. Not enough for radiation damage, but enough to take down the electrical grid and anything relying on a computer board."

"Nah, can't be," Emmett said. "That sounds like hocus pocus tomfoolery some sci-fi author would make up."

"Maybe so," Josh said. "It's only a theory, something we briefly touched upon in school. It's never been tested."

"If we're being graded, test grades are only pass or fail," Nico cut in. "I don't know about you two, but I've never failed anything in my life and don't plan on starting now."

* * *

An hour later, after a bumpy and extremely slow ride, the rancher stopped in the town's only grocery store's parking lot where he idled the tractor to a stop. Nico and Josh hopped off the tractor and stretched their legs.

"Will ya look at that?" Emmett said, his mouth gaped open at the scene.

The front glass plated doors of the grocery store had been shattered and the store looked like a bomb had hit it. Displays were knocked over, shelves had been picked clean, and sundry items lay scattered on the floor.

"Yesterday, it was still open for business."

"Don't you know the old saying?" Nico asked.

"What saying?" Emmett said.

"Society is only three meals away from anarchy. Today is the second day after the electricity went off, which means we're already passed three meals. People have realized resources are scarce and the government is incapable or unwilling to help. The citizens have taken matters into their own hands, including looting the grocery store. If their kids are hungry, parents will do anything to feed them."

"Lord Almighty!" Emmett exclaimed. "I better get home to my wife and tell her there won't be any store-bought milk anytime soon. I'm sorry, boys. I'm going to have to leave you here. Hope you understand."

"No problem," Nico said. "We understand. You've already helped us considerably." He reached up to shake hands. "Godspeed to you and take care of yourself."

"And the same to you." Emmett laboriously turned the steering wheel a hard right, lurched forward a few feet, then had to back up the ancient tractor. It groaned and creaked as if to protest the movements required.

Emmett throttled the tractor full speed to make a hasty exit, or as hasty as the tractor would rumble. The last Nico saw of him through the black smoke of the tractor was a hazy image of a man hell-bent on getting home.

"Want to check out the store?" Nico asked.

"Sure, why not?" Josh said. "I don't want to stay too long, 'cause it's getting dark. I want to be out of here when the looters come back."

Carefully, Nico and Josh stepped over the shattered glass and entered the store. They stopped near the front where customers normally checked out groceries. The cash register drawers had been ripped out and tossed on the floor. A few pennies were scattered around on the floor along with empty bottled water containers.

The stands by the cash registers containing impulse purchases of gum and candy were empty except for a few pieces of bubble gum. Nico picked one up, unwrapped it, and popped it in his mouth, chewing audibly. Getting an idea, he got on all fours and looked under the stands. As he thought, there were several candy bars accidentally kicked out of sight. In the looters' haste and melee, they had probably scooped up the candy bars by the handfuls, not mindful of any on the floor.

Stretching his arm as far as he could, Nico retrieved several Hershey chocolate bars with almonds, and once his eyes acclimated to the low light, he spied two Baby Ruths and four fun sized Butterfingers. Not exactly his favorites, but it would give him the added boost he needed and quell the empty feeling in his stomach.

Nico put the candy bars and gum on the conveyor belt, divided the stash equally, then handed half to Josh.

"Thanks," Josh said. He stuffed the candy in his pockets. "I'm going to check the courtesy booth for anything useful."

"Good idea," Nico replied. "I'll make a quick sweep of the store."

Nico grabbed a hand held basket and sprinted down the aisles, while Josh quickly opened the cabinets which appeared not to have been rifled through. There were office supplies, paper napkins, hand lotion, pictures of kids, books of stamps, a stapler, tape dispenser, then way in the back of one of the cabinets he spied a case of water. Josh pulled it out and lugged it on top of the counter.

Nico came back.

"Whatd'ya find?" Josh asked.

"Not much," Nico said. "The deli is empty except for spoiled meat and cheese. I found a box of crackers and a peanut butter sandwich which I guess was someone's lunch." Digging around in the basket, he pulled out a packet of baby wipes. "For, you know…necessities."

Josh gave a 'sup nod. "Gotcha."

"Let's check upstairs," Nico said.

"What for?" Josh asked.

"The manager's office should be up there." He pointed to the ceiling. "See all those mirrors?"

"Yeah."

"Two-way glass. Offices are up there. It's where they look for shoplifters. Stairs should be near the meat department. Bathrooms too, so if you need to go, now's the time."

"I could use a pit stop," Josh said. He grabbed two plastic bags, checked the magazines, then popped the latest gossip magazine into the bag. Reading about the latest Hollywood gossip and the A-lister star's shenanigans always entertained him. He'd had enough of calculus and trigonometry to last him a while. What he needed was brain putty reading and the magazine he held in his hands fit the bill.

Before Josh left for his maiden solo flight, he had dropped his car keys into his pocket. It had a small Photon flashlight on it, and flicking it on, he was surprised it still worked, casting a feeble, yet readable, light.

"See you in a few minutes," Nico said.

Josh opened the bathroom door and peered into the darkened space. He propped open the door using his foot. Other than Nico clomping up the stairs, it was eerily quiet.

"Anybody here?" Josh tentatively asked. He waited for an answer although he didn't expect one. He held the door as it shut, letting it click into place.

Flicking on the flashlight, he chose a stall on the end where he pushed open the door. The toilet was a household type instead of a commercial one. He peered in the bowl filled with water.

Good.

Meaning water was in the tank so he wouldn't have to waste any of his precious bottled water. He took a minute to squirt some pumper soap on his face then went to the tank and splashed cold water on his face and hair. He wiped his hands on his flight suit then sat down.

He shook open the magazine and thumbed to the story about an

A-list actor who had been caught red-handed fooling around with his leading lady. Apparently the A-lister's wife had hired a private detective and once she had the evidence, she said she was going to take the guy to the cleaners. There had been no pre-nup, so with the latest string of blockbusters the wife was sure to get the L.A. mansion, four vintage and very expensive cars, and—

A sneeze came from somewhere in the bathroom.

Josh had been so enthralled in the article he wasn't sure he had heard correctly. His mind might be playing tricks on him.

Another sneeze!

"Who's there?" Josh demanded in his most authoritative voice. In the cramped confines of the stall and the fact he was sitting on a toilet, he was aware of his vulnerable situation.

There was no answer.

"If you make another move, I'll shoot," Josh said. He ducked his head under the stalls and looked for another pair of feet. He shined the flashlight in the direction of the sound, but still didn't see anything. He quickly buttoned up and carefully eased open the bathroom door.

He pushed open each stall door and peered in, second guessing what he thought was a sneeze. Maybe it had been water in the pipes, or someone had entered the store. Maybe in his tired state of mind brought on by exhaustion he had imagined the sound, that was, until he opened the last stall door.

CHAPTER 13

Nope, he had heard it alright.

"Who are you?" Josh asked. He shined the flashlight on the girl's face full of freckles and childhood innocence. Ringlets of light brown hair tumbled around her cheeks.

The eight or nine year old girl looked at him as if he was a male lion and she was a hapless gazelle about to be devoured. She was sitting on the back of the toilet with her knees tucked to her chest.

"I'm not going to hurt you."

Still no answer.

"What's your name?"

The girl shook her head and crossed her arms. "You need to leave because you're in the ladies room. Boys aren't supposed to be in here. Only little boys are allowed, and only if their moms are with them."

Josh laughed at the mix-up and the spunk she displayed for such a small girl. "Sorry, I didn't know. I thought this was the men's room."

"It's not," she said, pointing him in the right direction. "It's over there."

Josh noted her voice was steadfast and didn't waver. She was a little pistol and a scrappy girl. "The lights were off. I didn't notice."

The girl looked at him with speculation.

Josh cleared his throat. "My name is Josh. I fly airplanes."

The girl immediately perked up. "You do?"

"Yes," he said, noticing the change in her demeanor. "Important airplanes that keep our country safe."

The girl's eyes got big and round. "Do you know my daddy? He flies those fast planes in the sky. I'm Tracey."

"Is your daddy stationed at Laughlin?"

She nodded.

"What's his name?"

"Bill Killion."

A breath of horror escaped Josh's lips. "Bill Killion is your dad?"

"Yes," Tracey said. "His nickname is Kill Bill."

"After the old movie."

"Right," Tracey said excitedly. "Do you know my daddy?"

"I did...I do. We worked together, and he always talked about you and how proud he is of you. We were about to get our..." Josh stopped in mid-sentence at the thought Bill was also taking his first solo flight. He recalled seeing Bill's jet lose power before his did. Helpless in the air, Josh followed Bill's jet and waited for him to eject. Images of the jet spiraling out of control to the ground, followed by the explosion knowing Bill would have been killed instantly, came to him.

"What's wrong?" Tracey asked.

Josh dropped to his knees so he'd be eye to eye with Tracy. He looked at her with a mixture of fatherly protection and utter sadness.

"Tracy," Josh said. "Your dad is..." Josh diverted his gaze, unable to make eye contact with Tracey. "Where's your mom?"

"I don't know. She didn't come home last night from night school where she's getting a master's in education and my sitter had to leave early and my phone isn't working and I couldn't text my mom or dad. The TV doesn't work and I'm hungry and the milk tasted yukky this morning and I didn't know what to do, so I came to the grocery store to get food, and I had to go to the bathroom—"

"Whoa, whoa, slow down," Josh said. "I'll take you home. Do

you live far from here?"

"No."

"Can you find your way back home?"

"Yes."

"I'll take you there. I'm sure your mom is probably home by now and is probably worried—"

The bathroom door flung open. Josh pivoted expecting to see Nico, instead two teen boys rushed Josh.

Josh pushed Tracey out of the way then ducked as one of the teens swung a metal bat at his head. The bat collided with a stall door, knocking it inward, banging the dividing wall.

Tracey screamed.

The hit which missed Tracey by inches was so powerful the reverberating metal bat sent shivers through the teen's hands and up to his arms. For a moment the teen was stunned, and he waited in surprised shock for the feeling to return to his arms.

Josh kicked his right leg out, making contact with the back leg of the other teen, some pimply, gangly kid jacked up on youthful bravado. The teen buckled to the linoleum floor, and when he was down Josh kicked him in the fleshy part of his thigh, not enough to do any real damage, only hard enough to leave a nasty bruise. The kid let out a surprised high pitched squeal as if having his swagger wounded was worse than a real injury.

The teen holding the bat lifted it high above his head, took a quick step forward, and as he was about to bring it down hard and fast on Josh, an opposing force jerked him back. Off balance and with his arms at a weakened position over his head, the teen struggled to get control of the bat and regain his footing.

Two hands had a stronghold on the bat and kept the teen at an awkward angle. A hard knee to the teen's kidneys forced him to release the bat. He bent at the waist and grunted in pain.

Another kick to the back sent him sprawling on top of the other juvenile delinquent.

"You came in the nick of time," Josh said.

"I don't think these jerks will be bothering you anytime soon." Nico cast a disgusted look at the teens who were cowering on the floor. "Who are you?" he demanded. When there was no answer, Nico decided to bluff them. "I'll crack your skull right now if you don't tell me your names." He held the metal bat high over his head, moving it as if he was about to hit a fast ball.

"I'm Stewart Kunkul. Don't...don't...hurt me," he stuttered. He held a feeble shaking hand over his head.

Nico took a commanding step forward. "Who's your friend?"

"Uh, uh, his name is Gene—"

"Shut up!"

"—Paulson."

"Well, Stewart and Gene," Nico said, "What should we do with you?" He ran a hand over his chin.

"Please," Stewart pleaded, "let us go. We were kidding. We weren't going to hurt you."

"Oh really? You and this metal bat?"

"I just found it. It's not even mine."

"You stole it?" Nico asked.

"No we didn't. Right, Gene?" Stewart elbowed Gene. "Right?"

"Yeah, right. We found it in the park, and we were bored and didn't have anything to do so we came to the grocery store. We thought this guy was a looter."

"You expect me to believe that?" Nico asked.

"It's the truth!" Stewart squealed, his voice rising to the pitch of an adolescent girl.

"Maybe you can pull the wool over your parents' eyes, but not over mine." Nico paused for effect. "Josh, what do you think we should do with them?"

"I swear it's the truth," Stewart said.

Rising, Josh stepped closer to Nico. Looking Nico straight in the eye, Josh winked. "We have a special new program at the base."

"So?" Stewart said. "What does that have to do with us?"

"It has everything to do with punk kids like you who get into trouble." Josh paced back and forth in front of the teen. "The program lets parents drop off their delinquent kids at the base no questions asked, so we can do what we want to with them."

"D-do what with them?" Stewart's voice shook with anxiety.

"Let me explain. First I need you to promise you won't tell anybody about it because the kids who graduated are sworn to secrecy." Josh glanced at Nico and winked. "Otherwise there are dire consequences to be paid."

"Right," Nico said, playing along. "It's a brand new program. Border Patrol got an email about that the other day." He could barely keep from laughing at the scared expressions on the teen's faces.

"You're joking," Stewart said. His gaze bounced from Nico to Josh to the exit.

Nico stepped in front of the door.

"Nope, it's called TBS," Josh said. "Stands for Teens Being Stupid."

"You're lying! TBS is a TV network."

"The network plays mostly teen dramas so the government can monitor who's watching it."

"I knew it!" Stewart said. "I knew the government was behind this!"

"You're a smart kid, Stewart. And you know what else? It's so covert and undercover that the local police don't even know about it. Only teachers know about it. It's a way for them to get rid of teens who cause trouble. And you," Josh said pointing a finger at Stewart, "have recently been in the principal's office."

"What? Those records are supposed to be private. I have rights!"

"Shut up!" Gene screamed. "They're playing you."

"We'll play with you alright," Josh said. "We know all about your school record. So you'll know what's in store for you, the TBS program allows us to strap you to the underside of a fighter jet. A microphone is hooked up to you so if you scream even once after the jet takes off, the pilot has the permission to press a button and drop you. Nobody will find you, except for the buzzards." Kneeling, he put his face close to Stewart's. "Do you know what buzzards do to a dead body?"

Stewart shook his head.

"First, they poke out the eyes. Then they devour the lips and cheeks until only the skull is left." Josh thumped Stewart's head. "A whole flock of those big, ugly, squawking vultures will tear apart a face in a matter of minutes. Later, at night, the carnivores come out, tearing and fighting over the corpse until the limbs have been torn off. They'll gut you and eat your insides." Standing, Josh said, "You don't even want to know what they'll eat next. The onions are their favorites."

Stewart closed his legs and a little bit of pee dribbled out, staining his pants. His face had gone white and he swallowed the bile in his throat. He cradled his flip flopping stomach with both hands. "I'm gonna toss." He dry heaved, then sprung up and stumbled to a toilet.

Nico bent down and got in Gene's face. "Think we're kidding now?"

Gene didn't answer.

"I thought so. I'm with the government, so if you ever get into trouble again I know how to find you."

"I promise I won't get into trouble. I promise." Gene's gaze bounced from Josh to Nico. "I promise."

"What do you think, Nico?" Josh asked. "Think we should let them go?

Nico thought for a moment before answering. "Yeah, I think they're good to go because if they get into any more trouble we'll know about it."

"Gene, you can stand up," Josh said. "Get Stewart some wet paper towels and tell him to clean his face. If I catch you here again, remember what will happen."

Jumping up, Gene said with all the enthusiasm of a kid waiting to get a cavity filled, "Yeah, I'll remember."

Josh took a step toward Gene, crowding him against the wall. "Yes sir, I will remember, sir!" Josh yelled in a loud, authoritative voice.

"Huh?" Gene's eyes darted around in confusion. "What?"

"Say it! Yes sir. Say it like you mean it! And straighten your shoulders when you talk to an adult."

"Okay, okay," Gene said standing taller. "Yes sir, I will remember, sir."

"That's better. You can go now."

* * *

After Gene and Stewart left, Nico and Josh had a good laugh. "How'd you come up with TBS?" Nico asked.

"I don't know. It just came to me."

"Good one!"

One of the doors to the stalls squeaked. Nico pivoted in the direction.

A quiet child's voice asked, "Are you telling the truth about TBS?"

"Who's that?" Nico asked, dumfounded anyone else was in the

bathroom.

"Her name's Tracey. She's been in here the entire time. I'll tell you about it later," Josh said. "Come on out, Tracey. It's okay."

Tentatively, Tracey pushed open the door and stepped out facing Josh and Nico. "Is TBS true? Will you really tape them to the jet?"

"No," Josh said. "We only wanted to scare them."

Puzzled, Tracey thought. "So they'll learn to behave?"

"That's right."

"Come on," Josh said. "Let's take you home. Your mother is probably worried sick by now about you." He took her by the elbow and escorted her to the door.

"Aren't you forgetting something?" Tracey asked.

"What?" Josh wrinkled his brow, not understanding what she meant.

"You need to wash your hands."

Josh laughed. "You're right, I do."

Standing at the basin, Josh squirted pumper soap on his hands as a trickle of water came out of the faucet. He whispered to Nico, "She's a little pistol."

Nico nodded. "In about ten or fifteen years she'll be more than a little pistol. More like a .357 magnum."

"Sounds like Kate is a .357 caliber."

Nico's thoughts went to Kate and how she must have been a pistol at that age too, probably giving her parents lots of gray hair and sleepless nights.

Picking up on Nico's silence, his faraway expression, and what it meant, Josh said, "You need to go to her."

"I know." Nico wondered if she was thinking about him or waiting for him, or what she would say to him when he pushed through door of the hotel. Would she be happy? Scold him for being so late? No, she wouldn't scold him. It wasn't her style. From the little he knew about her, she could hold her own at the bar and put the drunks in their place if they got out of hand. If dogs mirrored their owners, she was a survivor like Reload.

While it was obvious her soul had been wounded, she'd recover, and Nico planned to be the one helping her do it.

CHAPTER 14

A day after the incident at the Alamo Plaza where the policeman had been killed, Kate had risen early and was tending bar. From the shadows casting on the street, she estimated it was 11 a.m. Normally tourists filled the street along with buses and cars, or the guys working valet, zipping in and out of the valet area while horses clomped along the street carrying a carriage full of tourists.

Today was different.

The busy hum of the city had gone quiet. No honking cars or harried parents carrying crying babies or the influx of new hotel guests walking the halls dragging luggage behind them. No steady stream of sports news from the bar TV, only a black screen to reflect a changing scene when the door leading to the hallway opened.

There had been no news reports regarding why the electricity was still off, or why cell phones or cars wouldn't work. Without news, rumors started regarding the cause. Some thought it was some sort of conspiracy by the government to shut off electricity, therefore causing the good people of the United States to be completely dependent upon them. National elections were a year away, so now was the time to head off the competition by shutting down the media. If the current party swooped in and came to the rescue, they'd have the populace eating out of their hands and the election would be a landslide.

Although most bar patrons scoffed at the idea, it did lead to lively discussions.

Then there were the bikers staying at the hotel who came close to starting a brawl. One of them had challenged a drunk on the theory, saying, "I do believe you, sir, must be a student not of arts or philosophy, but a student who dallies in the grand platform of social media. Am I correct?"

Kate recalled it had been the biker known as Doc Holiday who had delivered the line with the finesse of a concert pianist, resulting in the drunk looking dumbstruck, trying to decide if he'd been insulted or complimented. He had nodded in agreement, to which Doc Holiday said, "Thank you, sir, for your agreement."

It had taken another guest to tell the guy he had been insulted in a grand way.

The night before, several of the Tombstone bikers who were stranded at the hotel stopped by the bar. Kate couldn't remember their real names, but their nicknames sure were ones she could remember. Doc Holiday had been there, along with Morgan and Virgil Earp. The others were Johnny Ringo and Ike Clanton. When she asked where Wyatt Earp was, she had been informed nobody yet had joined the group who they could crown with the revered name.

The bikers didn't need to give Kate a nickname since she shared the same name as Big Nose Kate, who was Doc Holiday's sidekick. At the time when Kate had been given the nickname, she absentmindedly touched her nose. They assured Kate she did not have a big nose.

"What can I get for you?" Kate asked.

"A beer will be fine." Virgil said.

"What kind?"

"Any will do."

Kate popped the cap and handed Virgil the beer. He took a long, satisfying pull, savoring the taste, albeit a warm one. Virgil had on the usual biker garb: leather jacket with the name of their group – Tombstone Gang – embossed in blazing black letters on the back of the jacket, faded jeans, and graying hair poking out of a doo-rag. His goatee lacked attractive fullness and Kate suspected the goatee was courtesy of the trip, and not one the man usually wore.

Guessing the profession of the bar's patrons was a pastime of Kate's. She could gather a lot of information about her customers by the way they talked, their vocabulary, their hands, manner of dressing or length of hair. From her observations she discerned this current group of bikers were professional men on vacation.

Take Doc Holiday, for instance. He sprinkled his conversation with words authors might use, but not ones which were pompous. Pretty words, she called them. Words giving life and meaning to his story. Perhaps he was an author and looking for another life experience, one he could use as fodder for a novel. He was a man who used his hands to make a living, but definitely was not a carpenter. His fingers were smooth and long, without scars or other blemishes. "What do you do for a living?" Kate finally asked.

"I'm a surgeon."

"Of course. That explains your hands and your nickname."

"These," Doc said, flexing his fingers, "are the tools of my trade. Two million dollars worth of insured tools to be exact."

"I thought you might be a concert pianist."

"I dabble a little in playing, but nothing special. I'm more of a science and math type of guy."

"Then you should play the piano. There's a big correlation between science and the arts. Isn't surgery an art?"

"Now that you mention it, I suppose it is." Doc thought about her statement. "The human body is my canvas, and the scalpels are my paintbrushes."

"Exactly." Kate retrieved another beer and handed it to Doc. "Compliments of the house."

"Thanks."

"What about the other guys in your motorcycle club? What do they do?" Kate asked.

"Bob, uh, I mean Virgil is a Federal firearms dealer. Johnny Ringo is an insurance executive in risk management, and Ike Clanton is an oil and gas VP."

"Hmm. I didn't think y'all were part of Hells Angels."

Virgil laughed. "Not by a long shot."

"Why are y'all still here? Didn't most of your group already leave?"

"The guys with antique bikes already left. Not sure why those are working and ours aren't. I guess the newer bikes are too modernized." Doc took a swallow of beer then set the bottle on the counter. "Besides, we can't leave Virgil's trailer unattended."

"I think I can guess what's in there. It might come in handy," Kate said.

"Any word on what's going on, or when the electricity is coming back on?"

"No. I hope soon because the natives are getting restless."

"Hotel guests?"

Kate nodded. "That's why the bar is still open. My manager wants to keep whoever is left happy. Besides, liquor doesn't need to be refrigerated, which frees up the generator to keep hotel food at the proper temperature."

"How much food is left?" Virgil asked. He was curious how much longer the hotel would serve food.

Kate looked left and right to make sure an eavesdropper wasn't within earshot. She leaned over the bar. "We'll serve food as long as we can. Right now we are only serving perishable food because the generators won't hold out forever. My boss said we are running low on gas. He sent one of the valets to the closest gas station to get gas for the generators, but he came back empty handed. The pumps work on electricity."

"Can I let you in on a little secret?"

"I'm listening," Kate said.

"If you need gasoline, take a sturdy knife and a container suitable to hold gas, then crawl under any car around here and poke a hole in the gas tank. You'll get the gas you need."

"Excellent. I'll be sure to tell my manager."

"Getting back to the food," Doc said, "what about the non-perishables? Got enough for a while?"

"We haven't dipped into non-perishable food yet."

"Such as...?"

"Chips, canned goods, pasta, rice–those types of food. We have a lot in storage, and since the majority of hotel guests have left, we'll have enough food for a while in case the..."

"In case what?" Doc asked.

"In case of a real emergency." Kate lowered her voice. "I've heard some rumors."

"Like what?"

"Something called an EMP."

"That's a bunch of bunk," Doc scoffed.

"No it's not," Kate shot back. "Military guys have told me about it. You know San Antonio has a big base, right?"

"I know."

"Those guys come in and when they start drinking, they start talking. Several years ago Newt Gingrich made a report to Congress about EMPs and how the United States is vulnerable to an attack."

Doc shrugged in speculation. "I read the report. It's fodder for science fiction writers."

"Maybe so, but science fiction has an odd way of coming true."

Doc acknowledged the statement with a nod.

"Those guys have told me the military is already EMP proofing some of their planes." Kate stood back from the bar. "Have you seen any Southwest planes lately?"

"Can't say I have," Doc said.

"Neither have I. The trusty orange and white has left the skies. The only plane I've seen was a military plane, flying low and fast."

The door leading to the street opened. A man stumbled in, laughing and tripping over his feet, filling the bar with a pungent mixture of old sweat and inebriation. His hair was sprinkled with gray, crow's feet lined his eyes, and he had the beginning of a middle aged paunch. He brushed past Doc then plopped down on a barstool. He gave the interior a onceover then pounded his fists on the bar.

"Excuse me," he said in overly punctuated syllables. "I heard this joint is giving out free beer. I wanna free beer."

"It's only for hotel guests," Kate said. She folded her arms across her chest.

The drunk straightened up from his slouched position. "I'm a guest."

"What room are you in?" Kate asked suspiciously.

"Uh, I don't remember." The drunk's head bobbed down. "604. Room 604." He lifted his gaze to gauge Kate's reaction.

"Sixth floor?"

"Yeah, yeah. Sixth floor," the drunk said. He let out a short-lived sigh of relief.

"We don't have a sixth floor so you need to leave."

"I'm not gonna leave. So there," the drunk said with increasing anger. "Get me a beer."

When Kate didn't move fast enough to the drunk's liking, he reached over the bar and grabbed her by the shirt, jerking her toward him.

Reload, who had been sitting quietly listening to the conversation, sprang up when the man grabbed Kate. In the dark corner he had been invisible, but it was soon evident he was large with an imposing frame and an impressive set of canines. He planted his front paws on the bar, bared his teeth and growled a low, guttural warning

The big dog surprised the man.

Kate thrust her arm up and wrenched it away from him.

"You got a dog in here? Dogs aren't allowed in bars! What kind of piss ant place is this?"

The man slapped both hands on the bar to try to scare Reload into submission. Undeterred by the man's bluff, Reload barked loud and throaty.

The man slapped the bar again.

Reload lunged at the man, jaws snapping together. The man quickly withdrew his hand.

"You better get your old cur to back down because if he bites me I'll sue this place out of existence. Then I'll sic the Department of Health on you and whoever gave you your bartending license to make sure you never serve liquor again!" The man stabbed an angry finger at Kate.

Reload stared dog daggers at the man and bared his teeth.

Kate said, "Down, boy. Down."

Reload acquiesced to the instruction. He took his paws off the bar and stood to the side of Kate. She was adjusting her shirt the drunk had pulled loose. Standing at five foot four, Kate was not an imposing figure, but when push came to shove, she'd give it her all. She squared her shoulders and said steadily, "You need to leave."

"Make me," the drunk said in a condescending tone.

One of the bikers who went by an alter ego, and who had been sitting quietly in the corner, observing, decided to get up. "I'd be happy to make you leave."

"Oh yeah? And who might you be? The bar police?" The drunk laughed at his cleverness.

"Let me introduce myself. I'm Ike Clanton and this is my friend

Johnny Ringo."

The drunk laughed. He looked at the guy sitting next to him. "I guess you're Doc Holiday."

"As a matter of fact I am. I would express my gratitude followed by pleasantries then say I'm pleased to make your acquaintance, but evidently you are a boorish man, thus precluding formal introductions. Instead I will say you are a dolt, a simple word which perhaps is in your vocabulary. Unless you want Ike or Ringo to rearrange your face..." Doc Holiday leaned into the drunk, "...which might make you even uglier if that's possible, this is your last opportunity to depart without physical discomfort."

The drunk slipped off the barstool, pondered a second, then took a wild swing at Doc Holiday.

Quick on his feet, Doc ducked.

Johnny Ringo rushed in and hooked his arm under the drunk's arm, twisting it behind his back. With the drunk under control, Johnny wrestled him to the floor and put a knee in his back.

Ike rushed in, jerked up the drunk, and shoved him into a wall, mashing his face into it. Ike made eye contact with Johnny, motioning to the door for him to open it. Johnny opened the door leading to the street, stood aside, and with a sweeping gesture said, "After you."

Ike manhandled the drunk toward the door, and flung the guy out onto the street where he landed on his butt. "If you come back, we'll be waiting." He slammed the door shut.

"Thanks," Kate said. She glanced at Reload. "If y'all hadn't helped, Reload might have been the one persuading the guy to leave." Reload thumped his tail, knowing he was being praised.

"Mind if I lock the door?" Ike asked.

"Can't." Kate shook her head and pointed to the sign above the door. "It's against policy. When the bar is open, the door needs to stay unlocked."

"It'll keep out riffraff," Ike offered.

"Sorry, still can't."

"Okay, I tried. We may not be here the next time something happens."

"I've dealt with worse customers. I can take care of myself. Thanks, though."

During the melee, Kate noticed Ike was carrying a 9 mm Glock.

And while the bar had a 30.06 sign indicating carrying a concealed weapon on the premises was barred, Kate decided to keep the bit of intel on Ike to herself. These were the good guys, and good guys didn't need to be barred from carrying. The sign never stopped the bad guys.

She carried, even if it meant breaking the rules, or risking jail time. Her own Glock was located in an inconspicuous place she thought nobody would suspect. Her eyes flicked to Reload then back to the bar. She shook her head, knowing it took a tragedy of epic proportions to change laws.

The defining moment for Texas happened in 1991 at the Luby's Cafeteria in Killeen located in central Texas where twenty-three innocent people had been killed by a deranged madman. A woman whose parents had been killed at the cafeteria while her life was spared had later spearheaded Texas lawmakers into action to pass a bill in support of concealed handgun laws. She said she would have liked to have had her gun but, "it was a hundred feet away in my car." She feared if she was caught carrying, she might lose her chiropractor's license.

Kate gave Reload a reassuring pat on the head. "You're a good boy."

Reload thumped his tail.

Even Reload recognized the Tombstone Gang were good guys. She thought it odd how dogs could sense whether or not people were good or bad, and Reload had indicated without failure or hesitation who the good guys were. He allowed Ike to pet him the first day he walked into the bar, otherwise he would have growled and bared his teeth, a clear indicator he wanted nothing to do with the person. Reload's reaction to some customers drove a few off, there were a few complaints and threats of lawsuits, but overall, Reload added to the personality of the bar. People from all over came to the bar specifically to meet Reload, which increased business, increasing profits for the bar.

The manager decided Reload could stay.

Reload had accepted Nico the first time he set foot into the bar. The big dog with expressive eyes had lifted his snout in the air, tasting the essence of the man. One sniff told him Nico was strong and confident. He spoke in tones Reload understood. He was an honorable man who looked after the little guy, and who spoke the truth through his actions.

Protective of Kate, Reload sensed the interest Nico showed her. He was excellent at recognizing body posture and the odd scent humans released around one another, scents as individual as their faces. Intermittently when the conversation became animated, and when both experienced spiking blood pressure and an increased heart rate, Reload became aware of tiny bursts of adrenaline, not enough to warrant action, only an observance he filed away in his brain for future use.

Kate had fought her reaction, while the man had not. Reload's first instinct was to go to Kate, to comfort her when he recognized the emotional release, yet he held back due to Kate's comfort with the man.

On the last day when Nico was at the hotel, Reload observed the unusual interaction between Kate, the Hispanic woman, and Nico. Subtle facial expressions, voice intonation, and the odd dynamic of ownership of Nico the woman claimed. Kate had obviously been annoyed.

Yet after the woman had left, and the brief conversation between Kate and Nico, Kate's body language indicated an understanding had been achieved. She had looked at Nico with the same longing and worry she bestowed upon Reload.

If Kate wanted this man, then Reload would also accept the man. They would be part of a new pack, one Reload would protect with his life.

CHAPTER 15

Nico, Josh, and Tracey left the grocery store while it was still light. They needed to reach Tony's house before dusk darkened the land, and before unsavory characters and looters claimed the night. They briskly walked along the blacktop, letting Tracey direct them to her house. They walked past vacant lots and a dollar store. A fast food restaurant sat dark and quiet, gas stations were deserted of cars and people.

A corner store was still open, the lights on and the loud rumbling of a generator filling the air.

As they neared the store, Josh looked at the mostly empty shelves, and what appeared to be locals shooting the breeze. He spied a few bags of pretzels and some candy bars. The isle with the paper goods was still stocked, though. There were a few cold drinks in the coolers, and suddenly Josh was aware of his unquenched thirst.

What he wanted was an ice cold Coke, the kind in the bottle, not a can, fresh out of the cooler. Bottled Coke tasted better, although he wasn't sure why. When he was at the grocery store, he had searched for cold drinks only to find warm canned Coke. If he had been starving or extremely dehydrated, he would have downed the warm Coke in a few gulps. Right now, it was a craving. Maybe it was the sugar he needed. Whatever it was, the urge to splurge overcame caution.

"I'd like to stop at the store." Josh said. He swallowed hard in anticipation of a cold drink.

"I don't think it's a good idea. Can't it wait? Nico asked.

"The cooler still works and I see a bottle of Coke with my name on it. I'm in dire need of a rush of sugar."

"My mom likes Coke," Tracey said. "She doesn't let me have any. She says too much sugar isn't good for kids. She says I have to wait until I'm 16 before I can have a Coke, because she says her parents made her do the same thing."

"Really?" Josh said dumbfounded. "I had a girlfriend in high school who said something similar to me."

"What's her name?" Tracy asked.

"It doesn't matter. You wouldn't know her." Josh's attention wandered as they walked past the store.

"Do you ever talk to her?"

"No. We lost contact a long time ago. I went to college, and she stayed here." For a brief moment Josh thought back to that time in his life. Eighteen years old. Del Rio, a lazy town near the border where the most excitement on Friday night was high school football, had become too constrained for him, too suffocating. He yearned for the big city, to meet new people, have new experiences, but the further he got away from his hometown, the more he realized it was who he was.

Small town America was completely different than the big cities where a million people lived, yet among all the hustle and bustle, loneliness was ever present. Here, in Del Rio, he remembered walking along the street and having people he knew wave to him. Friends, relatives, parents of his friends. He missed it, and it had taken him to leave for him to appreciate it.

His high school sweetheart said she'd wait for him; said she'd get a job at the bank and live with her parents until he came back. Josh was too impatient, too young, so like most long distance relationships, time and distance chipped away at it until the emails and phone calls stopped completely. There was no bad breakup between him and his girlfriend, or pleading to come home. Only a gradual, natural, parting. He couldn't even remember what their last phone call had been about. Every once in a while, when it was quiet, and when he was left with his thoughts, he wondered how she was and if she had married. Whatever had happened to her, he did not know. Perhaps it was better so he could remember her as that carefree seventeen year old, freckle faced and always smiling. She'd never grow old in his mind.

"We're almost there," Nico said. "My partner's house is the fourth one on the left. It's the one with the big mesquite in the front."

"After this, can you take me to my house?" Tracey asked. "I only live a couple of blocks away."

"We'll take you there," Nico said reassuringly, patting her on the shoulder. "I need to stop and talk to my partner's wife first."

"Tracy," Josh said, "when we get to your house I'll need to talk to your mom about something."

"What is it?" Tracey asked.

"Grown up stuff."

Coming to the house, Nico took a big breath to steel himself for what he needed to do. He reached into his pants pocket, feeling for Tony's wedding ring, making sure it was still there. He swallowed a big lump in his throat then rapped his knuckles on the screen door. A hound dog bellowed from inside. The click-clacking of nails on hardwood followed.

"Coming!" a female voice shouted.

Nico glanced at Josh. "This is going to be hard."

"I know. I'm sorry, man."

"Who is it?" a woman asked from behind the door.

"Vanessa, it's me, Nico."

The door swung open.

"Nico, I'm so glad to see you." Vanessa's eyes swept past Nico, then to his companion as she searched for her husband. "Where's Tony? I've been so worried." Before Nico could answer, a young woman in her late 20s came to the door and stood to the side of Vanessa. "Who is it?"

Tracey, unable to contain her delight at hearing her mother's voice, shrieked, "Mommy! Is that you?"

"Tracey?"

"It's me, Mommy!" Tracey squeezed in between Josh and Nico

113

and ran to her mother, who scooped her in her arms and held her tight.

"I've been worried sick about you," her mother said, smoothing down Tracey's hair. "Where have you been? And who are...? She trailed off when she locked eyes with Josh.

"Kristen?" Josh's voice was soft and low, and pained to the point he had trouble saying her name.

Kristen set Tracey down. "Josh? What are you doing here? What's going on?"

"You know him?" Vanessa asked.

"Yes, from a long time ago," Kristen said.

Vanessa looked at Nico. "Where's Tony?"

Nico glanced at the ground.

"Will someone tell me what's going on?"

"Can we come in?" Nico asked.

"Sure, I'm sorry," Vanessa said. "Come in." She held the door open while Nico and Josh entered the house.

Josh snuck a peek at Kristen then looked away.

"Can I get you anything? A sandwich?"

"If you could spare a sandwich that would be great. I'd appreciate a glass of water too if you don't mind."

"Of course. Come sit in the den. I'll be back in a moment."

Tracey and her mom sat on the loveseat, while Josh and Nico sat on the sofa. Nico folded his hands, clasped and unclasped them, scratched his head, cleared his throat, and generally showed signs of nervousness. Josh was unable to look Kristen in the eyes.

Vanessa was in the kitchen opening and shutting cabinet doors. Tableware clinked, and after a few minutes of uncomfortable silence she returned with sandwiches and water for everyone.

"Is everything alright?" Vanessa asked. She handed out sandwiches on paper plates, sliced apples, and a few potato chips. She kept her eyes on Nico.

Nico didn't answer her question, instead, he asked, "Where are the kids?"

"Upstairs playing card games."

"Would it be okay if Tracey played with them? Kristen, is it okay?"

"Sure, yeah." Kristen turned to her daughter. "Let's go on upstairs. Would you like to play with some other kids?"

Tracey nodded. "Can I take my sandwich?"

"Sure," Vanessa said. "And take Pepper with you."

"His name is Pepper?" Tracey asked referring to the dog.

"Yes. Offer him a bite of your sandwich and he'll follow you anywhere."

Kristen said, "I'll be back in a moment."

When Tracey and Kristen were out of earshot, Vanessa asked, "Is my husband okay? Nico, weren't you and Tony on an undercover mission?"

Before Nico had a chance to answer, Kristen returned and said, "The kids are all upstairs. I turned on one of the lanterns with the LED lights. It was getting dark up there."

"Thank you," Vanessa said. "Tony always made sure we had workable lanterns in case the electricity went off."

"Tony was a good man," Nico said. He immediately regretted the past tense he used.

Kristen sat down next to Vanessa.

"Nico...tell me what's going on. You're scaring me."

"I'm not sure how to tell you." Nico hesitated, glanced away, then back to Vanessa. "I'm sorry. There was nothing we could do."

"What? What do you mean?"

Nico took a big breath. "Tony was piloting the helicopter when it went down in the river."

"The chopper crashed? Where is he? Is he at the hospital? We have to go."

Nico shook his head. "I'm sorry."

"I don't like this, Nico. What are you trying to tell me?"

"Vanessa, Tony died from injuries he suffered in the crash."

Vanessa's eyes bounced from Nico to Josh then to Kristen.

"No. What are you trying to tell me? I don't understand." Her strain was evident.

Kristen reached to Vanessa and held her hand.

"He's *what*?" Vanessa's voice cracked.

Nico went to Vanessa, kneeled in front of her, and took her shaking hands in his. "The helicopter was hovering over the river when it lost power. It crashed in the river and sunk. It took me a few seconds to locate the chopper and to get him out. He had been knocked unconscious and wasn't breathing. I was able to get Tony to shore and perform CPR on him."

Vanessa gasped and put her hand over her mouth.

"He started breathing. He coughed, but I don't think he got any water in his lungs. I checked him for injuries and didn't find any. He said his side hurt. I figured he had a cracked rib or something and told him I'd get him to the hospital. After we got to the truck, we found out it wouldn't start. The radio was dead too."

Vanessa dropped her chin to her chest. Tears rolled down her cheeks. "What did you do?"

"There wasn't much we could do. About the same time, Josh ejected from his fighter jet and landed not too far from where we were. I left Tony at the truck and I went to find Josh."

Josh nodded.

"I helped Josh out of his harness and we raced back to the truck because the crash started a grass fire. At that point, we decided our best course of action was to head to the river. Tony was having trouble walking, so we helped him to the river where we had stay for several hours until it was safe. We made a fire on the riverbank and tried to keep Tony warm. When he went to sleep, he said he was okay." Nico paused to let Vanessa digest the information. "He spoke about you and how much he loved you and the kids. He passed away some time during the night."

Thumps on the ceiling and children laughing from upstairs interrupted the solemn moment. Pepper barked in excitement.

Vanessa swallowed and looked at Nico through eyes blurred by hot tears. "Where is he?"

"We buried him next to the truck and placed stones on his grave. I can give you exact directions to where he is buried."

"I think I'm going to be sick," Vanessa said.

As she rose from the sofa, Nico put a hand on her arm. "Wait. I have something for you." He reached into his pocket and retrieved Tony's wedding ring. "You should have this." He dropped the gold ring in Vanessa's hand.

Picking it up, she looked at it and silently read the inscription. "It has our wedding date on it and our initials." She reached behind her neck and unclasped the necklace she had on. She looped the necklace through the ring then fastened it back together. "I want to be alone." Vanessa left and headed to her bedroom.

"I'll go to her," Kristen said.

"No, you stay here. I'll go to her," Nico said. "Tony was my partner for years. I owe it to him."

* * *

After Nico left, Josh and Kristen were left alone.

"What are you doing here?" Josh finally asked.

"I was going to ask the same about you."

"I've been stationed at Laughlin. Nico helped me after my jet crashed, and he needed help with Tony. Since my parents' house was on the way here, I walked with Nico and Tracy. And you?" Josh asked. "How do you know Vanessa?"

"We were going to night school together and met in one of the required courses. I'm studying to be a teacher."

Josh thought back to their high school days. "You always said you wanted to be a teacher."

Kristen ignored the comment, suddenly aware of long ago emotions she thought she had buried. "I didn't think I'd ever see you again."

"I'm sorry it has to be under these circumstances."

"I've often wondered what I'd say to you if I ever saw you again. Do you remember what I told you?"

Josh didn't say anything.

"I said I'd wait for you," she said with a hint of anger. "I meant what I said."

"I'm sorry," Josh said. "I had to leave. I had to find out what the world was about outside of Del Rio."

"Did you find what you were looking for?"

"No. What I was looking for had been right here all along." Josh met Kristen's eyes. She glanced away.

"I'm married now. My husband was stationed at Laughlin also. Do you know him?"

"Everyone knows Bill. We nicknamed him Kill Bill."

Kristen furrowed her brow. She stepped away from the sofa and went to the window. She pulled back the curtains and glanced at the darkening street. Cars were parked curbside. A dog barked in the distance. A cat scurried across the street and disappeared into the bushes.

"What are you doing?" Josh asked.

"Looking for Bill. He knew I was coming over here. He knew

Vanessa and I carpooled together. He was supposed to have picked me up." She turned and faced Josh. "From what you've said, he probably was flying about the same time you were. Do you know if he was?"

"Kristen, I didn't know you and Bill were married. He always talked about how proud he was of you and his daughter. When he mentioned your name I never imagined it was *you* he was talking about. He's a friend of mine, and I want you to know I'm here for you."

Kristen eyed him with growing concern. "I don't understand. Why do you need to be here for me?"

"I'm sorry, Kristen. Bill's jet lost power at the same time mine did."

"Did he eject?"

"I don't know. I didn't see him, but it doesn't mean he didn't. It all happened too fast."

Kristen straightened up. "When we married I knew there was a chance of something bad happening, especially since he was training to be a fighter pilot. Until I have proof otherwise, I won't consider the alternative. I can't. I won't. We built a life together. I've moved on from being eighteen, Josh. I found what I wanted."

"I'm glad you did. Really I am, but I meant what I said. Bill was my friend, and I'm here for you if you need me."

"Thank you. I'll stay here with Vanessa so she won't be alone. I guess Nico will need to leave soon, and your parents will be worried about you."

"I'll stay with you and Vanessa and the kids as long as I need to."

CHAPTER 16

The night passed long and lonely. Josh took up residence in an armchair and intermittently nodded off. The kids and the dog were sleeping peacefully upstairs, unaware of the life-changing event.

Unable to sleep, Vanessa compulsively cleaned the house to the point Nico thought she might drop from exhaustion. Vanessa rebuffed all of Kristen's and Nico's offers to help with housework telling them, "I need to stay busy."

Using one of the LED lanterns Tony had purchased, Vanessa straightened magazines on end tables, dusted furniture and mini blinds, swept and mopped the kitchen, rearranged books in the bookshelf, then refolded the bed sheets in the linen closet. After she finished, she asked Nico to move the sofa so she could clean under it, and since the carpet couldn't be vacuumed, she took a wet towel and rubbed it in a circular motion to remove pet hair and dust.

Once she finished with the carpet, she began pulling the books off the bookshelf then set them on the floor.

"What are you doing?" Nico asked.

"I'm going to classify the books using the Dewey Decimal

system so they'll be in proper order. I've always wanted to do that."

Nico put a hand on her arm to get her attention. "Vanessa, that's enough. You're exhausted. You need to stop."

"People will be coming over once they hear Tony died. I need to have a clean house," she protested.

"Nobody will care." Nico placed the books back in the bookshelf. "Your house is clean enough. It must be three in the morning. You–*we*–all need to try and get some sleep. I have a big journey in front of me tomorrow and I need all the rest I can get."

"I'm sorry," Vanessa said. "I've only been thinking about myself."

"Under the circumstances you're entitled."

"I still need to clean the kitchen."

"Stop," Nico said.

After more cajoling on Nico's part, Vanessa agreed sleep would be good for everyone. She checked on the kids, were who sleeping on the floor in the playroom. She gazed lovingly at her two children, wondering how she was going to tell them their dad had died.

"Do you have anything to help you sleep?" Nico asked.

"Only a prescription for Valium a doctor prescribed Tony a couple of years ago. He was having trouble at the office."

"Take it," Nico said.

"It's not for me. It was for Tony."

"He won't need it, Vanessa," Nico said quietly.

Vanessa took one pill with a glass of water then crawled into bed next to Kristen. Having Kristen sleeping on Bill's side of the bed briefly comforted Vanessa. Maybe it was the warmth or the pressure on the mattress, but whatever it was, she was thankful Kristen stayed.

Exhausted, both mentally and physically, Vanessa put her head on the pillow and tried to reassure herself things would be better in the morning.

It was always better in the morning.

Before she could form another thought in her mind, she drifted off to a fitful sleep, full of dreams about Tony and their life, and the life they wouldn't have together.

* * *

Nico woke in the morning to the sounds of birds chirping and kids playing outside. He'd left the window open during the night to take advantage of the breeze. The corner room had two windows, one on the north side of the house, the other on the east side, which provided a cross breeze. Josh told him to sleep in the guest bedroom, while he would sleep on the sofa knowing he had a long way to go and would need the sleep. Nico didn't fight him on it, and once he stretched out on the bed and closed his eyes, he fell fast asleep. He hadn't moved from the spot he fell asleep in.

He woke groggily, yawned, stretched his toes to the bottom of the bed, and his first thought was it was too early for kids to play outside. He opened his eyes a slit, greeted by the morning sun filtering into the bedroom. From the position of the morning sun, it was probably 10 a.m. or later. He was blasted by a shot of adrenaline when he realized he had overslept. He threw off the sheet and dressed hastily.

Nico muttered an obscenity under his breath, chastising himself for sleeping late. He'd never make it to San Antonio on time. Nature was calling so he took the stairs two at a time, hurried through the den, and stepped into the kitchen.

She said, "You can go outside behind the tool shed." Nico hurried through to the laundry room and unlatched the screen door to the backyard. His eyes swept over the yard. He spied the tool shed, figuring the space between it and the fence was as good a place as any.

When he returned to the house, Vanessa was at the kitchen sink staring at the faucet.

"Are you okay?" Nico asked.

"I don't know. I haven't told the kids yet."

"You'll need to tell them. Do you want me to tell them what happened?"

"No. It's better if they hear it from me." Vanessa sighed. "This is so annoying."

"What is?"

"There's hardly any water pressure, only a trickle."

"Get the kids up and have them stand at each faucet and fill whatever containers you have with water. You're going to need it."

"We have a good supply of bottled water," Vanessa said.

"It's better to have more than less."

Vanessa nodded. "Can I get you anything to eat for breakfast?"

"I don't want to trouble you."

"It's no trouble and I need to stay busy."

"I understand," Nico said. "Do you have any coffee?"

"It's cold, but it's still coffee."

"I'll take it."

Vanessa poured a cup of cold coffee into a mug and handed it to Nico. "Do you need cream or sugar?"

"Black's good." Nico gulped the coffee then set the mug on the counter. "Can I ask you to do something else?"

"Sure? What do you need?"

"If you could pack me several peanut butter and jelly sandwiches, I'd be most appreciative. I didn't mean to sleep so long. I guess my body needed the rest."

"I think we all did." Vanessa retrieved a butter knife, put out six pieces of bread, and spread a thick layer of peanut butter on three of the pieces. She opened the jelly jar and spooned out a teaspoon for each sandwich.

"Vanessa," Nico said, "I've been thinking about something."

"I'm listening."

"Would you mind if I borrow Tony's bike? I need it to get to San Antonio."

"Not at all. It's in the garage. The automatic door doesn't open, so go in the side door. The bike should fit through it."

"Thank you so much," he said. "I'll be sure to return it someday."

"You don't need to. It will be ages before the kids are big enough for it, and it'll sit in the garage and rust. Take it. Tony would have liked you to have it."

"I'm so sorry about Tony."

"I know. I'm not the only one who lost him. You lost him too. I've been so consumed by my own grief I've forgotten his loss has affected not just me, but others."

Nico went to Vanessa and hugged her, not knowing how else he could comfort her. He patted her on the back and said, "He's with our Heavenly Father and I know he is watching over you. Stay strong."

Vanessa hiccupped. "I'm trying." She pulled away from him, swiped under both eyes, then stepped to the counter to finish making the sandwiches. Sensing that he hadn't left, she said, "If you don't want to waste any more time, you'd better go on and get the bike."

Nico headed to the garage where he found the bike. Removing it, he wheeled it through the door and onto the patio. The tires were low so he went back into the garage to find a tire pump.

Vanessa delivered a sandwich and a bottle of water to him, and he gobbled it while he worked at getting the bike ready.

After he fully inflated the tires he adjusted the seat to his height. With any luck he'd be in San Antonio in eighteen hours, on the day he promised Kate he'd be back.

That is, if all went well.

Something always went wrong, and Nico went over in his mind possible contingencies he'd have to deal with. Foremost was the bike. He'd be a target for anyone who wanted it, desperate people who would kill for it and dump his body in a ravine. On the other hand, Nico was armed and he wouldn't hesitate to kill to protect himself, having already made up his mind that it was easier shooting a man than a dog.

He figured it was 150 miles from Del Rio to San Antonio, and since he was tall with long legs, he could probably bike along at 15 mph, which made the trip 10 hours of non-stop riding.

Dream on.

Even if he had trained for a marathon, it would take him two days of rest stops, snacks, and a place in the shade to cool off. He was in good cardio shape, always finding time for a good run where he broke out in a sweat. Biking was something else altogether. He probably wouldn't be able to walk after he made it to San Antonio, but he'd cross that bridge when he came to it.

"I thought you might need this," Vanessa said. She shut the laundry room door. "A CamelBak. It holds two liters of water and will be easier to carry than a bunch of water bottles. I thought you'd need it."

"I can't," Nico said. "I've already imposed on you enough."

"Tony never even used it," Vanessa said wistfully. "He was always ordering stuff on the internet, stuff he never used, always said he would. I'd tease him that I'd have a garage sale to get rid of all that stuff. Some of it is still in the boxes." She dropped her chin. "I can't believe he's gone."

"If there is anything I can do—"

"I don't think there is anything anybody can do. Please take it," Vanessa said, handing him the CamelBak. "I've already filled it with water." She opened a paper grocery bag. "In here are sandwiches and some high protein snack bars. I put some dried fruit in a baggie, and a chocolate almond bar in case you have a sweet tooth. It was from a school fundraiser from last year. I'm not sure how fresh it is, but it's still good. And I also packed a fettucine alfredo MRE, complete with chicken and mixed veggies."

"Mmm," Nico said. "Makes my mouth water."

"It doesn't expire for five more years."

"Can't wait to dig into that over a glass of wine."

Vanessa laughed. "It beats going hungry."

Nico nodded.

"Also, your backpack is still in the den. Don't forget that."

"I won't." Nico cleared his throat. "I guess I better get going. If you need me to stay—"

"I'll be fine. Josh and Kristen are with me. I know where Tony's guns are and I know how to use them." She looked at the second story of her house. "I still need to tell the kids, so I'd better let you go."

"I left instructions on the coffee table where we buried Tony."

"Thank you. I'll be sure to notify the authorities. Tony said he wanted to be buried next to his parents." Vanessa paused. "Well, I have to go on upstairs and talk to the kids."

"Okay. I'll get my backpack, say goodbye to Josh and Kristen, then I'm leaving."

"I'll say a prayer for you."

"Say two if you don't mind," Nico said, looking skyward. "Something tells me I'm going to need all the help I can get from the man upstairs."

CHAPTER 17

Several hours later, Nico was reaching the point of exhaustion. He had to take more breaks than he thought was necessary so he could massage his legs to keep them from cramping.

He kept giving himself a pep talk for motivation to keep going and used landmarks along the road for guidance.

Once he reached the big oak a football field length away, he'd stop, or so he told himself. After he passed it, he'd find another goal to reach. Perhaps a road sign or a house, and before he knew it, he had biked another mile, then five, then ten. The mileage signs to San Antonio kept decreasing, a good indicator of his progress.

If he had trained for a marathon bike ride, the 150 miles from Del Rio to San Antonio would have been manageable. He had made good progress on the way to Uvalde, but once his legs started cramping, his progress slowed. Probably dehydration and lack of proper mix of carbs, electrolytes, low fat foods, and protein had been the cause. A good helping of risotto would have fit the bill, and given him that extra push he sorely needed at the moment.

Black, squiggly lines of tar used to repair weather cracks marred the road, and the more Nico looked at the lines, the more they acted like a sedative on his brain. He shook his head to clear the overwhelming fatigue.

The next mileage sign indicated Uvalde was within his goal for the day, and he estimated it would take thirty minutes to reach it.

Fields of the first growth of wheat and corn covered the landscape. A shiny green modern tractor sat still among the golden growth. Cows munched idly in pastures. Houses were silent. A rancher sitting tall atop a horse waved at Nico and called to him, but Nico only waved back, determined to stop only when necessary.

Whenever he rode past abandoned cars he'd slow down and check for anything usable. At one, he found an unopened bottle of water which he gulped greedily, thankful he found the extra water. At another car he found a baseball cap with the San Antonio Spurs emblem on it. He tried it on, adjusted the back of it, and decided to keep it.

Uvalde, known for its magnificent pecan trees, a result of the high water table in a land where everything stung or bit, was an anomaly in the quasi desert.

Not quite the Hill Country, and not quite South Texas, it had its own brand of notoriety and hailed as hometown for several famous people including John Nance "Cactus Jack" Garner, who was a former Speaker of the House and Vice President of the United States. Oscar winner Matthew McConaughey, actress Dale Evans, and Governor of Texas Dolph Briscoe were also born in Uvalde, and it was the final resting place for gunslinger King Fisher.

Nico had eaten one of the sandwiches Vanessa had packed, and polished off half of the dried fruit, along with a bag of peanuts Vanessa normally saved for squirrels. In desperate times like these, eating squirrel food wasn't beneath Nico. Water was running low, and fortunately a farmer had let Nico fill up his water bottles.

The wind brushed his face, reddened from the sun and wind, and he rode on, pedaling one rotation at a time.

Civilization showed its face with an increasing amount of mom and pop businesses and houses as Nico approached Uvalde. The speed limit decreased from 70 mph to 55, then 40, and finally 35. A dog dashed from the porch of a nearby house and bolted toward him, barking and snapping, nipping at Nico's heels. He had to shoo it away with a push of his foot.

He crossed a dry gulch and observed a group of kids playing kickball.

To his left a large gas station with sixteen pumps came into view. People were milling around the front of the convenience store and cast wary glances at Nico.

Vintage cars, decades old, puttered along the street. A shiny red 1964 Mustang, one that had probably been stored in a garage, had stopped at the gas station. The owner looked bewildered at the gas pump, until someone shouted, "It needs electricity to pump!"

Nico had been tempted to tell the guy that if he was desperate for gas, he needed a sharp knife and a metal tub. Crawling under a car and poking a hole in the gas tank was a lot safer than trying to siphon gas.

He disregarded the guy's conundrum, keeping his promise to himself to only stop for rest, necessities, an emergency, or to eat. So far he had been lucky and hadn't run into any trouble. Staying the course was his game plan.

Further along Main Street he chuckled at the sign on an old warehouse named Horners, advertising wool and mohair, obviously from the sheep and goat farming once so prevalent.

After crossing the Leona River, it was only a matter of minutes before he came to the edge of the town.

Nico mentally patted himself for making it this far.

On the flat expanses he gained speed only to be beaten back by a slow and torturous climb when he came to a hill. Garnering strength he didn't know he had, he put his head down and leaned into the incline. When the going got tough and when he didn't think he could go any farther, he told himself all he needed to do was to pedal one more time.

One more.

That's all. Just do it.

Over and over until he crested the hill.

With a final push, he took his feet off the pedals, straightened out his legs, and glided down the hill.

The glorious wind cooled him.

He was free, liberated by the struggle.

He had driven these roads many times in the comfort of a car while listening to his favorite CD to pass the time. He had promised himself he would reach San Antonio by early morning on the day he had told Kate he would be back. Nico was a man of his word, and unless he was dead, he was determined to keep that promise.

* * *

The sun slid beneath the horizon, casting long shadows on the land, offering a cool breeze to the weary, hot traveler, and the night came swift and fast, gobbling the last bit of daylight.

Clouds rolled in, obscuring the moon and stars, and without any ambient light, Nico squinted. He nearly fell when his bike hit a branch blown onto the road, and fortunately he was able to keep his balance. A fall resulting in a broken bone could be the death of him.

He desperately needed sleep.

A mile back, he had noticed a sign for a rest stop and was tempted to stop there, ultimately deciding against it. Drunk with fatigue, he'd be an easy target if he fell asleep.

He decided stopping on the far side of the rest stop was the safest thing to do right now, so after a mile or so past it, he glided the bike to the side of the road. Putting the kickstand down, he surveyed the spot.

It was a diminutive valley nestled between rolling hills. Scrub brush and mesquite dotted the dry land. A coyote howled long and lonely in the distance then fell silent, waiting. Soon another one joined in until a chorus of yips and barks filled the bleak silence.

Twenty feet from the road, an oak tree loomed dark in the low light, branches spread out into an even canopy, one magnificent enough for a wilderness painting. Nico decided it would be a safe spot to call home for the night.

From the road he wasn't visible and he had some protection from the tree in case of a sudden shower.

He hopped the fence and lifted the bike over. Like a true professional, he'd staged his pack so the first things needed were at the top of the main compartment or in one of the outer pockets.

He gathered dry, dead wood for a small fire, taking care not to select green or wet wood which could produce smoke that could be seen for miles. Staying undetected was a main priority. He wanted a few coals near him in case the night became cold, but he would extinguish the main fire so that he wouldn't be spotted.

He spread out the bedroll, sat down, and quickly ate the MRE.

Although it wasn't that bad, a candlelight dinner at a white tablecloth restaurant it would never be. He licked the container clean then dug a hole in the ground to bury it. Leaving the countryside littered with trash around indicted the person was trashy.

Nico licked the fork, wiped it with the bottom of his shirt, and put it in his backpack for later use. He spied the package that had originally sent him on the mission to the Rio Grande. Picking it up, he held it in his hand, trying to gauge the weight. Too light for drugs or gold, so what exactly would be so valuable to test his loyalty to Santiago? Santiago was perhaps branching out into diamond smuggling. Nico reached in his pocket and flicked open his clip-it knife. He held the knife to the package and thought about ripping into it to find out. If he did, he'd lose the trust of Santiago, so he flicked the knife shut and put it back into his pocket.

Still hungry, he dug around in the goody bag Vanessa had packed him and found a packet of instant coffee. Using his teeth, he tore off a corner, emptied it into a bottle of water, and shook it. While not exactly Starbucks worthy, it did the trick to satisfy his caffeine craving. He polished off half of the bottle then decided to save the rest for in the morning. After the day he had, he knew he'd need a jolt of caffeine for the last leg of his trip. Considering how tired he was, he had no doubt the caffeine wouldn't interrupt his sleep.

Fortunately bugs were at a minimum on this October day, and a hint of cool autumn air dried the day's sweat. The excitement of the day, and the grueling physical ride added to Nico's exhaustion. He needed a good night's sleep.

He brushed away twigs and rocks on the spot under the tree where he could put his sleeping bag, shook it out, then placed it on the ground. It wasn't cold enough to get inside the sleeping bag, yet if it did get cold, he'd want to cover up quickly so he unzipped it and laid it out, folding the top to make a pillow. He stretched his legs and his arms, yawned wide, and crossed his arms over his chest. He didn't even bother to take off his boots.

He thought about the day, about Tony and Vanessa, the fire, and soon his thoughts wandered to Kate. What exactly did he know about her, the woman who had occupied his thoughts for the past week, the woman he knew was for him? She was from Austin and had worked at the Minor Hotel. She had a service dog, but for the life of him, he couldn't imagine why. She hadn't been in the military, so that wasn't a reason. Some sort of assault maybe? Nah, that couldn't be it either.

There was so much he wanted to know.

When he got back, he'd make that steak he promised then ask her to go to Padre Island.

Nico knew all the good beaches and where the best sand dunes were located. He thought about the warm salty water and the waves breaking over him. It was a place that reinvigorated him, away from the problems and stress of the city, of the drug culture and dealers he dealt with. He needed to get away from that and take Kate with him. She'd feel safe with him and forget about whatever tragedy had forced her to rely on a service dog.

He'd feel the sand between his toes and the sun on his face. He'd dive for sand dollars, show them to Kate, then toss them back into the water where they could grow. So much he wanted to show her.

His eyes became heavy and the tree above him swayed in the breeze, rustling the leaves. Somewhere a coyote howled at the moon, another one joined from a faraway hill until a chorus filled the night.

While Nico slept, the stars became brighter in the sky, and the animals of the night emerged from their dens.

In a nearby pasture an armadillo used its powerful claws to dig for grubs and worms. A raccoon scurried in the brush, searching for insects and crawfish at a nearby creek.

* * *

In the tree above where Nico slept, an owl leapt off a branch and glided on silent wings to another tree. Its eyes were large and round as it observed the land of magnificent oaks and rolling hills; of cactus and cows; of a road cutting the land in half.

Movement caught its eyes and the owl swiveled its head in the direction.

The object was black, about the size of a field mouse, although the shape was different. It was low to the ground and moved over the land with jerky, yet deliberate ease and caution, navigating rocks and cactus, fallen tree limbs, and other obstacles.

The owl pushed off its perch and silently glided toward its prey, sharp talons and legs stretched out in position. Looking down on the hapless prey, the owl descended with the precision of a surgeon's scalpel, dispatching the prey in one deft strike.

Sitting over the crumpled body curled inward, the owl swiveled its head and looked over the gray land, searching for predators. Satisfied it was safe, the owl tore into the soft underbelly, devouring its meal until only fur and other unidentifiable parts were left. Minutes later the owl flew back to the tree it called home. The man sleeping on the ground snored softly. Uninterested in the man, the owl preened its feathers.

The night became darker and stars moved in the heavens. Clouds rolled in, obscuring the ambient light of the moon.

More movement on the ground garnered the owl's attention, and without wasting any time, the owl swooped in to dispatch its prey. It was of the same species it had dined on before and the owl tore into the flesh with ease.

Throughout the night, the owl feasted on the plethora of prey until its belly was full.

Unaware of the cat and mouse game being played out in the pasture, Nico slept soundly and had vivid dreams of Kate. She was splashing in the warm waters of the Gulf of Mexico, laughing and twirling in the surf. The sun was high in the sky and Nico squinted through the glare. She called to him and motioned for him to join her in the water. He went to her and splashed through the shallow, foamy water. She bent down and cupped a handful of water and tossed it playfully at him. He took her in his arms, kissed her fully on the lips, and she responded. They kneeled on the sand, letting soft waves wash over them.

This was how he dreamed of her. This was how life should be.

He whispered something in her ear then nibbled it, running his hands over her back and shoulders, bringing her closer.

Another wave washed over them.

It was warm and tingly.

He kissed her more, but the dreamy moment was interrupted when his leg began itching. In his sleepy state, he reached down to brush away the irritant. Probably seaweed which was prevalent on Padre Island. "Where were we?" he thought he asked. He kissed Kate again then moved his lips to her neck, but now his arm itched so he pulled back from her.

His entire body itched and suddenly the dream was over and he popped open his eyes. Drugged from the heady dream and deep sleep, he thought the imagined itching was from the salt water or microorganisms which could result in an allergic reaction.

But it wasn't a dream.

Something crawled up his arm and he casually brushed it away with his hand. In the moment it took for his mind to register what could have bristly fur, Nico's relaxed expression turned into one of bewilderment. He looked at his hand, and his former expression of bewilderment turned to revulsion. In the dim light he saw a...

A...

A tarantula!

He might have yelled or let out a surprised breath, or said, "What the hell!" but whatever he uttered, Nico shot up like a geyser at the same time he flung the tarantula away.

He looked down at his pants to find three more crawling toward his chest and frantically swiped them away with the back of his hand.

Another one was on his other arm.

One had crawled up on his shirt.

Like a wild man he stomped on the ground and shook his head. He brushed his chest and backside, and with furious hands, he slapped his head then tore off his outer shirt, flinging it to the low hanging branches of the tree.

The ground was alive with thousands of black tarantulas crawling over brush and rocks like something out of a horror movie.

Nico retrieved his shirt and quickly put it on. He grabbed his backpack and slung it over his back, shook out his sleeping bag, and flung it over his shoulder. Taking the handlebars of his bike, he sprinted to the fence. He heaved the bike over, hopped the fence, and navigated the ditch only to find more tarantulas covering the road. The closer ones reared up their front legs in defense while the others scurried across the road. He swore he heard hissing.

Wherever Nico stepped, he winced at the sickening crunch of a tarantula being reduced to a pile of slimy mush of limbs and organs.

He shuddered.

With his sleeping bag over his shoulders, he swung his leg over his bike, pushed forward, and rode through a hundred yard wide swath of tarantulas.

Sweating profusely and pushing the bike to its limit, Nico finally reached the end of the tarantula crossing.

He had completely forgotten about the coffee he had saved for in the morning to give him an extra boost.

He certainly didn't need it now.

CHAPTER 18

It was late morning and miles away from the tarantula migration. Nico had been riding for hours without breakfast or stopping to take a break.

The South Texas sun shined hot and bright in the clear sky.

Asphalt absorbed heat from the sun and released it like a radiator during the day and early evening. Nico became keenly aware of the heat cooking his feet and of the pedals being heated like a barbeque grill.

He glanced at the sky. There wasn't a cloud or a hint of one anywhere along the horizon, and he became innately aware of his thirst and fatigue. Determined to ride as far as he could, he trudged on.

Yards ahead, shimmering heat waves bounced off the road and mirages of puddles of water appeared.

Sweat formed on his forehead and he wiped it away.

He sucked on the CamelBak only to find it empty, and he hated the idea of dipping into his reserve of water with miles to go.

The smooth asphalt road would have been perfect if his journey was on level ground, but Nico was entering the famous Texas Hill Country where each blissful downhill glide was rewarded with an equally leg burning uphill ordeal.

He recalled his one and only time to volunteer for the MS-150 from Houston to Austin. He finished but was in so much pain he could hardly walk for three days. The potential romance with the girl who talked him into riding had fallen through, and he had not been on a bike since then. It had left a bad taste in his mouth. Like those who quit a hard physical activity then take it up again, he wished he had kept in practice.

The tops of his aching thighs reminded him of that with each rotation.

The longer he rode, the more difficult it became, like the bike tires were slogging through glue. Slowing down, Nico glanced at the back tire and swore under his breath. It was going flat. With his energy waning, he needed to stop, find water, eat, and also fix the tire.

So far the trip had been uneventful except for last night's excitement and he hoped it stayed that way. A flat tire was a minor issue, one that could be easily remedied if he had the right tools and materials.

As luck would have it, about half a mile ahead, he spied an old gas station. Coming closer, Nico observed it was made of wood and had probably been built at the time Model Ts were still on the road. Like most stations servicing small country towns, it had two pumps of the analog variety which would qualify as genuine antiques. Profits must have been lean judging by the peeling paint and rotting edges of the wood siding. Considering the events of the past couple of days, curb appeal wasn't a necessity at the moment.

What he needed was full service, and this station fit the bill.

"Welcome" was painted in large bold black letters on one of the wooden posts supporting the overhang, while a stamped metal sign in the window indicated the station was open. A handwritten sign saying, "We Fix Tires" caught his attention.

Excellent.

Regardless of what Nico had told himself he wouldn't do unless there was an emergency, he stopped. On a bike ride, a flat tire counted as an emergency.

He walked the bike toward the gas station. When he got closer an old man sitting in a rocking chair by the front door gave him a curious look then waved him closer.

"It's good to see someone on the road," the old man said. "I'm Wade Greer." He hocked a mouthful of chewing tobacco into a spittoon. With great difficulty, he got up out of the chair and extended a hand to shake.

The old man looked harmless enough in his stained blue denim overalls, work boots, and a short sleeved shirt. Nico reciprocated the welcoming gesture, shook hands, and said, "Nico Bell. Nice to meet you."

"You too," the old man said, grinning, showing a mouthful of tobacco stained teeth.

While shaking hands, that sixth sense Nico had relied on gnawed at his senses. Something wasn't right. There was hesitation in the handshake, not exactly firm or the kind of handshake an old-timer like this guy would offer. Nico discounted the feeling, trying to tell himself he was jumpy because of the tarantulas.

He certainly had the right to be jumpy. Or was there something off about this place?

Nah, it was the tarantulas.

It had to be.

"I was beginning to think I shouldn't have opened up at all this morning," Wade said. "What brings you here?"

"A flat tire. Can you fix it?"

"Sure. Set it to the side of the building and I'll take a look at it in a minute or two. Come in and sit down first. You look tired and thirsty."

"I am."

The old man led Nico into the store, pointing toward the snacks in wire racks. Nico stopped at the beef jerky display to grab half a dozen packages. He picked up a package of pecan sandies for a quick sugar boost when needed, and he selected a two liter bottle of water. He spotted a large bottle of Orange Crush in the cooler being powered by a generator. "I haven't had one of these in ages. Is it still as good as I remember?"

"Take anything you need. It's not like we have any travelers stopping," Wade said. He stepped behind the counter.

"Speaking of that," Nico said, "have you heard anything?"

"There's been talk of an EMP from the Russians or North

137

Koreans. Only old stuff works. How about you?"

"The same." Nico shrugged. While he didn't want to be rude, he sure didn't want to get into a long conversation about conspiracy theories. He was on a mission to get to San Antonio, and shooting the bull with this guy wasn't part of it.

Nico placed his haul on the cracked glass display counter. "I hope I can afford this since credit cards aren't working."

"No profiteering at this store."

Nico glanced at the corner of the store by the front door. A Winchester .30-30 lever action rifle, once the most common truck accessory in Texas, was leaning against the wall.

Wade noticed Nico looking at the rifle. "Don't worry about the rifle, it hasn't moved from that spot in years." On the ancient register Wade manually punched in the prices of the items Nico selected.

"That looks about as old as this place is," Nico said, referring to the cash register.

"Yes, sir, it is old. If it ain't broke, don't fix it, I've always said. I haven't even bothered to upgrade the pumps. It don't affect the bottom line one bit."

"No doubt," Nico replied.

"That'll be $21.98."

Nico pulled his wallet out of his back pocket. "I've only got twenties. Can you make change?"

"Nah, don't worry about it," Wade said waving him off. "A twenty will do. You'll probably need the rest of the money for your trip."

"I appreciate it." Nico handed the twenty over.

"It's nothing." Wade paused, thinking. "You can pay me the balance next time you're back this way." He put the items in a plastic bag.

"I'll take you up on that," Nico said. "I can't thank you enough." He unscrewed the top of the orange soda and took a long pull. Several gulps later, he set the empty glass bottle on the counter. "That hit the spot."

"Have another one," Wade said. "When you're finished, come on out with me and sit a spell while I fix the tire. I need to get a few things then I'll meet you out front."

Popping the top off another Orange Crush, Nico figured he could humor the old man while he fixed the flat. He could use the rest, and the old man would probably do most of the talking. Nico would nod his head every so often or say, "uh huh," pretending to listen.

Nico started for the door, then remembered he had put a five dollar bill in his shirt pocket. Since the old guy had given him a break, Nico decided to return the hospitality by leaving the five on the glass counter as a surprise tip for the friendly old guy. A gust of wind blew into the store, so Nico searched for something to anchor the five with. Spying a stapler, he leaned over the counter, reaching for it.

A look of shock overcame him and he wasn't sure he was seeing correctly. A body was laying lengthwise face down on the floor behind the wooden base of the glass case. Nico grimaced at the pool of brownish dried blood surrounding the dead man's head. He had on work clothes and a red rag stuffed in his back pocket. He was probably the gas station owner.

Nico needed to get out of here.

He looked to the front of the store to confirm the Winchester was still where he last saw it.

It was gone.

Crap. When did that happen?

The old man wasn't as laid back or as dotty as he pretended to be. He must have stealthily swiped the rifle on his way out.

Whatever was going on here, Nico wanted no part of this fight.

The best thing for him to do would be to walk away and pretend he hadn't seen the body. Nico chose which battles to fight and he didn't plan on fighting anyone else's.

He cursed himself. He should have listened to his sixth sense. This place was bad and he needed to get out of there fast.

When Nico turned to leave, he grunted then stumbled from a hard blow from a rifle butt to his head. It was like someone was using his brain for a ping pong table. He reached for his Glock, but his hands went limp at another skull-cracking hit to his head. Lights exploded in front of his eyes and he sensed an immediate foreboding that if he came out of this alive, it would only be because of his determination to live and to see Kate again.

"Kate," he mouthed.

He took a big breath, his eyelids fluttered, and as his eyes rolled into his head he glimpsed Wade. "You bastard."

Nico tried heroically to stay on his feet, but another rifle butt to his forehead caused the lights to go out. His body went limp and he crumpled to the floor with a thud.

CHAPTER 19

Nico woke to a throbbing head and a sick feeling in the pit of his stomach. He opened one eye a slit. He blinked and waited for his fuzzy head to clear. Instinct directed him to be quiet and still in case he was being observed. Taking in his surroundings, he realized his face was mashed into a floor, dirty and cracked from years of use. The rack of chips and candy looked familiar, and his peripheral vision told him he was still in the gas station.

The setting sun created the last long shadows of the day, and Nico figured he had been knocked out for hours. He moved his head and was immediately struck with intense throbbing in his head, a result of the wicked blows he had sustained.

He looked at his arms to find his forearms were duct taped together from wrist to elbow, while his legs were likewise bound from the knees to the ankles. Nico concentrated on his senses and realized his gun and knife were gone.

The door to the station squeaked open, the sound of footsteps echoed in the silence. Nico closed his eyes pretending to be unconscious. Whoever it was stopped inches away from him and kneeled. Nico got a whiff of chewing tobacco.

"You don't need to worry. I know you're awake so you don't need to pretend anymore. You've been moaning for the past half hour. Playing possum with me won't work."

Nico opened his eyes and threw an ice cold stare at Wade.

"Why so surly?"

Nico continued with the icy stare.

"When I come back, I'm going to ask you a few questions then I'll let you go."

Right, like Nico believed that for one second.

"I've got a few of my own. Why'd you kill that guy?"

"Him? That SOB is the grandson of the man who stole my grandpa's ranch, and ever since we've been poor as church mice. My daddy worked himself to death, leaving my mama to clean rich people's houses to feed us. I swore if I ever got the chance, there'd be payback."

"That was two generations ago," Nico said.

"It could be ten for all I care," Wade said. "The result's the same."

"I don't care about your family feud or murdering that guy, untie me and you'll never see me again."

Wade scoffed at the suggestion. "I may be old, but I ain't stupid." He stepped behind the counter, grabbed both feet of the man he had left for dead on the floor, and began the arduous task of dragging dead weight foot by foot across the floor. The old man had to stop midway to take a breather. Nico listened to his wheezing.

"You know the easiest way to get rid of a body?" the old man asked.

"I'm sure you're going to tell me," Nico said.

"Let the coyotes and buzzards do the work. They can pick a corpse clean in a matter of hours until only bones are left, then the coyotes will drag those back to their dens. The buzzards will clean up the rest. They are nature's garbage disposal."

After the short break, Wade resumed dragging the dead man to the front door. While the old man was obviously evil, he was in poor health and no match for Nico, even if he had a concussion and was duct taped.

He'd find a way to free himself.

Nico had been self-sufficient all his life, starting when he was a boy. With his parents working long hours, Nico amused himself by devouring comic books and survival magazines to the point of it being an obsession, much to the chagrin of his parents. He stored away survival tidbits in the recesses of his mind, perhaps thinking one day he might need the knowledge he gained from reading to save his life.

This was one of those times.

While the old man was gone, Nico began to formulate a plan. If he acted quickly, he might stand a chance. Nico flexed his arms to test for any wiggle room.

Zilch.

The duct tape tear trick only worked if there was enough room for movement to get some leverage, and the old man had taped Nico's arms tighter than a mummy being prepared for entombment. He looked around for anything he might use as a weapon. He glanced at the glass case and recalled that it already had a crack in it.

Old style glass, including windshield glass, tended to break into long, sharp pieces. Auto injuries before the 1960s were so horrific that public outcry led to the adoption of safety glass that broke into relatively safe squares of dull glass.

The same was true for display cases. Too many lawsuits of kids crawling onto glass displays, breaking it, and being cut led to safer glass for retail stores, and if this station hadn't even upgraded pumps, no way had the owner upgraded the display case.

Nico inched closer to the display case and swung his bound legs upward toward the glass. The first hit didn't do much so he repositioned himself then threw his legs harder against the glass. It was more durable than he expected. Undeterred, he tried for a third time. He swung his legs up and with momentum on his side, he smashed them into the case, shattering the glass. Large chunks fell inward into the display case while several shards clanged to the floor.

Using his bound hands, Nico picked up a razor-sharp glass icicle. He gingerly placed it between his lips and held it firm with his teeth. Sitting on the floor, he brought his hands to his mouth then began sawing through the sticky tape, fiber by sticky fiber until he was able to move his hands. Then with enough momentum, he jerked his hands to tear the rest of the tape from his forearms.

Working fast, he made quick work of his leg bonds.

Now that he was free, he needed a weapon to protect himself. His guns and knife were nowhere in sight.

Think!

Nico's gaze fell to the broken glass. He selected the longest glass shard from the pile of broken glass, then taking the duct tape he found behind the counter, he wrapped it around one end of the glass to form a makeshift knife handle. Not exactly a Ka-bar, but i would suffice in a pinch.

While Nico was busy freeing himself, Wade had dragged the dead man to a pasture behind the gas station and rolled the corpse between clumps of tall grass. He stood back from the dead man and admired his handiwork with morbid curiosity. Buzzards were already circling overhead, and by nightfall the corpse would be covered in squawking vultures, pecking at the softest parts of the face. If anyone saw the buzzards, they'd probably think it was roadkill the buzzards were after.

Satisfied the corpse couldn't be seen from the road, Wade headed back to the gas station.

The soil was dry and clouds of dust puffed up with each step the old man took.

When Nico heard Wade muttering to himself near the pumps, he scooted to the shadow of a filing cabinet, waiting for an opportunity.

Shuffling toward the front of the station, Wade held the Winchester Model 94 ready for action with the hammer back over a live round. He peeked in through the door and checked in all directions looking for Nico.

"Trying to hide or escape is useless," he bluffed. "Answer a few questions and I'll let you go."

There was no reply.

Frustrated, Wade racked the lever of his Winchester six times, emptying the shells onto the concrete, knowing that if Nico wrestled the rifle away from him, it could be used against him. He picked up the shells and pocketed them. The old man removed Nico's Glock from his pocket and held it close to his chest. A pistol worked better in close quarters.

"Come on, son. Let me cut you loose. This has been a misunderstanding. Here, you can have your gun back." Wade tightened his grip on the Glock.

Crouched against the filing cabinet, Nico held his makeshift knife tight in both hands, listening, waiting. A fly buzzed his bloodied head and face, and he shooed it away. Sweat dripped into his eyes and he blinked it away.

Nico noted the offer of the gun had been completely hollow. He needed a plan to get the old man without getting shot. A bullet wound, even a minor one, could get infected, and in a world where medical treatment was a day away, the wound might not be survivable.

He'd have to strike without mercy. Nico's body tensed, ready to pounce like a hungry lion.

The old man's eyesight and hearing were failing and he strained to listen for any unusual sound. Taking a chance Nico might have already escaped, Wade stepped around the metal filing cabinet, unaware Nico was hiding in the shadows.

In the half light of the darkened room, Nico jumped up and shoved the heavy filing cabinet against the old man.

The force of the cabinet, weighted with hundreds of pounds of receipts and files, slammed into Wade.

The old man lost his balance and fell to the floor.

Unbalanced, the cabinet teetered precariously.

Still gripping the Glock, Wade fired two wild rounds. One hit the ceiling, the other a wall.

With shaking hands, he maneuvered the gun and pulled the trigger again. The Glock fired, blasting through the metal exterior of the cabinet, and the round ended up driving deep into a thick folder of receipts.

Nico put his hands in front of him, leaned into the filing cabinet and gave it a forceful coup de grace shove. The massive filing cabinet fell hard on the old man, drawers opened, spilling papers on the floor.

Nico dove onto the cabinet, adding his weight to the already heavy cabinet, pinning the old man on the floor. Wade grunted under the weight. With the Glock continuing to bark out rounds, Nico jumped onto the old man and jammed his shooting arm to the floor.

Without hesitation or a second consideration, Nico plunged his makeshift glass knife into the old man's throat, twisting it to sever major arteries.

Resistance stopped, and Nico took possession of the now empty

Glock. A gun without bullets was about as useful as a car without gas, so Nico searched the old man, looking for the extra magazines.

Finding them, he took a moment to load the Glock, racked it once, then peered into the chamber to make sure it was loaded properly. He pocketed the extra magazine and the empty one in case he found more 9mm ammo.

Sweating profusely and with his head bleeding, Nico headed to the restroom to assess his injuries. Looking in the mirror, he was unrecognizable. His face was swollen, lips bloodied, his hair matted with dried blood.

He had been so jacked up on adrenaline he didn't realize he had cut his lips with the glass shard that freed him. He thoroughly scrubbed his hands and rinsed them until the day's dirt and grime had been washed away. He wet a paper towel and gingerly dabbed the blood from his lips. Bending over, he gently splashed water over his head to rinse away the blood. He slipped his hand inside his back pocket and retrieved a comb. A few swipes through his hair and he was good to go.

On his way out, he'd grab alcohol and other medicine he might need.

Advil was at the top of the list for his throbbing head, and Vaseline was needed for his bleeding and parched lips.

Nico exited the bathroom and searched the drawers of the counter looking for ammo. In the bottom one he found a box of .30-30 softpoints. He also found a hidden Smith & Wesson 686 .357 Magnum revolver. He put the 686 and the extra .357 ammo in a plastic bag.

A quick search of the station produced a short range 12 gauge stacked with a mop in the broom closet.

Holding the shotgun, he ran a hand over the stubble on his chin thinking about the practicality of carrying two long guns on a bike. He decided a long range response might be more useful in the country, so he placed the shotgun back into the broom closet, then loaded the Winchester to full capacity.

He swiped rubbing alcohol, Advil, and Vaseline. On a lark, he grabbed two cans of Spam and stuffed those in his pockets. He popped two Advil in his mouth and gulped an entire bottle of water. He smeared a copious amount of Vaseline on his lips and decided it was time to leave, except he had forgotten one thing.

The flat tire.

Mumbling, he searched the station for a bicycle tire repair kit. Finding it, he worked in the waning light and patched the tire. He pumped up both tires and decided he'd better go before he encountered any more problems.

He'd had enough excitement for one day.

It was time to finish the last leg of his trip.

Gathering his gear, he turned onto the highway and headed east. The night came swiftly and with it a welcome chill. Taking a chance, Nico rode the entire night, keeping an eye open for trouble. He stopped once when it was necessary to take a breather and to rest his legs. He allowed ten minutes to eat a quick meal and to take care of necessities. The time for sleep could come later because he was worried if he laid down he'd fall asleep, so he mounted the bike and pedaled onward.

At last, he crested a hill and the darkened city of San Antonio came into view. The downtown skyline loomed gray and quiet above the trees and houses of the west side of the city, and nestled among the buildings would be the Minor Hotel, where Kate was.

Where she waited for him.

CHAPTER 20

"Kate," Dan said, "why do you keep going to the front door? Are you looking for someone?"

Dan had made his rounds for the morning, checking rooms for a headcount of the number of guests still in the hotel. All the guests had left except for the Tombstone gang.

Kate was standing near the revolving doors which opened to the street.

Reload stood like a shadow by her side. He had sensed her rising anxiety level and had observed her gazing out the front of the hotel. He knew not what she was looking for, yet sensed a longing in her he had not observed before. Ever since the man had left, Reload had stayed close to her to the point she had nearly tripped over him several times. She opened her mouth to admonish him then changed her mind, talking to him in soothing words.

"He should've been here by now," Kate said.

"Who should've been here?"

"One of the guests who was here last week."

"Which guest?"

Kate didn't answer the question nor did she look to her manager. She kept scanning the street, looking for Nico. Worry spread across her face. "He said he'd be back."

"When?"

"Today."

"Kate, what's going on? Who are you talking about?" Dan asked. "I didn't even know you were seeing someone."

"I'm not."

"I don't understand. Then why are you so worried?"

Kate turned to face Dan. "Because he's worth worrying about, that's why. He said he'd be back, and if he doesn't come back, then something terrible must've happened."

"Do you know him?"

"I know him enough. When he said he'd be back I believed him."

"You have a boyfriend? You never told me."

"He's not my boyfriend," Kate said.

"I don't understand."

Kate opened her mouth to explain the situation when Reload barked loud and commanding. His tail thumped back and forth, and he loped to the door where he huffed a big breath.

The door opened.

Nico stumbled in, took one look at Kate, and collapsed on the floor near a sofa. His face was sunburned and whipped dry by the wind. The wound on his head had opened and blood oozed down the side of his face. His lips were swollen.

Kate ran to him. Bending down, she cradled his head in her arms. "Dan, go get water and some bandages. And antibiotic ointment if you have it. Quickly!"

"Nico, what's wrong? Are you hurt?" Kate asked. She gave him a quick once over looking for more injuries other than the apparent ones.

With great difficulty, Nico said through parched lips, his voice gravelly and raspy, "I tried to get back sooner, but I ran into trouble."

"Are you hurt?"

"No. I'm exhausted and thirsty." Dan came running over with two bottles of water.

"That's all?" Kate gave Dan a look of exasperation. "I need twice as much."

"We're getting low, Kate. We need to conserve water." Dan opened a water bottle and handed it to Nico. "Drink this. Not too fast, though."

While Nico sipped the water, Kate used a little to wash her hands then poured the remaining water on his head wound to wash away dirt matted into the blood.

"Go easy on the water," Dan cautioned. "We need to be careful with our remaining supply."

She patted the wound dry with one of the sterile bandages then gently covered it with the antibiotic ointment. "You've got a nasty gash. How'd it happen?"

Nico didn't answer.

"Nico?" Kate asked.

"I think he's fallen asleep," Dan said. "He must be exhausted, and from the looks of it, he's had a difficult time. Something bad must have happened to him. Where's he been?"

"He said something about going to the border to get tile for a client."

"I doubt that was why he went there. I'm not sure what his profession is, but I doubt a tile guy would be carrying the kind of weapons he has." Dan noted the rifle and pistol Nico had carried in. "You think he walked all the way here?"

"I don't know. Check the sidewalk if he has a bike or motorcycle."

Dan did as Kate asked, came back inside, shaking his head. "There's nothing. If he had a bike, he's lost it."

Nico jerked awake. "What, what did you say?" He sat up and leaned his back against the sofa. He rubbed his eyes. "How long have I been out?"

"Only a few minutes," Kate said. "You need to rest."

"I can't. I've got to deliver a package." Using the sofa for leverage, Nico pushed up into a kneeling position. He breathed hard then stood, unprepared when stars appeared in his vision. He put a hand to his forehead. "I'm so lightheaded."

Dan acted on instinct and looped an arm around Nico, holding him up. Kate did the same. "Sit on the sofa," Dan instructed.

Kate and Dan coaxed Nico to sit. Kate retrieved a decorative pillow from one of the chairs and told Nico to lie down. She put the pillow under his head then lifted his feet and put them on the sofa.

"You need to rest."

He nodded. "Don't let anyone walk off with my backpack."

"I won't. I'm going to stay here with you. I don't think anyone will steal it."

Dan added, "Only the Tombstone guys are left."

Kate studied Nico's face and wondered what had happened to him. Whatever it was, it must have been some kind of horrific battle for his life. She leaned closer to Nico. He had already fallen asleep.

"Kate," Dan said, "you need to rest too."

She waved him off. "I'm not sleepy. I'll stay here with him until he wakes up. From the way he looks, he might sleep for long while."

* * *

While Nico slept on the sofa in the lobby, Kate didn't leave his side. She sat on the sofa and cradled his head in her lap.

Reload sat quietly at Kate's feet and when one of Nico's arms dangled to the side of the sofa, Reload licked his hand, gaining valuable information about him. He tasted the struggle Nico had been through, some type of herculean effort of a life and death fight, exhausting the man into a state of deep sleep Reload had not known was possible. Reload licked Nico's hands again and waited for a response. When there was none, he looked to Kate, who had calmed down while in the presence of Nico. It strengthened her resolve, a characteristic Reload hadn't sensed before.

Occasionally, Nico mumbled in his sleep and when he did, Reload perked up his ears, trying to discern the meaning of the garbled words. Finding none, he put his muzzle back onto his paws.

During the week that Nico had been gone, Reload had become accustomed to the Tombstone Gang, and while he did not know the names they answered to, Reload recognized each from their own unique scent.

They had qualities similar to Nico in the sense the men worked together for a common goal. There had been no quarreling or posturing for dominance, only a respect for each other, the same respect Nico and Kate showed each other. During the time Nico slept, the Tombstone men filed past Kate and Nico, greeting her with a dip of a chin or speaking in quiet tones. Kate indicated no adverse reaction to their presence, so Reload acted accordingly, letting them pass without interference.

* * *

Later, Dan came up to them, stopped, and asked Kate how things were going.

"Okay, I suppose. I think Nico is starting to wake up."

"I'm awake. How long have I been out?" Nico yawned long and wide.

"A while," Kate replied.

"Do you need anything?" Dan asked.

"Another bottle of water would be great," Nico said.

"Fresh water is becoming a real problem. We've gone through it faster than I thought we would."

Sitting up, Nico rubbed the sleep out of his eyes and ran his hand through his hair. "I can make a filter system."

"You can?" Dan asked incredulously.

"Yes." Nico yawned again and rubbed his eyes. "I need as many five gallon plastic buckets you can find. Several dozen would do. I'll also need door screen, gravel, fine fabric, sand, charcoal, and unscented bleach. I'll stage it so it'll be ready for boiling."

"That sounds labor intensive."

"It will be," Nico said. "First you filter out the big impurities with the screen wire mesh. Then you drill a hole in the bottom of several buckets, place the fine fabric over the hole, and make a multi-stage filter by adding alternating layers of charcoal, fine sand, coarse sand, and gravel. Each layer will catch impurities so that the water that flows out of the filter is ready for boiling. If you want to store it for an extended period, just add eight drops of bleach to each gallon."

Dan mulled over Nico's suggestion. "I feel like I just got a doctorate in hydrology, but we still need to find another source for water."

Nico thought a while and suggested it might be possible to use some of the Riverwalk water.

It was river water, channeled in from the San Antonio River into a three foot deep, twenty foot wide concreted channel which snaked through the tangle of restaurants and hotels lining the Riverwalk. It created a tropical atmosphere suitable for magnolia trees and vines, and provided a perfect tourist attraction.

Dan nixed the idea. "Too much runoff from oil and transmission fluid from cars. Every time it rains, the runoff contaminates the water. Plus I've seen dead bats floating in it."

"Dead bats!" Kate exclaimed. She had a look of disgust on her face.

"Yeah," Dan said, "they roost under the bridges at night and when they die, they fall into the water. Mostly the fish eat them."

"That's so disgusting." Kate wrinkled her nose at the thought. "Come to think of it, I've seen a drowned rat a time or two."

"Me too," Dan added. "No Riverwalk water for us. If you have any ideas about where to get water, I'm all ears."

"What about the water channeled down from one side of the Hyatt then to the other? It's the area on the other side of the plaza. I think it's self-contained and doesn't flow into the Riverwalk."

Dan ran a hand over his chin, thinking. "The water does have a green tint probably due to chlorine. The other day I noticed the ferns and larger plants had been torn out along the walkways. Someone planted vegetables there."

"So unless there is a no trespassing sign, I don't know why we can't use some of the water. Chlorine will eventually evaporate."

During a lull in the conversation, the man who went by the name Virgil Earp stopped to inquire what everyone was talking about.

"I couldn't help but to hear y'all talking about water," Virgil said. "Maybe we can trade with the Hyatts and Crocketts. I think the water you're talking about now is under the turfdom of the Hyatts."

"Who are the Hyatts and Crocketts?" Nico asked.

"Possibly gangs from what we've been able to scout. We believe it's the name they are calling themselves. Both hotels have been taken over, and all the management has left."

"Really?" Nico was all ears hearing about the offer to trade.

"They have signs posted saying trade/barter is available at the Hyatt mall level, but to leave long guns at home."

"What do we have to trade?" Nico asked.

Virgil explained after hotel guests had left, they went through each room looking for items of use. In one of the rooms, a guest had left a shipment of Photon keychain lights used for marketing purposes. He estimated a thousand lights were not yet activated, explaining that, in order to activate the lights, the only requirement was to remove a plastic tab, which activated a light powered by a lithium coin cell. "Considering most of the flashlights aren't working, I think we can use the Photon lights to trade."

After some discussion, they decided to trade several hundred Photon lights. Virgil told everyone to stay where they were while he retrieved the lights.

While Virgil was gone, Nico snacked on food he still had left in his backpack. He also noted the package he had been sent to collect at the border was still in his backpack.

Although he had promised to deliver the package to Marisa the moment he returned, he decided it could wait.

CHAPTER 21

Marisa Sanchez was sitting on a vanity stool in the master bathroom of her house, located in a trendy gated community in San Antonio. The shower had been running a while, filling the bathroom with hot mist. Marisa didn't like cold baths, so she had elaborately prepared for any type of contingency that might force her to take a cold bath. Money was no problem for her so she had bought an industrial sized generator, had it trucked in, and placed in the backyard. She also had a private well dug on her property, much to the dismay of local officials.

One side of her lips tilted up into a wicked grin. Everyone could be bought, and city officials were some of the easiest, especially when dangling thousands of dollars in front of them.

By the time the well would be shuttered, Marisa would be long gone to another bigger and fancier house.

They had lived in a two room shack in a barrio slum where Marisa shared a mattress with her mother and brother, younger by a decade. The father had never been in the picture. Money was scarce and Marisa and her brother never had enough to eat. School lunches were her favorite part of the day, the part where she would finally get enough to fill her.

Her mother toiled long hours as a maid at a seedy hotel. Tips were left in nickels or dimes, when they were left at all. To supplement their income, Marisa's mother had taught her children how to look for loose change under vending machines and under cars, and on Saturdays the three would take a bus to a big mall where they scoured the parking lot looking for dollar bills a careless shopper had dropped. A twenty dollar bill would feed the family for a week, and once when Marisa had found money but had not turned it over to her mother, Marisa had been beaten.

Marisa had grown up looking at the ground. Although she now had millions in the bank, she couldn't force herself to stop looking at the ground for a coveted twenty. Old habits died hard.

A bath back then consisted of a tub of cold water and a flimsy bar of used hotel soap her mother pocketed when cleaning rooms at the hotel where she worked. She collected slivers of soap, then melted them together to form a useable bar.

Marisa now only used expensive soap she bought from an upscale department store.

After a particularly harsh winter when her childhood home had stayed damp and cold, Marisa vowed right then and there she would do whatever was necessary to escape her pitiful existence. Since drugs were rampant, Marisa learned how to grow marijuana and to run drugs in her neighborhood. She quickly earned a reputation as being ruthless with anyone who tried to infringe on her territory.

There were rumors if anyone got in her way, they disappeared.

The operation from a backyard marijuana farm turned into buying a remote property where she farmed the illegal crop. Then she moved on to deal harder drugs and even harder people. Her territory grew.

Nobody messed with Marisa.

She looked fretfully at her hairbrush and the amount of hair in it. A long ago memory flashed in her mind of her mother brushing her hair, telling her it was part of her beauty. "Don't ever cut it short, Marisa," she had said in a thick Spanish accent, "because if you do, it will never grow back to the way it was. A woman needs her beauty regardless if she is eight or eighty."

Maybe the amount of lost hair was a sign she was getting a little older. Or was it a sign of something else? She wouldn't consider the "something else", she couldn't or wouldn't. She was only in her mid-forties. There was work left to do, especially with the hotels near the Alamo.

Removing her plush bathrobe, Marisa stepped into the shower where she could forget about the past and plan for the future.

Her spies at the Alamo had told her Nico had made it back safely to the Minor Hotel, somewhat worse the wear, but still carrying a backpack. The spies had been given strict instructions not to intervene or harm him in any way.

He had something she needed, and was the type of man who could help her accomplish her plans.

Her empire was still growing, she had work to do, and Nico was shaping up to be the man she needed.

She was tired of being alone, having to run the operation all by herself. She trusted no one except her brother, who she had taken care of after her mother passed away. Marisa was like a second mother to her brother, but regardless of how much she pleaded with him, he always got into trouble. And the scar on his face made him too recognizable. How foolish it was of him to rob tourists in broad daylight. If he didn't straighten up, he might disappear too.

Family or not, Marisa had an empire to protect.

Loyalty only went so far.

CHAPTER 22

Virgil returned with a couple hundred Photon lights. "I think this'll do it," he said holding up two bags of the lights.

"You ready, Virgil?" Nico asked.

"As ready as I'm gonna be."

"I'll come too," Kate said.

"No, absolutely not. It's too dangerous." Nico looked to Virgil for reinforcement.

"Kate, listen to Nico." Virgil put a hand on Kate's shoulder. "We can't afford to have anything happen to you. Besides, I think there will be plenty of action later. If something happens to us, you can come rescue us."

"Don't make fun of me."

"I'm not. You'd be the best person to organize a rescue." Virgil gave Kate a reassuring smile.

"Alright. I'll stay here. Dan and I will keep an eye out for you."

Nico cast a serious glance at Virgil. "We are going into the unknown and we don't know what to expect. I need you to watch me like a hawk. If I draw my gun, you do the same. If I start shooting that's your signal to start shooting. We're not looking for trouble, but we should be prepared."

"I'll follow your lead, but don't underestimate me."

Nico wasn't sure what to think about the statement, but decided to keep his thoughts to himself. Virgil appeared to be a competent man.

Virgil said, "Let's step over to the check-in desk. I've got something to show you." Walking in step, Virgil had noticed Nico's belt was heavy with loaded magazines.

"What are you packing?" Nico inquired.

"SIG P220 in .45 ACP loaded with Federal HST rounds."

"Good choice. The SIG is eight plus one isn't it?" Nico already knew the answer to the question, he was only making small talk. Nico's Glock held seventeen plus one of law enforcement grade ammo.

"Yes," Virgil confirmed. "That's why I carry two of them." Virgil didn't know if Nico was trying to be sarcastic with the eight round magazine remark, but he knew he had won the exchange. Virgil was carrying two large caliber guns to Nico's single high capacity gun. "By the way, you look a bit light. How about some extra magazines for your Glock plus an extra Glock for those magazines?"

"Sure. I can always use extra ammo."

"Be back in a moment."

While Virgil was gone, Kate and Nico talked for a while about nothing of any real consequence. It was small talk normally saved for cocktail parties. Pleasantries and other meaningless chatter meant to put the other person at ease or to elicit a laugh. It worked because by the time Virgil reappeared, Kate was laughing.

"What do you have there?" Nico asked.

"Eight loaded Glock magazines in Kydex pouches." Virgil handed them to Nico.

"Man! I had no idea you were so well supplied. Did you raid a gun shop before I got here?"

"No. I'm a Federal Firearms License holder," Virgil explained. "FFL for short. San Antonio is a great place to shoot with its world class ranges. I bring my best inventory here and usually sell out by the end of our club's annual rally. A lot of the members are accomplished shooters."

"I would have never guessed it," Nico said. He finished threading the last magazine pouch Virgil gave him onto his belt then plucked out a magazine and popped out a round. "This is Cor-Bon. You like the good stuff. Many thanks!"

"Glad you like it. Guess money's no good anymore, so you'll just have to save my life someday to make it even."

Nico was uncertain if Virgil was serious or only kidding. It took time to get to know a person, but from first impressions, Virgil was a stand up guy.

"Here's the little extra I promised. It'll use the same magazines you have on your belt." Virgil handed Nico an item wrapped in cloth.

Taking it, Nico suspected what it was by the weight and feel of it. Carefully, Nico unwrapped the item to find a loaded Glock 26, 9mm, in a DeSantis pocket holster. Christmas had come early. The Glock 26 was surprisingly accurate despite its size. Nico placed the holstered Glock into his front left pocket. It was a tight fit, but he could draw it quickly if he needed to in an emergency.

Kate had been standing to the side with Dan, watching the entire transaction. She was quite comfortable around guns, having grown up shooting with her dad and brothers, yet she didn't have a good feeling about any of this.

"Let me come with you," Kate pleaded.

"No, Kate. We've already gone over this," Nico said.

Kate's shoulders shrunk down at the thought she'd be left behind.

"You stay here with Dan."

"I can't stay," Dan said. "I told my wife I'd come home. I've done what I can for the hotel. All the guests have left except for you two and the Tombstone guys. There's really nothing left for me to do."

"You got kids?" Nico asked.

"I do."

"Then you need to go to them. Don't waste any time and don't make any excuses for what you need to do. We all understand. You've already gone above and beyond what any hotel manager would've done in a situation like this."

"Thanks, I appreciate it." Dan turned to Kate. "I have to leave now."

163

"I know. It's okay."

"Good luck to you, Nico." Dan extended a hand. Nico grasped it, gave him a firm handshake, and patted him on the shoulder. Without another word, Dan slipped out of the hotel and disappeared along the sidewalk.

"You and Virgil better get going," Kate said. She turned away, afraid her expression would betray her thoughts. The last thing she wanted to do was to distract Nico. She called Reload, who was sniffing a potted plant for some reason. He loped over to her and waited for instruction. Kate scratched him on the head and said, "Come." They left the lobby and headed to the front desk.

* * *

Standing at the front desk, now deemed the "Ready" table set up for anyone who needed to grab a few loaded magazines in an emergency, Kate removed a sheet placed on top, folded it, and set it aside. Morgan had the idea for magazine resupply so he commandeered the marble check-in desk, filling it with fully loaded AR-15, SIG, Glock, 1911, and a few CZ magazines.

She scanned the table and picked up three Glock 17 magazines, tested their combined weight, then placed them in the left pocket of Reload's service dog vest. She tilted a long 40 round Magpul Pmag into the right side pocket for balance.

She patted Reload on the head. "Now you'll live up to your name." The big dog started to roll his body from side to side like he was shaking water off from a bath, but Kate put her hands on his sides to prevent him. "No," she said firmly. "You'll get used to it."

Kate checked her own Glock 19, a mid-sized fifteen plus one round 9mm pistol that used the slightly longer seventeen round magazines of the Glock 17 as well as the less common thirty-three round Glock 18 magazines. Interchangeability of magazines between the three was an added bonus to the Glocks.

Virgil and Nico headed to the hotel bar then exited the side door, which led to the street facing the south side of the Alamo. They crossed the empty street and traversed the stone steps leading to the Alamo Plaza. The walkway ahead of them contained various tourist shops peddling clothes and other wares, including a place for the well-heeled to rent Segways. Beyond was the Hyatt where their plan would take them to the Riverwalk level mini-mall.

"Hyatt Trade Fair" was crudely painted in large capital letters on the faux stone walls. The "No Long Guns" warning had been spray painted in big black letters on the face of a mural, destroying its beauty. Whoever painted the signs had no respect for art, property, or the law, and probably didn't think before acting, resulting in Nico's resolve to act decisively increasing a few notches.

Stepping away from the street, they came to the stairs leading down to the Riverwalk level. A voluminous amount of water cascaded over several concrete steps, emptying into a larger concrete pool located below street level. The water was then channeled to the Hyatt before being recycled. Tables had been placed curbside so tourists could have a leisurely meal or beverage. Planters, formerly decorated with ferns, now showed the first growth of vegetables.

Nico took in the pleasant smell of clean water, a definite improvement over the foul looking Riverwalk water in the canal. Both men nodded to each other in an approving way. This was the water they needed.

Nico and Virgil navigated the stairs adjacent to the cascading water, then headed to the mini-mall below the Hyatt.

They stopped short of the glass wall and doors, noting the Hyatt men were heavily armed, including with the long guns Nico and Virgil were prohibited from carrying.

Nico made one last remark before he opened the glass door. "If things go bad, I'll handle the left and you handle the right."

Virgil gave a slight nod, indicating he understood.

* * *

A large man leaning against a wall watched Nico and Virgil enter through the doors. He took a last drag of a cigarette, tossed it to the floor, then rubbed it out. At first look, the guy appeared to be a teenager, but on closer inspection he had a hardened expression of a man who had seen and done things…bad things.

Nico didn't take his eyes off him for one second.

It became a duel of matching of eye contact to determine who would back down first, and while Nico never backed down from a challenge, he decided to let the other guy feel like he was in control.

Nico casually flicked his eyes in another direction.

"I'm Manuel. You here to trade?"

"We are," Nico confirmed. "We saw your signs and are interested in the water." In the moment the seedy-looking guy digested the information, Nico was mentally running through scenarios on how he would handle Manuel if the situation required it. The Cold Steel Tanto on his belt indicated Manuel was the kind of guy who could handle knives deftly.

Nico was on full alert.

There were three more men to the left and four men on the right. They were armed with military styled weapons such as AR-15s, AKs, and Galils. Manuel appeared to be armed with twin .44 Magnum revolvers.

"Come on over," Manuel said, disarmingly pleasant.

Nico and Virgil took a few steps toward the table while keeping an eye open on the rest of the thugs.

Virgil placed a package on the table, opened it up, and handed a Photon light to Manuel. "Squeeze the top button towards the bottom."

"I'm not stupid. I know what these things are." Manuel roughly grabbed the light.

Virgil flicked a quick glance at Nico.

Manuel tried out the light. "I've seen better."

Nico said nothing, recognizing the guy was posturing for a better deal. "Here, take a few more."

Manuel passed the lights to his men who played around with the new toys, shining the blinding beam into each other's eyes until he said, "Enough!"

Nico started his pitch. "These lights use lithium batteries so they'll last ten to twelve years. It's also possible to replace the batteries by—"

"I've heard enough," Manuel said, cutting off Nico. "What do you want for them?"

"I need access to the water without being harassed. I'll trade—"

"I make the deals here, not you. And I also run the Hyatt. I'll give you two gallons of water for all your lights. And I want your pistols too."

Nico took a step forward. "Those aren't for trade. The lights are for trade. Each one is valuable and worth more than gold."

"Gold?" Manuel said laughing, exposing a broken tooth, probably a casualty of a fight. He held a hand up and gestured with it. He had been studying the occupants of the Minor Hotel for some time and had planned for attack if the occupants looked weak. Severe need for water indicated the best time for attack.

Thirty armed Hyatt soldiers stationed outside the building next to the river snapped to attention when Manuel signaled them.

Nico's instinct kicked in and he took a step back. Virgil mirrored his movements as he observed an army of men by the river ready themselves for some kind of attack.

CHAPTER 23

After Nico and Virgil exited the Minor Hotel, Kate had scrambled to a ledge hidden by trees at the Alamo Plaza. Safely hidden, she used binoculars to track Nico and Virgil walking to the place designated as the trading area.

Scanning the area in front of the men, a man standing in the shadows came into focus. What was he doing there? Was he a lookout or something else? Kate scrutinized him through the binoculars and when he turned around, she jerked back. He appeared to be looking straight through her. Instinctively, she ducked, trying to comprehend his face. She furrowed her brow and flashes of memories came to her.

The scream, the shot, the blood.

She couldn't be wrong. But maybe she was. She had to be sure. She peeked her head above the ledge and took another look through the binoculars.

Even at the long distance, her gaze went directly to the scar.

That scar.

The one she couldn't forget. The one burned into her memory

on that fateful day.

For a moment she froze, captured by the helpless feeling and memories, and how those memories had been a scourge on her life. At first she wanted to flee, captured by the flight response of fight or flight. She wanted to get far away from here and from the man, but something washed over her, a powerful force which activated the fight response.

Damn him! From this moment on, she was determined not to be the gazelle. She was the leopard now and he was the prey.

It was an empowering feeling, and she embraced it completely.

Instead of fleeing for her own safety, she thought of Nico and what he had gone through to come back to her. He would expect her to act accordingly.

The man was still standing in the shadows so Kate swiveled the binoculars to where Nico was.

With steadfast fortitude, she steadied her gaze, intent on observing so she could help Nico. His life would depend on it.

She tracked back to where the man with the scar had last been. He wasn't there! She scanned the area looking for him. He must have slipped away. She turned her attention back to Nico and Virgil.

While she couldn't hear the conversation, she inferred from body language the trade was not going as planned. She observed the subtle gesture the leader made, and saw two rifle-carrying snipers appear on the rooftops adjacent to the walkway leading to the Hyatt.

Kate eased off the ledge and ran low to the ground, keeping close to the Alamo side. She dashed across the street, hugged the wall of the Minor Hotel, then slunk around the corner until she was at the main entrance. Rushing through the revolving door, she quickly got the attention of Johnny Ringo and Doc, who were sitting in the lobby near the front desk.

Breathless, Kate blurted, "Nico and Virgil are in trouble. They are in danger of being rushed by a small army and are about to be ambushed by snipers."

Johnny rocketed up like an Army officer. He snapped out an order. "Weapons hot. We'll have full discretion."

Like true riflemen, Johnny and Doc had their rifles with them.

"On it now!" Doc yelled.

Johnny carried a five shot bolt action Remington Model 700 heavy barrel .308 with a Leupold scope. Doc used a Les Baer Target

AR in 5.56 with a Nightforce scope. For his rifle, Johnny used 168 grain Federal 308M while Doc used Black Hills 77 grain Open Tip Match. Both of their guns used Sierra MatchKing bullets.

"Kate," Johnny said, "I have an extra AR-15. Take it. Do you know how to use it?"

Kate nodded.

"For a good hit from your position, raise the reticle up to the second crosshair and fire."

"Thanks," Kate said. She slung the rifle over her shoulder.

The two men sprinted to positions on the short wall of planters on the Alamo Plaza. They had good cover, although they would have to use a sitting shooting position to best utilize it. They decided to wait for some sign Nico and Virgil were exiting the building before making their shots. An early shot might cause the Hyatts to put more men on the roof.

Kate sprinted down the hallway and headed to the bar where she asked Morgan to tell everyone to get ready for a major attack. Morgan quickly gathered the men, assigning them to defensive positions in preparation for an attack.

"In case of a prolonged attack, be sure to get extra food and water. Ammo too!" Kate yelled. "We don't know how long this will take. It's better to have extra than not enough."

The Tombstones filled their magazines and put packs together to prepare for an evacuation. Morgan filled a large duffel bag with freeze dried meals, bottled water, gun oil, magazines, Ka-Bar knives, and ammunition in order to meet the needs of Nico and Virgil if they made it back. This duffel had rollers so he could move it himself with one hand if needed. He got two men to carry extra rifles for Nico and Virgil.

* * *

The sun beat down in soaring temperatures on the two Hyatt snipers positioned on the roof, which acted like a conductor for the sun, and shimmering heatwaves danced their misery on the roof. Unprepared for the heat, sweat stained the snipers' shirts and stung their eyes. Thirst became a problem and a distraction for the two men, both unaware Tombstone snipers had been assigned to punch their tickets.

While waiting, Johnny Ringo's mind started to wander. He wasn't a real sniper, rather someone who had won more than his share of NRA rifle matches. A one hundred and ten yard shot would be ridiculously easy for a man with his marksmanship ability, so worry about missing did not enter his mind. For Johnny, time passed agonizingly slowly, especially since his legs were cramping, and he silently cursed himself for being too zealous over conserving water. He licked his parched lips.

Positioned next to Johnny, Doc was thinking about the shot and how it could go wrong. His mind raced with different scenarios of potential last minute problems, including the arrival of more snipers, or his targeted sniper moving to a position with more cover. Doc had prepared with thirty rounds of the best ammunition available for his quick firing semi-automatic action, allowing him to help Johnny if he became overwhelmed with additional targets.

* * *

Nico had to come up with a plan fast. The Hyatt men on each side were positioned to take out Nico and Virgil without endangering Manuel with their fire. Nico decided to reset the table.

"Manuel," Nico said, "we'll take you up on your offer. Shall we put everything over here on the table?" He moved toward it, not waiting for Manuel to answer.

Virgil stepped inward with Nico.

Manuel was dumbstruck at the ease in which Nico had accepted his deal. "Lightweights," he muttered under his breath. His men swung their rifles, following Nico and Virgil, not realizing they and Manuel were now in a crossfire situation.

"Stop!" Manuel yelled. "Don't you idiots know what you're doing?"

His men came to stiff attention, waiting for the next order from Manuel. They were essentially frozen in confusion.

Nico recognized adding to his enemy's reaction time could give him a decisive advantage. Without any further hesitation, he drew both his guns, brought them up, and bullets started to fly. Virgil followed suit and drew both his SIG P220s.

Manuel regretted his previous choice of words and the blind obedience of his men taught to act on command instead of by their own volition as they were now taking fire.

"Kill them!" Manuel ordered.

Most gunfights were won or lost based on a half second of time. Virgil and Nico had the advantage of the slight lead. Manuel's men had all taken at least one hit, and they pulled triggers wildly in a futile effort to hit their targets. Caught in the crossfire, several of the Hyatt men went down.

Nico yelled, "Head shots!" In the melee and confusion, tunnel vision took over. Nico carefully aimed at each of his targets, taking a mere second or less to sight the opposition with his gun.

Before Manuel could pull the trigger on his Smith & Wesson .44 Magnums, he took a 9mm round between the eyes. He crumpled to the floor.

Standing over the big man, Nico said, "No matter how much muscle you have, your skull is till the same thickness as everyone else's."

"I got four of them with my .45s," Virgil said.

"The big guy counts as two," Nico said. He stopped to collect the .44s and the shoulder holsters. "These are some of my favorites."

Nico and Virgil had to leave quickly before reinforcements came. With their packs on, they turned their attention to the rifles of the fallen guards, several of which were damaged in the crossfire. Virgil found an AR-15 clone with holes in the handguard, but otherwise fully functional. Nico collected the only remaining functional rifle, a Galil ARM. It looked like a well-built milled AK-47, firing 5.56 ammo and had a bipod in its forearm.

Virgil's ears picked up sounds that were getting closer. "We've been made. Hurry!" Virgil and Nico adjusted the combat slings and opened the glass doors. They looked around cautiously, moving slowly into the outdoors. It was quiet. Too quiet.

A speedy exit sounded like the best plan, and they had to find cover fast.

Both men burst through the glass doors. Virgil jumped into the freshwater pool on his right, while Nico followed suit. A volley of shots filled the air, peppering the glass doors, disintegrating them into a pile of broken glass and bent metal frames.

Virgil and Nico made themselves small, submerging in the shallow pool, with only the topmost portion of their heads vulnerable to incoming fire.

Shots rang out.

Puffs of concrete particles raining down on them indicated the aim of the Hyatt reinforcements was improving.

Johnny Ringo and Doc Holiday saw the Hyatt snipers snap to attention as if they had seen a target of opportunity. With their scopes trained on their targets, all they needed was a trigger press. Johnny and Doc shot in tandem with perfect precision. The Hyatt snipers disappeared, leaving a trail of pink mist wafting in the air.

Johnny and Doc exchanged satisfied glances.

* * *

"Wait," Virgil said. "Did you hear that?"

"I think we just got our asses saved." Nico caught movement out of the corner of his eye and turned around. "Run!"

Armed men appeared near the obliterated glass doors of the Hyatt hotel, shooting while they walked.

Nico and Virgil rocketed out of the shallow pool and dashed to their friends.

Johnny and Doc were now standing in the open to get a clear shot at the Hyatts to cover Nico and Virgil's suicide dash to them.

The two men ran for their lives across the plaza. When they came to where Johnny and Doc were, they slid into position, taking cover behind the low concrete wall.

"Glad you made it," Johnny said while Nico and Virgil caught their breath. "Next time you should duck so we don't have to expose ourselves."

"Point taken," Virgil replied. "We need to get to the hotel and help with the defense."

"No objection, although I'm about out of ammo," Nico said.

Johnny and Doc confirmed they were low too.

"Now you're going to find out why having an FFL can be helpful," Virgil offered. "Follow me to the parking lot."

* * *

During the lull in shooting, a second wave of the Hyatts took cover along the facade of the hotel. The remaining Hyatt gang was progressing toward the Alamo.

The Hyatt group at the front of the Minor Hotel was preparing to enter the hotel.

A man known only by the name of Brick had taken charge after Manuel was killed. The big man who lived on the fringes of society and who only took orders from Manuel gave mercy to no one.

A woman who had been observing the charge from a safe corner of the plaza, emerged. She wore tattered clothes, had her face covered with a scarf, and at first glance she had the appearance of a homeless woman. The ease with which she walked indicated otherwise.

She came up to Brick. "Have you found him yet?"

"No, but we will."

"These will help you." The woman handed Brick a wooden box. Brick's powerful hands ripped off the top to expose a box of grenades.

"Where'd you get this?" Brick asked.

"I have my sources."

"Are they good?"

"Would you expect anything else of me?" the woman said coyly.

An evil grin spread across Brick's face. "These are worth at least five men." He threaded four grenades to the front of his belt.

"Find him and bring him to me."

CHAPTER 24

Brick gave the order to storm the hotel. Shots echoed from inside the hotel lobby as the group breached the revolving door. Two Tombstone guards were killed immediately with overwhelming fire.

Frank, Jesse, and Billy took over the firefight while the other Tombstones retreated to the bar.

Kate and Reload were with the group in the bar. Her eyes darted around the room, mentally counting heads looking for Jesse and Frank. Confusion and panic gripped her, momentarily unaware Reload was by her side, nudging her with his nose. When Kate didn't respond to his nudging, he took her hand gently in his mouth. She let out a heavy sigh and patted the big dog on his head. "It'll be okay. Stay by my side. Okay?"

Reload sensed the gravity of the situation and didn't break eye contact with Kate. Not the kind of dog to be gun shy, he still needed her instruction.

Putting on a brave face, Kate hid the fact she was fighting off both the demons of her past and the demons at the door, while taking the time to comfort her dog and give him direction.

Kate stood to address the group. "Does everyone have their packs ready?"

A chorus of low mumbled affirmations followed Kate's question.

"Good."

More shots rang out.

Kate screamed, "To the Alamo! Now. Grab what you need!"

Kate slung a pack over her shoulder and grabbed two large white food grade buckets, already filled with necessities.

The group hastily filed out the door leading to the street, ran low to the ground keeping to the south wall of the Alamo, then darted around the corner and to the main entrance. One of the men heaved open the heavy wooden doors and ran inside. Like a true leader, Kate waited at the entrance until all the group was safely inside. She instructed Reload to follow the men.

She took one last sweep of the plaza and stopped in her tracks when she saw the man with the jagged scar standing in the shadow of a tree. He was the same man she had seen earlier. In the moment it took her to recognize him, she relived the absolute terror of that day, the life lost, and a life she would never lead. It had nearly destroyed her, and she had rehearsed in her mind what she would do if she ever saw him again. What would she say to him? What would he say to her? Would he even remember her?

Knowing Nico was fighting for her and for the lives of others awakened in her courage and determination hiding deep in her essence. It had been there the entire time, waiting to reappear, to break through the avalanche of emotions burying it.

In the moment she recognized him, she knew what she had to do.

In the moment it took her to act, he recognized her, and she saw terror flicker in his eyes, the same terror she had experienced and was about to unleash on him.

In one deft movement, Kate brought up her rifle, sighted the man, and pulled the trigger. Known to be a crack shot with any type of pistol or rifle, the man was dead before he hit the ground.

"That was for Ben," she whispered.

Gathering a new resolve and determination, Kate shut the heavy wooden door and entered the main building of the Alamo, a revered historical symbol of sacrifice and honor of brave men fighting for what they believed in.

The cavernous space, two stories high, contained little in the form of amenities. Limestone walls more than three and a half feet thick kept the space at a constant temperature year round. An empty desk sat to the side of one wall where normally an officer in uniform was stationed. The stone floor was hard and dusty, along with the walls. Several small rooms containing artifacts abutted the main room. Light from windows near the ceiling illuminated the scaffolding still in place from recent repairs.

Kate recognized the spirituality of the Alamo, but as of right now, she needed a refuge to protect them from rifle fire.

"Barricade all the doors," she directed. "Put riflemen at the windows. And watch for Nico, Virgil, Johnny, and the others. Be ready to let them in."

* * *

Nico, Virgil, Johnny, and Doc had made a mad dash to the offsite parking garage not far from the Minor Hotel. They swept the multi-story garage, and Virgil noted the condition of the cars. It appeared the cars had not been searched for supplies which meant his trailer, about the size of a horse trailer but squared off, probably hadn't been ransacked.

Good luck was still on their side.

During the preparation for the Tombstones' yearly ride, Virgil's wife Madge decided to ride the Harley while Virgil drove the trailer. None of the other wives accompanied their husbands, deciding rather to have several girls' nights out while the guys were doing their thing. During the confusion, Virgil had lost track of his wife's whereabouts. He recalled seeing her walking back to the room so if she was hunkering down, she'd be okay. She had a weapon and knew how to use it. He prayed to the Almighty to keep her safe.

The two men entered the stairwell and proceeded with caution. Coming to the fourth floor of the parking garage, Virgil cracked open the door and looked at the plethora of cars and trucks. There was no movement and they inched toward the trailer. Virgil retrieved a pyramid shaped key out of his pocket and inserted it into the huge lock partially hidden by a metal hood. He opened the trailer and Nico stood there looking in awe at the contents of the trailer.

Glocks were in plastic boxes. There were rifle racks on the side of the trailer filled with semi-automatic rifles including LaRues, LWRCs, and Colts. There were cardboard cases and metal boxes containing various forms of military and police type ammo.

"Everybody but Nico use AR-15s," Virgil said. "I keep a good supply of loaded AR-15 magazines for 3-gun competitions. I've also got an M16/AR 15 Maglula BenchLoader that loads a 30 round magazine in seconds. I liked it so much I bought the Galil version." Virgil motioned to the Galil Nico was holding. "Did you look closely at your gun?"

Nico inspected the Galil, looked at the left side, and noticed the three position fire control. A big grin stretched across his face. Christmas had come early again. "This is full-auto."

"Thought you'd like it," Virgil said.

Virgil loaded Nico's 35 round Galil magazines and a few others, including 50 rounders he had in stock on the BenchLoader, a large rectangle of hard Delrin plastic. It was machined to accept the top of a magazine and a full magazine's worth of ammo with a plastic slider to load the magazine.

"Y'all finish topping off your handgun mags," Virgil instructed. "We have to get moving or nobody good will be left alive at the Minor."

Minutes later, the group ran hard to the front entrance of the hotel. Huddling close together, they listened to the firing inside.

"Stay behind cover to avoid friendly fire," Virgil instructed. "Begin shooting at the Hyatts and I'll let them know who is here."

Shots rang out, and Virgil yelled, "This is the Tombstone rescue party! Virgil says we will be partying tonight!"

The firing across the lobby intensified from Jesse's position. All but two of the Hyatts kept firing at Jesse. They were the first to go.

Nico, Virgil, Johnny, and Doc each took a quadrant and let loose a volley of combined firepower. A few minutes later the lobby fell silent.

"Virgil and company coming in!" Virgil yelled. "Don't shoot!" Virgil had issued orders before when he was the range safety officer, so everyone knew him.

Nico was quite surprised and impressed about how plugged in and squared away the Tombstones were in the face of danger.

While the group united, Jesse taped a bandage around Billy's side. "Frank was killed about an hour ago," he said. "Y'all arrived just in time otherwise we would've been goners."

"We should be thanking *you*," Virgil responded. "Let's grab a few more items and move to the Alamo."

While Virgil gathered medical supplies, Jesse found a wheeled portable bed large enough to hold Billy and two ammo cans. Nico showed up with several fire extinguishers in pillow cases. They prepared to go to the side door of the Alamo using a circuitous route.

"Nico, you take point and lay down automatic fire if we encounter resistance." Virgil turned to Jesse and his patient. "Let's go."

Nico had inserted the rare 50 round magazine into his Galil and had the selector parked in the middle position.

The group ran unchallenged to the Alamo.

Coming to the side entrance of the structure, Nico leaned into a wooden door. The aged, hardened wooden door was thick enough to stop anything short of a .50 caliber round. The sound of metal scraping on the floor was followed by a partially opened door and Kate pointing a Remington 870 12 gauge at the group. Satisfied no bad guys were in the group, she opened the door wide and motioned for them to come in fast.

Nico was impressed regarding the preparations.

"What does it look like out there?" Kate asked.

Nico responded with a quick analysis which impressed Virgil. "About fifty Hyatts are dead. We have one dead, and are equipped for a short siege. I can only assume the reason the Hyatts are confused is because they have lost their leadership. As soon as they find new leaders, we will be attacked. The dilemma now is do we return to the Minor Hotel or do we fight it out here? Anybody have any ideas for what—"

Automatic fire sprayed the thick wooden doors of the front entrance and the group ducked. Fortunately nothing breached the heavy wood. The few rounds hitting the stone structure bounced away harmlessly.

"Well, I guess your question has been answered," Kate said. The whole room broke out in nervous laughter. Kate was pleased the group could laugh at their dire situation. She hoped the morale stayed high.

UNWANTED WORLD

* * *

Working together, the group reinforced the wooden doors with display cabinets and excess scaffolding panels. The second floor of the Alamo had been partially restored, giving the snipers secure footing near the upper windows.

The foot-thick wooden crossbeams filled the indentations in the stone all the way down the main hall. The floored section created great support for the snipers using the high windows. Some windows had heavy wooden bars that worked well in 1836, but now partially blocked the sniper's field of view. The existing scaffolding was moved in front of the remaining second floor windows to give those snipers a steady foothold. The thick stone walls were all but impenetrable to small arms fire.

"You've done a great job, Kate. I really enjoyed the 'Men' and 'Women' white bucket latrine solution."

"I like to be prepared."

He got serious then. "Our snipers have a decent view of the courtyard and surrounding buildings, but we could control the area better with some snipers on the roof. Is there a way up there?"

Kate thought for a moment. "There are some windows under the roofline, but swinging up there would be tricky and dangerous. If someone saw you trying for the roof, even a novice shooter will hit you. It's too bad we don't have a large ladder or a stick of dynamite to make a hole in the roof."

"If the Hyatts choose to occupy the Long Barracks and put snipers in the tall trees, they can make it dangerous for us to set foot outside. I worry about getting starved out." Nico's expression turned worrisome.

"I had everybody get water and freeze-dried meals. I inventoried them and figure we can survive about three weeks." "It all depends on what happens in the next few days. There are just too many variables to consider."

* * *

Two hours later, a booming voice thundered from the front of the Alamo. "This is Brick. I am the new commander of the Hyatts. Turn over all the men and women who fired at us for their due punishment. I'll be sure they are treated fairly. In return, you will be given a chance to lay down your arms and return to the Minor Hotel without molestation. We want twenty-five percent of all supplies you have or collect in the future. For this, you shall be safe from us. You have one hour to reply."

The group looked to Virgil for guidance. Being the oldest of the Tombstones, command naturally fell to him. "Gather around, it's time for a vote. Anybody here want to give up your guns and twenty-five percent of everything you ever get in exchange for a flimsy promise they won't hurt you, say aye." There was total silence. "Everybody who wants to kick their sorry asses to Hell where they belong, say aye."

This time the roof vibrated from all the "ayes".

Nico was already using time to his advantage. He borrowed black clothing from several men and taped down all his loose equipment to his body, including the Galil, with electrical tape.

The setting sun cast long shadows outside, and the Hyatt soldiers lit torches for light.

Nico checked the view from several second story windows, scanning the area for torches the Hyatts were holding. He selected the window exhibiting the best point of egress and the least amount of nearby Hyatt torches.

With catlike grace, Nico silently slid out of the window and pulled himself to the roof.

He was painfully pulling off some of his gear when the top of a head appeared just above the roofline.

"Don't shoot. It's Jesse. I need a hand," he whispered.

Nico heaved Jesse to the roof and stood back.

"How do you get this off?" Jesse asked, referring to the electrical tape.

"Very carefully. Fast is the best way."

Grimacing, Jesse ripped off the electrical tape from his arm, taking with it a good amount of arm hair.

Nico laughed silently. "What kind of rifle do you have?" he asked. He already knew, but he wanted to be sure Jesse knew what he was doing.

"Colt H-BAR, slightly used, semi-automatic. I wished it was full-auto, but it's okay since it has a heavy barrel and bipod." Jesse patted a pack full of loaded 30 round AR-15 magazines.

"You've come prepared," Nico noted. "Here's the plan. I'll take the section with the most torches, because it has the most people at the time we moved from dusk to darkness. You take the side door because I think they will make an attack there. Always keep your eyes and ears open, because they may send someone to the roof from any direction. Remember to aim two feet to the right of the torch since most of them will be right handed."

"I don't quite follow."

"They'll have to hold a torch in their left hand away from their body." Nico held a bottle of water in his left hand and a gun in his right as an example so Jesse could absorb what Nico was saying.

"Got it," Jesse said. "I thought Virgil was the master when it came to gunfights. It might be Virgil could learn a thing or two from you. Thanks." Jesse moved into his position, using the lip of the roof as cover.

* * *

Brick decided the Hyatts had waited long enough. "War!" he screamed. Dozens of rifles from all directions fired on the Alamo, including two belt-fed machine guns pointed at the Alamo's main entrance. In the darkness, the muzzle flash was sufficient to illuminate the two machine gun operators.

"Move away from the door. It won't last long." Kate realized the Alamo was good in its day, but it could not withstand the concentrated pounding from automatic weapons. "Snipers, open fire!" she commanded.

With Virgil and Nico out of sight, command fell to Kate. She was well known and respected at the bar for holding her own against unruly customers. Her background of descending from a Russian woman sniper from WWII added to her ability, and the fact she had competed with her older brothers on the shooting range rounded out her competency. She had earned the right to lead.

Sitting on the roof, Nico put twenty rounds of full-auto mayhem on the left gun operator, then emptied the magazine into the other operator. He regretted he could not see well enough to dispatch the operators without hurting the guns. He assumed the guns were the exquisite Model 240 7.62 x 51 machine guns designed by FN (Fabrique Nationale) of Belgium. If the guns could be salvaged, they would be a great asset for the Minor's defense in the future.

Two new operators got back on the guns. Nico put a fresh 35 round magazine into the Galil, racked the charging handle, and pushed the selector lever down to the semi-automatic position. He had the operator positions in his memory, so he could preserve ammo and allow his gun's barrel to cool by using the Galil's flip up night sights to put one bullet into each man.

Inside the Alamo, people had moved to each side of the heavy wooden doors. Wounded, Billy had been placed behind a toppled display case that would supply some cover. "Remember the Alamo!" he shouted.

"Yeah!" someone yelled.

"Remember Goliad!" came another, honoring the war cry from the same time period when Colonel Fannin and his troops were massacred at Goliad, a frontier town near San Antonio.

A few people snickered, but most of them were filled with new resolve and a desire to win.

The defenders at the windows were kept busy by Hyatt soldiers trying to sneak up to the Alamo. The closer the Hyatts came the easier it was for the Tombstones to shoot them from the wooden barred windows.

Nico had been forced to go full-auto a number of times. He had to reload his magazines by hand and he wished they had taken the bulky Galil BenchLoader with them. "Jesse, can you cover all four sides while I reload all these magazines?"

Jesse nodded. "You bet."

CHAPTER 25

Fire from the Hyatts was noticeably dissipating. No one was volunteering to man the M240 machine guns due to the fates of the previous gunners.

Nico took turns moving from wall to wall to find targets who were still shooting. The Galil's night sights were deadly out to seventy-five yards. Jesse gave the thumbs up indicating he was doing well, so Nico concentrated on the remaining three sides of the building. It bothered Nico that Brick had disappeared.

"Jesse, have you seen any sign of Brick?"

"I haven't—"

Two grenades landed on the roof and rolled, coming to a stop a few feet away. Jesse acted on impulse, catapulted up, and ran to the grenades.

"Noooo!" Nico yelled. "Don't!"

Jesse threw his body on top of the grenades and pulled them to his chest.

As Nico went to pull Jesse away, the blast threw Nico eight feet back. It felt as though every inch of his body had been slapped with a giant log. When he came to his senses, he turned to Jesse, but there was nothing to be done.

On ground level, Brick yelled, "Knock, knock!" He tossed two more grenades at the main wooden doors of the Alamo then sprinted back toward the Hyatt machine guns.

Nico shook off the effects of the grenade blast. He pushed the selector lever to the middle and gave Brick an eight round burst. The roof vibrated under his feet and smoke from the second explosion filled the air.

"Kate, is everyone all right?" Nico waited for an answer. He balled his fists and silently cursed in frustration when no answer came. He picked up Jesse's pack and rammed all the loaded magazines into it, leaving the top flap open. He jumped off the side of the building and rolled. No fire came from the Alamo, which intensified his anger.

Nico walked the grounds, emptying magazine after magazine. He covered all four sides, emptying his Galil completely. Drawing his Glock after seeing some movement, he yelled for the Hyatt to show himself. Something did not look right.

Debris had been pushed to the side and Reload ran up to Nico. The large dog was panting and wild-eyed. Nico holstered his gun and patted Reload on the head.

"Is it safe to come out?"

Nico crouched and whispered, "Kate, is that you?"

"It's me."

"Come on out. It's safe."

Kate walked out with her hands up. When she reached Nico, she hugged him. She leaned back from him. "Are you okay?" She reached up to his face and gingerly touched his ears. "You have blood coming out of your ears."

"I might need some first aid. Let's go on back inside."

The wooden doors had been knocked down, but the lower hinges had held and angled the doors upward to direct some of the grenade's explosive force toward the ceiling.

Virgil emerged and slapped Nico on the back as he walked by. "Guys, pick up all the loose guns and ammo. Make sure the Hyatts are dead and not playing possum before you get too close." Virgil looked at the two heavily damaged M240s. "Well, I can cobble one working gun together from two junkers." Virgil looked around, waiting for his clever line to be appreciated.

* * *

Later, Kate peered through binoculars and noticed some activity over at the Hyatt Hotel. She saw a man looking back at her through his own binoculars. The man started walking toward her position. She briefly thought about telling Nico then decided against it so he could get some rest, knowing Nico's adrenaline dump would make him tired for several days.

"Virgil, can you give me some cover?" Kate asked as she passed the group cleaning the courtyard in front of the Alamo.

"Sure. Don't take any chances. If you hit the dirt, I'll unload on whoever I need to." Virgil pulled back the charging handle on an AR-15 to load the weapon, then pushed the forward assist to make sure the bolt was fully seated.

Kate walked up to the man approaching her. He was tall with white hair.

"You don't have to worry. I'm Randall. I represent the Crocketts."

"I'm Kate." She eyed the man, watching for any indication of his intent. "Are you with the group that took over the Crockett hotel?"

"I am. We had been planning to fight the Hyatts ourselves and I'm here to tell you we're cleaning up the remaining ones, and also to tell you we appreciate what you've done."

"We were forced to go to war over trading for water," Kate replied. "We have wounded and dead."

"I think we can spare medical supplies if you need it."

"I appreciate it," Kate said.

"If water was all you wanted, you can have it for free, anytime you want. You will have no trouble from us."

"Thank you."

"If you don't mind, I have work to do," Randall said.

"Not at all."

Randall left as quickly as he had appeared.

"We'll have to trust you on that promise!" Kate yelled. "Please make sure all your guards know the Tombstones can draw water at any time from your pools." Kate's hands were down, near her gun.

She still wasn't one hundred percent this guy was on the up and up.

"I promise, your people will not be bothered when they go for water. We don't want to repeat what just happened."

"Fair enough. Give us a few days to clean up and we'll have you over for supper." Kate motioned with a friendly wave indicating the conversation was over.

They both went back to their home bases.

* * *

Nico was up and walking around to calm his nerves. He emerged from the Minor Hotel's front entrance and walked onto a street no longer busy with traffic.

A woman wearing baggy gray pants and a hoodie walked toward him. "Carlos, or should I say Nico? I hear you go by Nico around here."

Nico whipped around, immediately recognizing the voice. It was Marisa Sanchez.

"We had a deal remember?"

"I remember."

"Do you have my package?"

"Coincidence or timing, you're here after all the excitement is over?"

"Maybe a little of both. Package, please."

"I'll get it. I also want to get paid. Remember that part of the deal?"

"I remember," Marisa acknowledged.

"Give me a moment." Nico turned and was about to leave when Kate showed up.

"Who's this?" Kate didn't recognize the woman in the tattered clothes and hoodie.

"A business acquaintance."

Kate's radar was showing all the colors of an impending storm. Whatever this woman was up to wasn't good. Beneath the tattered clothes and dirty shoes, Kate noticed the pale French manicured nails and salon worthy eyebrows.

Anticipating questions he did not want to answer in front of Kate, or to leave her alone with Marisa, Nico said, "Kate, could you bring me my backpack? It should be in my room. It has something I need." Nico flicked his eyes sideways indicating it was okay for Kate to leave.

"I'll be back in a moment."

Watching Kate leave, he got a nagging feeling about the man he was really after. Louis Santiago. Taking a chance, he asked. "Couldn't Santiago come?" Nico was back in his Border Patrol role.

"Not so fast. First the package."

Kate arrived with the backpack.

"Thanks, Kate." Nico patted Kate's shoulder in an effort to move her along. Getting the message, Kate left and disappeared around the corner.

Nico unzipped a secret zipper on the side of the pack. A package in brown waxed paper fell out. He handed it to Marisa.

She unwrapped the package and used her hands to spread the white powder out over the brown waxed paper. Three vials appeared and Marisa quickly pocketed them, leaving thousands of dollars of cocaine to blow away in the wind.

"I've done my part," Nico said. "Introduce me to Louis Santiago."

"Ah, the infamous Louis Santiago," Maris opined. "You're not the only one with many names. Let me introduce myself. I'm Marisa Louisa Santiago Sanchez." She gave him a catlike smile.

To say Nico was surprised was an understatement. He hadn't planned on the elusive Louis Santiago hiding in plain sight. He wasn't even sure what to say other than, "Is that all you need?"

"Not quite. I've been observing you for a long time Nikolai Belyahov."

"How do you know my real name?"

"Do you really think the leader of a cartel wouldn't know who she's doing business with? Although there isn't much available public information about you. It makes me wonder what you really do. Only the government has the power to erase identities."

Nico thought quickly. "I am Nikolai Belyahov."

"Do I detect a hint of apprehension? Hmm?"

Nico said nothing, only stared at her.

"Don't underestimate what I can do or the power I have," Marisa said. "The Hyatts were under my command. And if it wasn't for you, all this would be my territory. That's why I want you to work for me. You showed incredible fortitude under tremendous pressure and overwhelming odds, you—"

"Work for you?" Nico was incredulous.

"Yes! Why not? We'll put our heads together and the possibilities would be endless. Who knows? There might be other things in it for you, if you know what I'm talking about."

Nico knew exactly what she was talking about, and had zero interest.

"How much money does your employer pay you?" Marisa asked. "The government is notoriously stingy."

She had done her homework alright. Nico was lucky to be alive. He needed to be extra careful.

"That bad, huh? Perhaps a measly few thousand dollars a month? I could pay you a thousand times what they pay you." Marisa walked around Nico, eyeing him up and down. She touched him on his arm. "I've seen you in action. I've been watching from over there." Marisa pointed to a window high in an adjacent building. "You impress me, Nikolai." She lowered the hoodie and stood inches away from him. "Come work for me."

"You're the kind of people we try to put away for a good long time," Nico said.

"You and a lot of other people. I'm not kidding when I said I can pay you well."

"It's not the money that interests me."

"Everybody has their price," Marisa countered. "Name your price."

"Suppose I did come work for you. How long would that last? A year or less."

"What are you talking about?"

"Do you really think I risked my life for a brown package? I knew something else was going on with the infamous Louis Santiago, I just didn't know what." Nico leaned in closer to Marisa. "You hired me because you don't want anyone else to know your secret. You don't have long to live, do you?"

"I have no idea what you are talking about." Her previous seductive smile vanished into a petulant frown.

"Sure you do. The vials aren't illegal drugs. The writing on them is Russian. And since I can speak and read Russian, I know those are experimental drugs for cancer. Your secret is out."

"I want to live. Is that so bad?"

"No, but as soon as people learn you're sick, they'll be on you like a pack of wolves on a rotting carcass."

The heat in Marisa's face rose along with a Walther P22 she took from her waistband. She pointed it directly at Nico's forehead.

Nico was startled at the speed in which she drew the gun. There was no time for him to draw his Glock. Though he was fast on the draw, he couldn't beat the gun pointed at him. His mind raced for a solution.

"I don't like you knowing my secret," Marisa said.

Thinking quickly, Nico asked a question knowing it was difficult to talk and shoot at the same time. He needed to throw off Marisa's concentration. "What was your question earlier? Something about price?"

"I said name your price."

"My price is a million dollars plus control of this sector of San Antonio."

Marisa laughed. "You expect me to believe you now? No deal. My secret goes to the grave with you."

When Nico took a step back to put distance between him and the Walther P22, the report of a gunshot pierced the silence. He flinched, and his ear tingled at the vibration of the bullet slicing the air inches away from his head.

Marisa's head snapped sideways, followed by an instantaneous spray of brain matter. Her arms flew backwards and her body collapsed in a heap. There was a large, gaping hole in the side of her head. Nico had seen a lot of carnage in his days, but had never witnessed a woman having part of her head blown off. He grimaced. Nobody could survive a wound like that.

Kate walked up to Nico, still pointing her rifle at Marisa. "Is she dead?"

"Quite dead. I didn't know you were such a good shot."

"I've had some practice lately."

"What clued you in?" Nico asked.

Kate lowered her rifle. "I get suspicious when a thoroughbred dresses down to skid row. I thought I had met her before, but couldn't exactly remember. Then it hit me. She has a French manicure, the same kind the woman had who met you in the hotel last week." Kate knelt and picked up the Walther. "A micro .22 long rifle is about the only gun a woman could use with long nails. She was the woman in the bar, wasn't she?"

"She was," Nico confirmed.

"I didn't trust her from the moment I met her."

"Guess I don't have women's intuition."

Kate playfully punched him on the arm.

"You saved my life and killed the biggest drug lord south of the border. Did you know there's a huge reward for what you did?"

"No, I didn't."

"Last time I checked, the reward was at least one hundred thousand dollars."

Dollar signs danced in Kate's mind. She slowly repeated what Nico had said. "One hundred thousand dollars?"

"That's the going price."

The thought of the money made Kate woozy and she teetered on unsteady legs. Nico caught her and guided her to a spot away and out of sight from Marisa's corpse. He helped Kate sit in the shade of a big oak tree. They both ended up on the ground.

Reload appeared and nudged Kate's hand. She blinked open her eyes, and said, "A hundred thousand dollars. Are you kidding me?"

"Nope. Whenever the electrical grid boots back up, when and if it happens, I'll be sure you get it."

"What's my reward for saving you?" Kate asked playfully.

"Something priceless."

"That's even better."

Nico ran his finger down the bridge of her nose then tapped the end of it. "You're something else." Kate returned a smile. "Close your eyes," Nico said. This was the moment he had been waiting for. This was the woman he had been waiting for all his life.

As he gazed upon Kate, Reload wiggled in between them and stuck his snout on Kate's face, planting a smelly, slobbery dog kiss. His glee at being next to Kate was unadulterated and he wiggled from side to side.

Kate scrunched her nose and opened her eyes to a big hairy face with a black nose staring straight at her. She broke out laughing and nudged Reload away. "At first I thought that was you. I was going to tell you to brush your teeth."

Nico fell to the side and laughed. "This isn't going how I wanted it to. You need to tell Reload to beat it."

Kate propped herself up on an elbow. "Reload and I are a team, a package deal. I will never tell him to beat it. I'll never be with a man who doesn't want Reload."

Nico turned serious. "I know that, Kate. We – you, me, and Reload – are a team starting now. Wherever you go, I go. Wherever Reload goes, I'll be right there with him."

"That's all the reward I need," Kate said.

"Told you it would be priceless."

EPILOGUE

(One week later)

When it was all over, the Crocketts piled the bodies in an empty lot near an abandoned building and set them on fire. It had been a gruesome, yet necessary task to prevent the spread of disease. The pyre burned for days until only a pile of ashes was left.

One of the Crocketts informed Kate she had killed Marisa's brother, a killer in the drug trade known to be merciless.

"He deserved what he got," Kate had responded coldly, "along with his sister."

Nico had wanted to ask her if she knew him, but decided it would wait for another time.

After the shootout and the resulting fallout, Kate and Nico decided to stay at the Minor Hotel. They had all they needed to survive the winter so the decision had been a fairly easy one.

Of the Tombstone biker bunch, Doc Holiday was the only one who had engineering experience. He had minored in engineering at college, so after the excitement of the shootout he put his knowledge to use and tinkered with his bike hoping to start the engine.

He used the valet parking bay for his makeshift garage, having found basic tools in the valet's office. The bikes had all been gassed up prior to when the electrical grid went down, not in preparation for an emergency, rather for convenience. When Doc and the others were ready to get back on the road, the last thing they wanted to do was to stop and get gas.

There were four other bikes Doc had to repair, and while it had taken a lot of tinkering, jerry-rigging, praying, and good old fashioned engineering, the other four he fixed didn't take long.

"Won't you come and stay at my house?" Doc Holiday asked. He was sitting on his Harley ready to make the trip back home to Houston. He throttled the engine. "Kate can ride double with me, and Nico, you can ride with Johnny Ringo. It's only a few hours back to Houston from here."

Nico shook his head. "I promised Kate I'd get her back home to Austin."

"How?" Doc asked. "It's too dangerous to walk on I-35. Winter is around the corner too, and you're not exactly prepared for a long hike."

"I'm not sure how she'll get back." Nico put a protective arm around Kate and brought her closer. "I'll think of something. I'll find a way to get her home."

"I can't believe you're staying here."

Nico shrugged. "We'll be fine. The guests are gone, there's plenty of food to last several months, and we've got water."

"You'll be okay," Doc said. A gust of frigid northern air blew in, scattering leaves. A chill captured Doc and a cold shiver tingled down his spine. He pulled his collar up around his neck. He pensively looked at the road, mentally planning the quickest way to the freeway.

Nico gazed skyward at the dark clouds rolling in. "The cold front will be here soon. If you leave now, you can beat the front before it gets to Houston. These blue northers can drop the temps thirty degrees in an hour."

Doc and the others throttled their bikes. "It's time," he said. "Here's a list of rooms where Virgil and I hid the extra guns that we couldn't carry." Doc handed Nico a piece of paper with the room numbers penciled in. "Feel free to take anything you want, it's quite an arsenal."

"Thanks for everything," Nico said, "and Godspeed to all of you.

How will I ever find you? I don't even know your real name."

"The next time you see a bunch of middle aged graying bikers with Tombstone Gang on their jackets driving down the road," Doc said, "well, that'll be us. We've got a website, so hopefully one of these days, the grid will come back up and you can check us out."

Virgil added. "Just to let you know, we've decided to make you an honorary member of our gang. My wife Madge will get a jacket made for you. We've decided to crown you Wyatt Earp."

"I am honored." Nico shook hands with Virgil. "I've been meaning to ask you where your wife was during all the excitement."

"Madge," Virgil said, "tell him what happened."

"I got locked in an elevator."

"An elevator?" Nico asked. "How?"

"One of them was open so I went in it to brush my hair in the mirror. Next thing I know the doors closed. I guess it was a short or something, or maybe one of the infamous Minor ghosts. I was on a ghost tour before the grid went down and I could have sworn I saw one of the ghosts in there with me. The ghost was lonely and I think only wanted company."

"An overactive imagination, honey," Virgil said.

"Perhaps. I still had the willies the whole time I was stuck in there. I'm never coming back here."

"Me either," Virgil confirmed.

"Well," Nico said, addressing the group. "It's been a real pleasure to fight alongside you. Godspeed to all of you."

Doc put his helmet on, tightened it, dipped his head, and saluted Nico. The Tombstone Gang rode out of the valet bay, turned right, then followed Doc to the interstate. Nico and Kate watched them disappear around a building. The roar of the motorcycle engines became fainter and fainter until they could no longer hear them.

"Let's head on back inside," Nico said. "I need to check the doors to make sure the locks are holding."

"I'll meet you back at the bar."

Kate opened the door leading to the bar. Reload followed silently behind. The bar sat quiet and empty. Chairs were askew and lamps had been knocked over, courtesies of the previous fight. A few broken bottles of liquor lay scattered on the floor. Kate tapped Reload on the shoulder to get his attention. She led him over to a corner of the bar. "Sit," she instructed. "It'll hurt your paws if you step on glass."

Reload sat on his haunches, waiting for additional instruction.

Kate stepped behind the bar, retrieved a broom and a dust pan, and swept up the broken glass. She emptied the glass in a trash receptacle in the back room. "Reload, come." She tapped the window then said, "Guard it."

Reload went to the door leading to the street and put his paws on the window. A plastic bag rolled along the ghostly empty sidewalk. Low, heavy clouds had rolled in, casting a wintery pall on the land. He huffed a warm dog breath on the cold glass, sniffing and taking in the smells of the deserted street. He caught the scent of a possum which had crossed the street the night before. It had stopped at the door, picking up the scent of food inside the building. The possum had reached his snout up along the door, searching for a way in. The door was shut tight so the possum left the area to patrol the rest of his territory.

Reload's eyes roamed over the deserted street looking for any sign of an intruder. If there were any, he'd bark a warning to alert Kate of danger.

Kate picked up the chairs and set them in their proper places around the tables. She made sure lamps were plugged in the outlets in case the electrical grid booted back up.

Without any customers, she wasn't quite sure what to do. To busy herself while Nico made sure the doors to the hotel were secured, she dusted the shelves holding the liquor, tightened caps, wiped down the counter, and placed the liquor bottles so the labels could be seen.

The wind whistled around the eaves and up through the spaces in the walls, making a peculiar whining sound.

The sound of approaching footsteps in the hallway startled Kate. The doorknob squeaked open and a breath caught in her throat.

Sensing Kate's increasing apprehension, Reload went to her side. His muscles were tense.

The door opened.

It was Nico.

Kate breathed a sigh of relief and Reload padded to Nico, tail thumping, his body wiggling from side to side. If a dog could be sheepish, Reload was.

Nico reached down to Reload and took handfuls of fur, running his hands over the big dog's back.

"You both look like you've seen a ghost."

"We're still jumpy."

"It was some sort of adrenaline rush, wasn't it?"

Kate nodded.

Nico came in, slid into a barstool, and put his hands on the bar. Deep, weary lines furrowed his brow, and he had the posture of a tired man.

"Can I make you a drink?" Kate asked.

"Seven and seven," Nico said. "Hold the ice."

Kate laughed. "I think I can do that." She retrieved a tumbler, splashed in a few ounces of Seagram's 7 blended whiskey then topped it off with fizzy warm 7 UP.

Nico downed the drink in two big gulps. He set the tumbler on the counter. "I needed that. Another one, if you don't mind."

"I'll make us both one." Kate handed the stiffer of the drinks to Nico. Instead of gulping it, he took his time, sipping it.

"How's Reload doing?" Nico asked.

Kate glanced at Reload, who was in his dog bed behind the bar. When he heard his name, he canted his head.

"He's fine. Probably tired and wired up like we are. As soon as you came in, he relaxed. I bet he'll be asleep in no time at all."

"What about you?"

"Me?" Kate said. "I'll probably sleep good tonight."

"That's not what I mean. I mean, how *are* you?"

Kate shrugged. "I guess I'm okay."

"Are you?"

"Maybe."

It was quiet in the bar. Somewhere a faucet dripped slowly and far away voices echoed outside. Nico held Kate's gaze, and during the long moment a silent understanding happened between them. If they were to go forward, Kate would have to drop the invisible shield she had used to keep people at a distance.

Don't get too close.

Don't let anyone in.

Kate's heartbeat slowed down and she was keenly aware of her breathing. Nico hadn't broken eye contact, and she was afraid to glance away, as if looking away would break the connection.

"I think it's time you told me why you need a service dog," Nico said.

For a moment Kate froze and a breath caught in her throat. She waited for the debilitating onslaught of emotions she had fought for so long to keep buried. She did as she always did: she concentrated on her breathing to keep her calm.

Without realizing, she put her hand down to her side and waited for Reload to nudge her with his warm nose and muscular body. So many times he had come to her right before she had a panic attack. He'd nudge her until she petted him with long strokes on his back while she absentmindedly took handfuls of fur. It was like he was a sponge, absorbing those emotions she couldn't handle. He'd stay with her until her heart rate slowed down and until the chemical reactions in her body returned to normal.

When Reload didn't come to Kate, she looked at him, worried something might be wrong with him. He had curled into a little ball and was sleeping peacefully in his dog bed. He yipped once and his paws moved like he was having a dream. It's not that she didn't need him, but when he didn't come to her, it puzzled her for a moment.

"Kate?" Nico asked with concern. "Is Reload okay?"

"He's sleeping," Kate said.

"He needs to sleep. He's tired."

"It's not that. Whenever I think about what happened to me in the past, Reload is always there for me."

"I'm here for you now."

A sprinkling of rain fell against the door and a blustery gust of wind rattled the glass. Leaves scattered on the road. Reload snored softly.

"I think the cold front is here," Kate said. "I'll go get a blanket."

Nico reached across the bar and put his hand on her arm, stopping her. He met her eyes and shook his head. "No, Kate. Don't run away from whatever it is. You can never run away from what's inside," he said, putting his hand against his chest, patting it. "You need to face what happened to you."

Kate dropped her chin. "I'm afraid to face it."

"You need to, or you'll never be able to move on with your life."

"I know, but it's so hard. I've wanted to forget it." Kate absentmindedly rubbed the ring finger on her left hand, where a ring should have been, where she had worn one before.

Nico noticed the movement but didn't say anything.

Finally Kate spoke. "His name was Ben." She took a big breath then let it out. "I met him the first day I left home. I didn't know what to do when I got here, so I decided to go visit the Alamo. It was a Saturday afternoon, lines were long and he was in line behind me. He started talking to me about stuff...I can't even remember what he said. I thought he was some guy that was trying to make a move on me, and at the time I had no interest. When I left home I had a big fight with my parents so I was in no mood for guys."

Kate paused, letting her thoughts go back to the moment she had met Ben. She took a big swallow of the whiskey drink.

"He said he was there for some class he was taking at a local university. He was in architecture and he said he needed to sketch the inside. Anyway, the line moved quickly and before I knew it, we were inside the Alamo and he went one way, me the other.

"I didn't think much about him. I had my purse over my shoulder instead of my chest, which was a stupid thing to do. I was outside on the grassy area and before I knew it, someone knocked me to the ground and was trying to steal my purse. It happened so quickly and the guy managed to get my purse. I was panicking because I had all my money and my phone in my purse. I screamed for help and Ben was the only one who ran after the guy. He tackled him, punched him until the guy let go of my purse. If Ben hadn't helped me, I don't know what I would have done. There was no way I was going back home."

"He sounds like a great guy."

"He was," Kate whispered. Her gaze dropped to the floor. "We started dating soon after, and before I knew it, a month went by, then a year. We fell in love. We got engaged. He had started his own business and had signed a contract to design houses for a new planned community on the outskirts of the city. He was so excited and wanted to celebrate by buying a house for us, for the children we talked about having."

Nico put a hand on hers. He wanted to take her pain away, to turn back the clock, to erase whatever trauma she had endured. It pained him to listen.

She pulled her hand away from his. "It was a gorgeous day when it happened. We went to the bank to get pre-approved for a loan.

"We were sitting down at a loan officer's desk when some guy burst into the bank, shot a round in the ceiling, and ordered everyone to get down on the floor." Kate turned her back to Nico. A lump caught in her throat and she croaked, "I don't think I can continue. I can't talk about it anymore."

"Kate, please. You need to. You're safe with me."

Kate pivoted to face Nico. Her face was scrunched up with anger and confusion. "I thought I was safe with Ben."

Nico was taken aback by her sharp tone.

"I, uh, I'm sorry," she said. "I didn't mean to lash out at you."

"It's alright. I understand."

Kate dropped her gaze and stared at the floor as old memories came flooding back. Thoughts bounced around in her head and she took another drink to steady herself. She swallowed audibly and set the drink down.

"Nobody knew what to do. We were frozen. Then Ben reached over to put his arm across me and it happened so fast. There was a shot and something wet and warm splattered my arms and my face. I didn't know what it was. I thought it was coffee until I looked at my hands. They were covered in blood."

"Ben was shot?"

Kate nodded. She sniffled and swiped under both eyes. "Nothing made sense. It was like I was having an out of body experience. I was so focused on Ben I had no idea what else was going on. I remember him slumped over in his chair and making these awful gurgling sounds I'll never forget. He was trying to say something to me so I leaned in closer to hear him."

"What did he say?"

"I don't know. I'll never know. He was fading in and out of consciousness. I took his hand and I told him to stay strong and to hold on, that help was coming. He squeezed my hand so I knew he heard me. I was afraid to touch him, afraid I might hurt him. By then, the guy had left. Some of the people ran out of the bank while others were still hiding. One of the tellers came up to me and asked if I needed help. I said I was okay, but Ben wasn't. We slid him to the floor and someone put pressure on his wound. All I could do was to hold his hand until help arrived. Before the ambulance got there, I knew he was gone because when I told him I loved him, he didn't squeeze my hand."

"I'm so sorry," Nico said. "I have a question for you."

"What?"

"What happened to the man who shot Ben?"

"I killed him last week."

Nico looked oddly at her.

"He was Marisa's brother. I first saw him when you and Virgil had gone to make the trade. I recognized him by the scar. He was standing in the shadows of the Hyatt. I tried to keep an eye on both him and you, but somehow he disappeared. Then I saw the snipers go into position so I went to get help. Johnny Ringo gathered the troops to help you. When we decided to regroup at the Alamo, I saw him again. We made eye contact and I'm sure he remembered me. I shot him dead. I did it for Ben." Kate's voice cracked when she said Ben's name.

She looked at Nico through blurry, tear-soaked eyes. Her face was flushed and her brow was furrowed.

"You did right, Kate. You honored Ben's death. He died trying to protect you. He gave his life for you."

Kate swallowed the lump in her throat. "I know. And look what I've done to honor him. I'm barely able to cope since it happened, and can't do anything without Reload."

"That's not true. You know how Reload senses when you aren't able to cope, when you needed calming?"

Kate nodded.

"Look at him now. He's sleeping." Nico reached across the bar and invited Kate to take his hands. She took his hands and he held them tight. "You did this all on your own. Don't you realize that?"

"I guess I didn't."

"Reload would have come to you if you needed him."

"He's never let me down."

"I'll never let you down, Kate. Never. I promise."

Kate straightened up, took a paper napkin, and patted her face dry. With a renewed sparkle in her eye she said, "I'm going to hold you to that."

"You can hold me to that for a lifetime," Nico said sincerely.

Kate hopped up on the bar, swung her legs over and planted them down on the floor. "There was one thing you promised you'd do for me when you came back."

"What?"

"You said you'd make me a steak."

"Ah, yes, I do remember saying I would." Nico diverted his

gaze, thinking.

"Well?" Kate asked.

"Since I said I'll make you a steak, I will."

"How? The grocery stores are empty and any meat we have here at the hotel has spoiled."

"Do you like pork?"

"I do. Are you making pork chops? I'll eat one of those instead of a steak." Kate was suddenly aware of her growling stomach.

"I'm not exactly making a pork chop."

"Then what are you making?"

Nico didn't answer Kate's question. "Can you start a fire in the grill—the one on the patio?"

"Of course."

"Good. Get one going and I'll meet you on the patio in about an hour. Bring a bottle of wine and two glasses."

"Okay," Kate replied, suspicious of what Nico was planning.

"I'll be in the kitchen."

They walked out of the bar and when Nico opened the door, Kate said, "What about Reload?"

"He can come too. There'll be a little extra for him."

* * *

An hour later, coals in the grill had formed and were glowing red. Rain from the cold front had blown through leaving puddles of water pooled in the low lying sections of the patio. The sky was clear and cold.

Kate was sitting on a lawn chair on the patio, a rectangular green space located in the middle of the hotel grounds. There was no access to it from the street, and the landscaping still looked good. Hedges had been trimmed prior to the electrical grid going down, fall flowers had been planted, and the bird bath had water in it.

Kate shivered in the chilly night air, rose, and went to the fire to warm her hands. She looked skyward at a bright star twinkling in the dark sky. Without lights from the city, the stars shined brightly. She thought it might be one of the planets. Jupiter was a likely guess, but she wasn't sure since she wasn't familiar with the planets.

She pulled the collar of her jacket up around her neck and fluffed her hair to cover her ears in the chilly night air. She took a sip of wine then placed the glass on the patio table situated between the two chairs. Reload sat quietly by her side.

The door to the patio opened and Nico stepped out.

"I was beginning to worry. What took you so long?" Kate asked.

"It took me a while to find the cast iron skillet and a spatula that wouldn't melt on the grill, and," Nico paused, "I had to prepare the food."

"Would you like a glass of wine?"

"I sure would."

Kate poured a glass of wine for Nico while he put two covered pots on the grill.

"What's on the menu?" Kate asked. "I'm starving."

"Green beans with almonds and thyme, mashed potatoes—"

"Real mashed potatoes?"

"Sort of. They *are* from a real box."

"Good enough," Kate said.

"I also found some rolls, but they're on the stale side so you may not want to eat them. For the main entrée we have a delicious and moist steak, cooked medium well, which is how you like it if I recall correctly."

Kate smiled. "You remembered."

Nico removed the lid from the cast iron skillet and presented it to Kate. She suspiciously eyed the rectangular, breaded slices of some type of mystery meat. "What exactly is that?"

"May I present to you Spam steak."

A big smile spread across Kate's face. "Spam steak?" A laugh escaped her lips. "I didn't know there was such a thing."

"Spam can be eaten in many ways," Nico said. "In fact, Hawaii consumes more Spam than any other state."

"Why?" Kate asked.

"During WWII, the GIs ate a lot of Spam because it didn't require refrigeration. Surplus Spam made its way into the native diets of Pacific Islanders. Even to this day, it's a favorite."

"What exactly is Spam?" Kate asked.

"Mostly pork and ham."

"Well, when someone cooks for me, I am grateful. Thank you."

"My pleasure. Dinner will be served in about ten minutes."

Nico removed the breaded Spam to another plate then placed the cast iron skillet on the grill. Once it was heated, he spread a thin coating of oil in the bottom. He spooned each piece onto the skillet, waited a few minutes, then flipped the pieces over. Kate sat to the side and sipped on wine, dubious of how the Spam would taste. She had seen ads on TV when the economy had tanked, but had never eaten Spam.

"The steaks are done," Nico said. "Green beans and potatoes are hot too."

Nico placed two plates on the patio table then spooned food onto them. He sat down for the first time in days. It had been a long time since he had sat down for a proper meal. Normally he ate on the run or in his government issued vehicle. Tonight was different, and it deserved to be honored.

"Let's bow our heads." Nico cleared his throat. "Come, Lord Jesus, and be our guest, and let this food to us be blessed. Amen."

"Amen," Kate said softly. She lifted her chin. "That was very nice."

Nico nodded. "It was my dad's favorite. Dig in."

Kate speared a piece of Spam, cut off a tiny bite, and tasted it. She chewed it slowly, mulling over the salty flavor diluted by the breading. She took another bite then a sip of wine. "It's actually quite good. It's been a while since I had a hot meal. This is perfect."

Reload, who had been sitting quietly, had drool dripping from his jaw. He eagerly watched Kate take every bite. She slipped him several pieces of Spam, which the big dog scarfed down.

After she had her fill, she dabbed the corners of her mouth with a paper napkin, folded it, and placed it by the side of the plate. "The meal was delicious."

"Thanks," Nico said.

Kate scraped a few leftovers into a pile and offered the scraps to Reload. He greedily gobbled the tidbits. She stacked the plates and put the silverware on top. "What's for dessert?"

Nico cracked a sly smile. He put his hands around her waist and brought her close. "Whatever you want."

Kate dropped her gaze and grinned. She knew exactly what she wanted. "Let's take the wine and go upstairs. We can sit on the balcony and watch the stars. Or the clouds."

"Have I ever told you I stargaze?"

"I would have never guessed. There's a lot I don't know about you, Nico Bell."

"What do you want to know?"

Kate thought a moment before asking, "Why did you come back?"

"I came back for you, Kate. I knew from the moment I saw you that you were the one for me."

"I knew it too," Kate said. "I didn't want to admit it because I wasn't ready. I'm ready now though."

"Come on," Nico said, "Let's go watch the stars."

* * *

Nico and Kate left the patio and walked hand in hand back to the second floor where the guest rooms were.

Reload was on the patio, sitting on his haunches, tail thumping, waiting for Kate to instruct him. With growing apprehension Reload watched them leave, torn whether or not to go to Kate to comfort her like he always had. He waited eagerly for her to turn around, pat her thighs indicating he was to go to her.

Earlier, in the bar, Reload had listened to the conversation and had been keenly attuned to Kate's every sniffle, cough, shuffle, moving arms, growling stomach, and even her wobbly knees at one point. Then the man reached over to her and took her hands in his big warm hands, never lashing out in anger at Kate, and who looked at Kate with a longing Reload had noticed before. Whatever it was they were communicating about, Reload was satisfied in knowing the man would protect her.

During dinner on the patio, the conversation had been relaxed and Reload sensed the attraction between the two, noticing it in body posture, a smile, a laugh, or how Kate reacted when Nico put his hand on her shoulder. She, in turn, put her hand on his. It was a natural movement, not forced like some humans did.

Reload stood poised, ready to bolt at a moment's notice to be by Kate's side. When Nico and Kate disappeared around the corner, Reload instinctively wanted to go to her, but he held back. Kate was now a pair with the man, and she was safe with him.

Reload put his nose in the air, sniffing. Various aromas wafted in the air. There was the distinctive odor of meat, some type of vegetable which didn't interest him, and two rolls left on the table.

He sat on his haunches, waiting for Kate to reappear. After a few minutes, Reload's interest turned to the table and the uneaten food. The aroma was too enticing and he did what he had been taught not to do. He went to the table, put his paws on the sides, and if he turned his snout just right, he could reach the food. He licked the plates clean, including the leftover Spam. He pawed the rolls until they fell off the table and onto the ground. He greedily gobbled them down, then sniffed the ground, searching for anything he missed. Satisfied the food was all gone, Reload padded to the door, nosed it open, and followed the direction Kate and Nico went.

He put his nose to the ground to follow Kate's scent, taking him past sofas and chairs in the foyer, the grand piano, and glass-encased shelves holding knickknacks and various other memorabilia of a bygone time. Reload padded to the next space, a cavernous and dark room, loped across the worn rug past the elevators until he came to the stairs. He scampered up the stairs and followed the scent trail to the room where Kate and Nico were.

Reload stopped and canted his head, listening to the laughter coming from inside the room. He put his nose to the door and sniffed, taking in the smells of the room in which Kate's scent now mingled with the man's.

He stepped back from the door and sniffed the carpet for any signs of other people. Satisfied they were alone, Reload scratched the carpet, twirled a couple of times, then pillowed into it.

He let out a big breath and put his snout on his paws. There would be more to do, and tomorrow would be a new day.

He closed his eyes and sleep soon came to him. He would wait for the sun to rise. He would wait to walk by the side of Kate and Nico.

That's what a service dog did.

That's what he would do.

The End (almost)

DARK WATER

(a bonus scene)

The winter months passed without incident. There was something comforting about living in the city with people all around, the noises, chatter, the energy. Even though a city could have a million people, it was still easy to become lonely, to be invisible. Since the grid had been down and people had thinned out, it wasn't as lonely. Community had come together to survive and Kate and Nico traded whatever they had at the Minor Hotel in order to be comfortable. They had made friends and alliances with the neighboring Crocketts, and they passed the winter peacefully. Leaving it would be more difficult than she thought.

Spring showed herself by warming the land and brightening the dull colors with splashes of vibrant hues. Dandelions showcased a bright yellow flower which grew to full height since lawns and freeway embankments had ceased to be mowed. Trees sprouted new growth.

The air was lively with flitting butterflies while songbirds sang their melodies.

The swimming pool at the Minor was filled halfway with water that had turned brown, and a bullfrog had taken residence in the shallow end, croaking long and lonely during the warm nights. Somehow a goldfish entered the scene and darted among the soggy brown leaves.

Nico had made the rounds during the morning making sure the hotel was secured while Kate inventoried their remaining food in the bar.

"Nico," Kate said, "we're getting low on food."

He shut the door to the bar and walked over to where Kate was standing. "How much is left?"

Kate's eye's roamed over the remaining cans of spaghetti sauce, green beans, ranch style beans, canned tuna, bags of chips, packages of noodles, and a plethora of other canned goods she swore she'd never eat again if things ever got back to normal.

"About two weeks, possibly three if we ration carefully. We're running low on dog food too," Kate added. "The extra dog food the hotel had for the pets is almost gone."

"You know as well as I do it's time for us to leave."

"Where would we go?"

"Kate, I promised you I'd get you back home. Let me take you there."

"My parents have probably forgotten about me by now. I left on such bad terms I'm not sure my mom wants to see me again."

"I doubt it."

"How would we get there? Walk?" Kate thought about the daunting prospect of walking from San Antonio to the west side of Austin. "I don't want to walk a hundred miles."

Nico moved closer to Kate. "Who said anything about walking?"

Now that got Kate's attention.

Reload perked up his ears at the intonation of Nico's voice. The man was up to something.

"Do you have a bathing suit?"

"I do."

"Pack your suit and whatever items you can fit into a duffle bag. I'll pack my gear and a few days worth of food for us and Reload. We're going to the beach. We'll need a couple of towels and—"

"Huh? The beach?" Kate was dumbfounded. "The beach is farther from here than Austin is. How are we going to get there?"

"I'm going to steal a helicopter."

"If you know how to steal a helicopter, why didn't we leave during the winter?" Kate put her hands on her hips in a show of displeasure.

"I only learned the other day a nearby small airport has a few helicopters stored in hangers. The owners must have left them."

"Oh. So is stealing a helicopter like stealing a car?"

"It's a whole lot easier." Nico spied the inventory of liquor on the shelves behind Kate. "Bring a couple of bottles of wine." He looked at Kate's hair. "And be sure to wear several bobby pins in your hair."

"What for?"

"Just do it, please."

"Okay," Kate said, curious why Nico wanted her to wear bobby pins in her hair, although not asking questions. "When do we leave?"

"In one hour."

"We're going to the beach then to Austin?"

"You got it."

"On what? Fumes?"

"You can leave the logistics to me. I've got it all planned out."

* * *

By late afternoon, and after several hours of walking, Nico, Kate, and Reload stood outside the barbed wire rimmed fence protecting one of San Antonio's privately owned public use airports.

Thick woods surrounded the airport, and Nico had guided them to a place in the woods where he could study the layout and not be observed.

Standing in the shade of a large tree, Nico swung his backpack on the ground, retrieved a bottle of water, and chugged down half of it. He poured the rest into a plastic bowl for Reload. The dog drank thirstily.

Kate surveyed the airport containing hangers, a VIP lounge, airplane covers, and the two story terminal building. Nico said the airport had a radio shop, and was an FAA license repair and Cessna repair facility. There was also an upholstery shop for aircraft interiors.

"What's the plan?" Kate asked.

213

"See the helicopter over there?" Nico said, pointing to a Bell Jet Ranger helicopter.

"Yes."

"I'm going to steal it."

"It looks old."

"It probably is," Nico confirmed. "It could date from 1966. But if I know pilots, and since I'm a pilot too, I'm betting the chopper is in better shape than most of the newer ones. And it wouldn't have been affected by the EMP."

Kate was skeptical. "How are we going to get in?" She was looking at the razor sharp barbed wire which topped the high fence.

"I brought bolt cutters. Found them in the utility room at the hotel," Nico said. "Stay here. Once I finish cutting a hole large enough for us, you and Reload hightail it over to me."

"Then what?"

"You'll see."

Holding the bolt cutter in one hand, Nico slung his backpack over his shoulder, tentatively emerged from the woods, and bolted to the fence. He worked quickly and expertly, cutting the links starting at the bottom and working his way up. Kate winced each time the bolt cutter clanged though a link. In the quiet of the woods, the sound might as well have been a locomotive barreling along a railroad line.

Nico cut across the links at the bottom, then up and over, leaving one side intact until he had made a rectangle big enough to squeeze through. He held the piece of chain link fence then waved to Kate it was time to hoof it.

Holding Reload by the leash, Kate sprinted toward Nico. When she reached him, he motioned for her to squat down.

"Go on through," Nico said hastily. He checked in both directions making sure no one had seen them. After Kate and Reload were on the other side, he heaved his backpack through the hole, crouched over, and slipped through himself. Once inside, he leaned back through the hole and positioned the piece of chain link fence loosely in the cut out space.

"Why did you do that?" Kate whispered.

"If anyone takes a quick look this way, they won't notice the fence has been cut," Nico explained. "We're going to run as fast as we can to the hanger where the helicopter is. Stay low and keep Reload quiet. On three, okay?"

"Okay," Kate said.

"One, two, three."

Kate and Nico sprang up and bolted to the hanger. Reload followed behind. Hugging the side, they inched their way into the hanger. It was dark and quiet in the cavernous space.

Nico's eyes swept over the space, looking for any sign another person might have taken up residence or an owner had come to check on their plane or helicopter.

So far so good. The place was void of human activity.

"Hand me two bobby pins," Nico instructed.

Kate reached into her hair, pulled out two bobby pins, and handed them to Nico. Reload stood panting, looking around while taking in the unfamiliar surroundings.

"Stay close to me," Nico said. Putting the bobby pins in his mouth, he went to the chopper and slung his backpack to the ground. He reached in his pocket and flipped open a clip-it knife. Using both the bobby pins and knife, he worked his magic and picked the lock on the chopper. The door clicked open. "I told you it was much easier than breaking into a car."

"I wouldn't know," Kate said. "I've never stolen a car before. Have you?"

Nico winked. "Only when I needed to."

"You're a bad boy."

"Yeah, but you like bad boys."

Kate grinned.

Nico heaved his backpack on his back and mentioned for Kate to do the same.

"Should I put Reload in there?" Kate asked, motioning to the interior of the helicopter.

"Wait until we're in the open. In case anything happens to us, I don't want Reload locked inside."

"Good thinking," Kate said.

"We need to work quickly. While I'm pulling it, I need you to keep an eye out for anything unusual. If you hear or see anything out of the ordinary, tell me."

"I will."

Nico flexed his arms, planted his feet near the tow bar assembly, cursing the fact the tractor normally used to pull the chopper out onto the tarmac wasn't working. He took a big breath and heaved to pull the three thousand pound chopper.

Kate kept her eyes open, scanning the airport for intruders.

Nico straightened his back and stretched.

"You can do it," Kate said. "Put your back into it."

Nico laughed. "You sound like my dad."

"That's what mine always used to say."

Nico took several breaths and called upon all his strength. With a mighty heave the chopper moved.

"Keep going," Kate said. "You can do it."

Nico kept pulling and Kate kept up the rah-rah, that-a-boy, you-can-do-it cheerleading.

The roller assembly worked and gradually, Nico pulled the chopper away from the hanger and to where they could take off.

"Hop in," Nico said, "and put Reload in the back."

Sitting in the cockpit, Nico familiarized himself with the controls. It had been a while since he had flown a Bell Jet Ranger, but he was confident he could fly this baby. He turned on the master switch, then the fuel pump, and depressed the starter button. The electronics came to life. He flipped the fuel pump switch and the rotor blades groaned, thumping slowly at first then faster until the noise was deafening.

Nico yelled, "You ready?"

"As ready as I'm gonna be!" Kate yelled back.

"Let's find out what this baby can do!"

Taking the controls, Nico eased the chopper off the ground. Kate held on tight to the seat while her stomach flip-flopped. She had failed to tell Nico she got seasick, airsick, and didn't like to fly or be on a boat where she couldn't see land. She swallowed and prayed she wouldn't heave. Reload sat wild-eyed and had squished himself against his seat.

Gaining altitude, Nico turned the chopper to the east, throttled the engine, and guided the chopper away from the hangers.

Kate bent over and wrapped her arms around her stomach.

The chopper climbed higher until Nico decided they had reached enough altitude to safely clear the trees. He looked down at the ground where a man ran after him shaking his fist. Nico saluted the guy as if to say, She's a beauty. Thanks.

Five minutes later they were far away from the airport, flying over the outskirts of the city void of activity. The freeways were a congested mess of cars and trucks. An eighteen wheeler had been gutted of its cargo. A few cars had been burned and people ran out into the street to gawk at the chopper. Some waved, others stood awestruck like they had never seen a helicopter before.

Kate leaned into Nico. "How are we going to get there?" she yelled.

"We're going to follow I-37 all the way to Corpus then take the highway to Padre Island. It's not much to look at, but it's the quickest way to get there."

"How long will it take?"

"About an hour and a half. We'll get there in time for the sun to set," Nico said.

Kate rubbed her hands together in excitement. "I can't wait."

* * *

Less than two hours later they had passed Corpus Christi and when the highway changed, Nico guided the chopper to the east, toward the gulf.

They flew over the Laguna Madre, a long and shallow lagoon and one of the most hypersaline lagoons in the world. Looking at it from the shoreline, there wasn't one physical attribute which could distinguish it from another body of salty water.

Its wind-tidal flats and barrier island beaches remained the largest suitable habitat in North America for migrating and wintering shorebirds. Threatened and endangered species of birds including the peregrine falcon and brown pelican relied on the Laguna Madre for its protective status, accounting for eighty percent of Texas sea grass beds.

Kate looked down from the helicopter to what appeared to be a wasteland of shallow salty water and scant beaches.

"Is that the beach?" she asked.

"No," Nico said. "That's the Laguna Madre. We still have a little farther to go. Up ahead is the John F. Kennedy causeway. It's the landmark which means we're close to the beach. On the other side is Snoopy's. It's my favorite place to eat seafood, but I doubt it's open."

Kate took in the vastness of the Laguna Madre and the Intracoastal Canal which included the bridge on the John F. Kennedy causeway.

"We have to make a quick stop," Nico said.

"Why?"

"I'm looking for the Home Depot. There has to be one here because of all the development." Nico scanned the horizon, trying to spot the familiar orange and white sign. "There it is," he said, pointing toward it. "Let's hope it hasn't been looted too much."

Nico guided the helicopter to an empty part of the parking lot. He set down on the blacktop, told Kate to stay with the chopper and not let anyone in. "If anyone tries to open the door," he said, "show them this." He handed Kate a Glock. "Point it directly at them. It should scare anybody off."

"Okay."

"If all else fails, sic Reload on them."

When he opened the door, a blast of humid, salty air filled the cabin, blowing around strands of Kate's hair. She tucked it behind her ear. It had been a long time since Kate had been at the beach. In fact, she had been a child the last time her parents took the family to the beach. A lot had changed since then.

Various restaurants lined the highway. She saw several pizzerias, a sushi place, there was a Walgreens, a grocery store, a school, everything to indicate civilization, yet it looked deserted. Whatever Nico needed at Home Depot must have been important.

Reminiscing on the decision to leave, Nico was right: she needed to reconnect with her parents and family. There was so much she had missed out on, and whenever her parents had gotten on her case, Uncle Billy had come to the rescue. If only every teen had an Uncle Billy, there wouldn't be so much trouble in the world. Uncle Billy had a way of diffusing a drama-filled situation with his wisecracks and a unique way of looking at things. The family coined it "Billyisms."

Going home was definitely a good decision.

Jolted out of her reverie, Kate spied Nico pushing a cart filled to the brim with containers of some sort. She had no idea what he was up to.

Kate opened the door and leaned out. "Do you need help?"

"Yes," Nico said. He positioned the cart to the side of the helicopter. "Help me open these."

Kate read one of the labels. "Why do we need kerosene?"

"It's fuel for the helicopter. We're running low."

"You're using kerosene?"

"Yes. Helicopters use jet fuel, which is basically kerosene with additives. The chopper might not run quite as smooth as it would on jet fuel, but this will do."

Kate scratched the side of her cheek. "Okay, if you say so."

They worked together, Kate opening each container and standing ready to hand it to Nico. He poured each container of kerosene into the fuel tank. It had taken longer than he had liked, knowing a helicopter would attract unwanted attention.

"Okay, we have enough." He tossed the last container back into the cart. "Let's get outta here and head to the beach."

Nico started the chopper and as he lifted off, a man came running up to it. "Wait for me!" he yelled. Nico threw a look of contempt his way and shook his head. Undeterred, the man looped an arm around one of the landing skids.

The chopper lifted off, wobbling from the man's weight.

The man thrust his legs upward and wrapped them onto the landing skid, dangling from it like a monkey.

The chopper listed to one side, and Nico struggled to level it.

"Nico!" Kate yelled. "Can't you knock him off?"

Nico tossed Kate a grin. "Yeah, watch this. Hold on!"

Banking toward the west at a good clip, Nico piloted the chopper toward the Intracoastal Canal and hovered about twenty feet over the darkest blue water he could find. He spied down below at what looked like a school of some kind of large fish.

Nico took the controls, making the chopper toss violently left and right, and soon the man lost his hold, dropping into the water.

Looking down at the splash the man made, Nico said, "Back to school for you, buddy."

Kate craned her head and tried to find the man. "Do you think he'll be okay?"

"Sure," Nico said. "If he can swim. What's the use in going to the beach if you can't swim?"

"Got a point there."

Turning to the east, Nico guided the chopper to the four lane road leading to Mustang Island, of which there was no demarcation from it to Padre Island. Only a sign on the highway indicated the transition. When they came to a bridge, a man holding a fishing rod waved at them.

The land was flat and dotted with pockets of salty lagoons and vegetation which thrived in the inhospitable land. Grass and some type of low growing weed were the only green in a sea of white sand and blue water capped by breaking waves. A bulldozer sat idle in the tract of land that had been razed for some future development. A deserted hotel loomed on the gulf side of the island. Electric lines ran parallel to each side of the road. A seagull perched on one of the poles. Several cars were disappearing in the sand.

Kate tapped Nico on the arm. "Look," she said, pointing to the east, "there's the beach. Let's go over there."

"I'm going to look for a suitable spot to set the chopper down. I'm looking for the next access road leading to the beach. There it is." Squinting, he read the green highway sign, Newport Pass, indicating he needed to hang a right on the blacktop leading to the beach. "I'll set the chopper down on the road as close as I safely can to the sand dunes."

Kate could hardly contain her excitement. There was still about an hour left of daylight, and with any luck she could take a quick swim. She wore a bikini she'd snagged from the hotel gift shop under her clothes so she wouldn't waste any time changing.

Reload sensed the trip was coming to an end. He stretched his cramped legs, put his nose to the door, and sniffed, tasting the unusual scents of the ocean and land. Fish, dead fish, seaweed, jellyfish, grass, dunes…so many different odors he had never processed before. Invigorated by the new odors, Reload barked in anticipation of investigating the new surroundings.

Brain stimulation Kate called it. She reached back and patted Reload on the top of his head. "Are you ready, boy?"

Reload thumped his tail upon hearing Kate's phrase which he knew meant it was playtime.

Nico slowed the chopper and set down on the blacktop. Kate opened the door, invited Reload out, and before Nico could power down the helicopter completely, Kate and Reload were making a dash to the ocean.

"Watch out for jellyfish on the sand!" Nico yelled. "Even dead, their sting still bites!"

Kate didn't hear a word of what Nico had said. She was running full speed along the road, while Reload had stopped to sniff the scent of an unidentifiable animal that had stopped the night before. It was a strange scent, not quite a dog's, but some similar species. The animal had been running, come to a quick stop, nosed the ground, then left its mark. Reload left his own scent on top of it then dashed after Kate, legs gobbling the distance.

Nico could only shake his head at Kate and Reload acting like a bunch of kids. He supposed this little bit of diversion from what they had been through was good for the soul.

It seemed like yesterday when they fought off the Hyatts. Only by the grace of God had they survived.

Nico unloaded items from the helicopter and locked it. He swung their backpacks and the tent over his shoulders, positioned two jugs of water on the top of the cooler, and proceeded to the beach.

It was windy and a bit overcast, with low clouds rolling in over the gulf. It didn't look like a storm was coming, but one could never know for sure without a reliable weather forecast.

By the time Nico reached the beach, Kate had stripped off her shorts and T-shirt, and set them on top of her tennis shoes. Wearing only a bikini and the biggest smile, she skipped through the shallow water while Reload splashed along the shoreline.

Nico selected a spot near the sand dunes to make camp where the dunes sculpted by the wind and the water offered some protection from the west. Different types of grasses dotted the dunes and a vine of some sort with pink flowers which looked like overgrown morning glories snaked along the sand.

He went about setting up the tent above the high tide line. He put down the cooler and water jugs, then collected driftwood to make a campfire, all the while keeping an eye on Kate and Reload. When he thought Kate had waded too far into the surf he yelled for her to come back. Reload had the sense not to get in too deep.

Smart dog.

Nico stripped down to his swimming trunks and set his clothes and boots on the cooler. He breathed in the warm, fresh air and proceeded to the water where Kate was.

She had on a green polka dot bikini, and though she had lost a little weight, she was a sight for sore eyes.

Whatever extra fat Nico had on him before the grid went down, he had lost too. What remained was lean muscle.

He jogged to the shore, dodging broken shells washed up by the pounding surf. He went to where Kate was in the water and before he could get to her, she took handfuls of salty water and splashed him. He laughed, scooped up a handful of water, and returned a spray.

Kate laughed and playfully ran a few steps, splashing in the water.

Reload barked and ran after her.

"I'm going to dive in. Come with me," Nico said.

"No," Kate said. "I'm staying here." She sat down in the shallow water and dug her toes into the sand. Reload stood behind her and when the water brushed his paws, he skidded back out of the way.

Nico waded into the water and when it reached his thighs he took a deep breath and dove in, head first into a breaking wave. He dove to the bottom and opened his eyes. The water was murky with churned up sand, making visibility close to zero. He closed his eyes tight and stretched out his hands feeling for sand dollars. His feet dangled upwards and the tumbling water washed over him like a jet stream from a hot tub.

He relished the moment.

The power of the wave dissipated and Nico catapulted up. He shook the water from his head and held up his hand in the waning light. "Kate, look what I found!"

"What?" she yelled, trying to be heard over the crashing waves.

"A sand dollar! There's more. Come on in and then we'll body surf back in."

Kate stood up to get a better look. She brushed the sand off her legs and shook her head. "It's too deep for me, and it's getting late. Come back."

"What?" he yelled.

"Come back."

"In a moment." Nico waved to her, and tossed the living sand dollar into the water. He waded into the surf which was now up to his chest. He could still feel the sandy bottom and when he reached the next sandbar, the water was shallower, about waist high.

He stood on the sandbar and waited for a good wave, watching the swells rolling in from the deeper water.

Something bumped his leg, startling him. Nico did a 360 and checked the water looking for a fin breaching the murky water. He whipped around again, looking, searching.

His mind started playing tricks on him and he thought he saw...a...and his muscles tensed in anticipation of a shark strike.

A fish jumped out of the water, then another. His shoulders, which were about up to his ears, relaxed, and he let out a breath he had been holding, thinking it had been a shark. It was only a school of mullet, confirmed when several more jumped out of the water, a common behavior of the species.

Nico ran a hand over his forehead. Even a bite by a small shark could be deadly without proper medical treatment, and the hospital he saw closer into the city looked to be deserted.

He decided he'd better head back in. The sun would be setting soon and with darkness the sharks came closer to shore.

Kate yelled and Nico turned to look at her.

She was waving her arms and yelling. He couldn't quite understand what she was saying. Maybe she cut her foot on a broken shell. Reload was at her side, barking.

As he took a step in the waist high water, something powerful bumped his leg. Nico whipped around.

That was no mullet.

Adrenaline flooded his body and he scanned the dark water in the dimming light.

He shivered in the suddenly cold water.

His pulse raced.

Nico pounded the water with his fists to try to confuse or scare away any sharks in the water. Deciding he'd better get to shore, he tried to high step out of the water, but the water was too high and his legs were like lead weights.

He glanced at the shore.

Kate was yelling and racing into the water, and his mind tried to comprehend why she was acting as if she was in a slow motion movie. He reached his out hand and waved her away, to her to tell her to stay out of the water.

His words were garbled.

Something was terribly wrong.

An odd tingling sensation came over him and his leg felt odd. He reached to it, but couldn't feel anything.

Nico became woozy and he blinked through the hazy dense air clouded by sand and surf. The sand dunes, majestic and bleached white by the sun and water, shrunk away into the misty horizon.

A seagull swooped low along the water, and Nico followed its zigzagging flight until it became a speck in the sky.

Reload barked, an echo gobbled by the sea.

Nico looked quizzically at Kate. She was so fragile against the imposing beach, solid and steadfast, pounded incessantly by the sea since the beginning of time.

With his strength waning, an overwhelming need to protect her captured him. He took a step toward the shore as a powerful wave crashed into him, sending his body spiraling in the surf. It pushed him down and he hit his head on the bottom.

Disoriented, he rolled listlessly with the power of the wave.

His thoughts went to Kate. He was supposed to take her home where her parents waited for her, where her brothers and uncle were. If he didn't take her home, they'd never know she was still alive.

I'm sorry, he thought. He valiantly fought the muzziness clouding his brain. Thoughts bounced around in his head and he sensed the comforting presence of his deceased mother by his side. He thought she said something, but wasn't sure.

It was quiet and peaceful while Nico floated in the watery universe. His arms and legs were splayed out close to the surface, and he listened to the soft gurgling of the surf tumble over him. He watched a tiny sea creature, no larger than a wisp of a fairy wing, float in front of his eyes, its little fins fluttering like a hummingbird's wings.

It looked at him curiously then flitted away.

He didn't fight the power of the sea, and instead he joined with the authority of the water and sand, gliding him along the current in his cocooned universe.

There was no pain.

He was vaguely aware of being dragged through the water, but in his drugged state of mind he couldn't discern if the water was getting deeper or shallower.

Perhaps the tide was taking him back into the ocean, back to where his body would be reclaimed by the sea.

He wanted to see Kate one last time, to tell her he was sorry. If only he had the strength to go to her.

Suddenly he was cold and a shiver captured him, and no longer did the water and sand envelop him in a protective warm sheath.

He was aware of the hardness of the wet sand, and of a shadowy figure next to him. Something wet and warm licked his face. Reload? Something else? He couldn't be sure.

The pounding of the waves crashing to shore came again and again; he shivered and gulped a hard breath.

He willed his eyes to open. Kate was standing over him and the low sun was behind her. He reached up to her. She was so beautiful, her hair blowing in the wind. Her fair skin touchable.

He wanted to get up to hold her once more, but when he tried, it was like his legs were glued to the ground.

"Kate," he whispered. "I can't feel my legs."

She sounded far away, like she was deep inside a tunnel.

Mustering what little strength he had left, he wiggled his toes, all ten of them. He relaxed a bit, realizing he still had his feet. Perhaps he was bleeding profusely from a massive bite from the shark and had gone into shock. He had to look and he steeled himself for the sight.

Propping himself up on one arm he looked at his legs.

One was swollen and covered in blistering welts. Long stinging tendrils had wrapped around his left leg, topped by a translucent, puffy, iridescent jello-like blob sporting a puffy blue Mohawk.

Nico muttered, "Man 'o war. Get it off me. Hurry." Kate reached down. "No! Not your hands."

Kate looked for something, anything to remove the tendrils stinging him. She spotted a piece of driftwood, grabbed it and pried the man 'o war from Nico's leg.

His head dropped back to the wet sand, and he gasped for air. "Kate," he croaked. "I can't breathe, my throat is closing…"

"What did you say?" Kate asked. She leaned in closer to hear him. She thought quickly about what could be wrong. "Are you allergic?"

He nodded and pointed to his throat.

She expressed a look of horror.

"I'm going into…into…" Nico coughed and tried to focus. "Anaphylactic shock," he muttered. "EpiPen. Backpack. Get it and…" He was unable to finish the sentence.

Kate sprang up and raced to the camp only yards away. She tore into Nico's backpack and searched for the EpiPen. Finding it, she sprinted back to Nico.

Kate jostled him awake. "Wake up. How do I use this?"

He opened his eyes to a fuzzy and incomprehensible world. The dull sky weighed heavy on his chest and the wind moaned in the low light. He was unable to speak.

Kate ripped open the package and read the instructions. Following the diagram, she forcefully stabbed the EpiPen into Nico's upper thigh. She sat back, unsure what to do next.

Nico gasped a difficult and shallow breath. His chest rose and fell. He gasped a deep breath and another until his breathing became normal.

"Nico," Kate said, "are you okay?"

With tremendous effort Nico propped himself up on an unsteady arm. "I will be. Give me a moment."

"I didn't know you were so allergic."

"I'm allergic to anything that stings like bees and wasps. I didn't know that included a man 'o war."

"I got stung once by a jellyfish when I was little. I don't like swimming in the ocean. Things can eat you," Kate said.

Nico laughed. "And sting you."

"For the future, how many EpiPens do you have left?"

"A few. Next time we come to the beach, I'll stick to sunbathing with you."

"How are you feeling?"

"Better. I can breathe now."

Kate put her hand on his arm. "You're so cold, Nico. You need to get warm. Can you stand?"

"I'm not sure."

"Let's try."

While Nico pushed himself into a kneeling position, Kate hooked an arm around his waist and helped him up.

"Lean on me," she said.

With Kate's help, Nico stumbled through the sand back to their meager camp. Kate helped him into the tent and put a towel over him to help him warm up.

"Reload," Kate said. "Come here."

The dog trotted over to the entrance of the tent and looked at Nico. He lifted his snout and tasted the air, laced with salt and sweat and a fight for life. The man, known for his strength and courage, was weak. The man needed Reload's help. The dog gingerly stepped into the tent and padded over next to Nico. He lowered himself to the ground and pressed his warm body next to Nico. It was all he could do to comfort him.

"Good boy," Kate said. "Stay."

"I'm sorry, Kate," Nico said.

"Why? What are you sorry for?"

"I was supposed to protect you."

"You already have. We're all here for each other," Kate said. "We're a team. You, me, and Reload. We'll always be a team."

He reached his hand to hers and held it. "I'll be better in the morning, and I promise to take you home. It's time you go home."

"I know. It is time." Kate paused. "All this excitement has made me hungry. Are you hungry?"

"I could eat. Not a whole lot, but something."

Kate looked toward the beginnings of the campfire Nico had started. "I'll get a fire going so we'll have something hot to eat." Kneeling by Nico's side, she said. "You rest now."

"I'll try."

Kate kissed Nico on the forehead. "I won't be long."

* * *

Later, after the sun had set, and after they had eaten, Nico lay awake in the tent, thinking and listening to the comforting sound of tumbling surf. It was dark and the chilly night air brushed the tent filled with the scent of the dog, and of a man and a woman. A coyote howled long and lonely somewhere among the dunes, and Reload growled low in his throat.

Kate was sleeping curled into a little ball. Occasionally, she shivered. Nico took the beach towel she had given him and placed it over her to keep her warm.

He thought about his parents and how they were no longer alive. He thought about his life up to this point and how Kate had grown in these past few months. No longer was she afraid to live or to face the vagaries of life thrown her way. What was it she had said? "I'll face life as it comes. And I want you to be part of that."

Nico closed his eyes, lulled to sleep with the knowledge the woman he loved was next to him.

Tomorrow he'd fly her back to Austin and to her home where her parents waited for her, to a safe place where they could both rest and recuperate. She had told him so much about her home that he could picture it in his mind. A grand two story house sitting on the banks of the Colorado River, lined by century old pecan trees and where her mother's cooking was food for the soul. A place where her father had taught her to stand up for herself and to always stay true to herself. A place where she grew up with two brothers, Chandler and Luke, who had protected Kate from bullies when she was young. And Uncle Billy, Kate's favorite.

Memories of her life were there. Pictures, drawings from her childhood, her room with her favorite blanket, stuffed animals, clothes, shoes she had left behind. She needed all that now. She deserved a sense of normalcy in this unwanted world after what she had been through.

In a few hours, as soon as the sun gleamed the first morning light over the ocean, they would leave, and Kate would have the homecoming she had dreamed about.

What the next day would bring, Nico did not know, but one thing was for certain – whatever he faced, he and Kate would face it together.

The End

BEHIND THE SCENES

A Note from the Author

Hi Readers, this is Chris. After finishing Book 3, I knew I needed to write the story about Kate Chandler and Nico Bell. I wasn't sure where the book would take the characters, but it needed to do justice to San Antonio, its culture, and people. Growing up and living in Texas, I'm well acquainted with city life, country life, the dusty back roads, and since my parents retired to Goliad country, I've read the stories about Colonel Fannin and his troops.

During the Battle of San Jacinto in present-day Harris County, Texas where Houston is located, the men yelled the battle cries, "Remember the Alamo!" and "Remember Goliad!". During the Battle of San Jacinto, the Texan army led by Sam Houston defeated Santa Anna, thus establishing independence from Mexico.

The battle cry "Remember Goliad!" paid homage to several hundred prisoners of war from the Republic of Texas Army executed at the hands of Santa Anna at Goliad on March 27, 1836. Colonel James Fannin was the commander and was also executed along with his men. A quick Google search can provide much more detail and accuracy of the horrific event. Despite pleadings of clemency by other Mexican leaders, Santa Anna gave the order to execute the men.

For research, I traveled to San Antonio and stayed at the Menger Hotel (which the fictional Minor Hotel is modeled after), located across the street from the Alamo. I tried to stay true to the historic hotel, its layout, grand entrance, the bar, and other amenities. We also toured the Riverwalk and visited the Alamo where visitors are required to be quiet and respectful of the spiritual place. No photographs are allowed, and even children grasp the significance of the old mission.

UNWANTED WORLD

* * *

For some parts of my books I take experiences from my life, expand upon them, and fictionalize them. For example, the tarantula scene was taken from an experience I had many years ago. I was driving north on Highway 183 heading toward the city of Gonzales, east of San Antonio. I crested a hill, and on the other side there were thousands of tarantulas crossing the highway. I didn't even know there were tarantulas in that part of Texas, much less the sheer numbers of them. Cars whizzed by, and if the tarantula was lucky, it raised its front legs in defiance or protection or whatever the reason tarantulas raise their legs, then scampered across the highway to the other side. If they were unlucky, as many were, they became a squished black blob on the highway.

I researched the phenomena and learned male tarantulas migrate to find a female tarantula to mate with. Not surprisingly, females outlive their male counterparts by many years.

Fortunately, I was in my car and not camping on the side of the road so I did not have to experience the tarantulas crawling up my body.

Another scene taken straight out of my life was the one for the Bonus Story. My teenage years were spent in Corpus Christi, where every Saturday in the summer we went to the beach on Padre Island. We body surfed the waves, dove for sand dollars, and when adventuresome we swam to the second sand bar. I never made it to the third sandbar, because it was too far out and the water was too deep. Many times while swimming, things bumped into me, which was always unnerving. In the back of my mind, I would think about a shark and would look around to see if I could find any. I'd breathe a sigh of relief when I saw mullet jumping out of the water. Other times the bump was stronger, and as I look back on it now, it might have been a juvenile shark.

The Portuguese man 'o war (according to the National Geographic and Wikipedia) is a marine hydrozoan of the family Physaliidae, found in the warm waters of the Atlantic, Indian, and Pacific Oceans. It's not a jellyfish, rather an animal made up of a colony of organisms working together. It uses a "bladder" that resembles a sail which sits above the water line and is the only means of propulsion. The bottom line is, the animal floats around the sea, capturing prey using long, thin, venom-filled tendrils to paralyze small fish and other creatures in the ocean. A human can experience an excruciating sting from one of the tendrils, but rarely is it deadly. I've seen many man 'o war washed up on the beach and we were always careful not to step on the tendrils. If we saw them in the ocean, we would get out.

In the scene where Nico is floating semi-conscious in the surf, he sees a tiny sea creature. This is the sentence: *He watched a small sea creature, no larger than a wisp of a fairy wing, float in front of his eyes, its little fins fluttering like a hummingbird's wings.*

I saw something like that in Lake Travis near Austin one hot summer when we were scuba diving at Windy Point. I got separated from the others so I swam to the platform (about 15 feet underwater) and sat there until I thought I had decompressed enough to surface. There's not much to see in Lake Travis due to the poor visibility so I sat there staring at the murky water and listening to myself breathe. In front of my mask, a fluttering little fish, I'm not sure what it was, swam up to me, looked at me, then skittered away. I was mesmerized by how small it was and the ease with which it swam. When I was writing that scene, the memory came to me and I decided to add it.

* * *

On a recent Facebook post (I can be found at Author Chris Pike), a friend asked me how long I resisted writing. I said it wasn't that I resisted writing, it's that I didn't realize until a few years ago it's what I wanted to do. The seeds were planted a long time ago, I just never paid any attention to them.

I look back on it now and know there were a couple of defining moments. One was in college where I had to write a term paper in an oil and gas class. My topic was dull. Regardless, I thought about how I could write it to make it interesting. Since I was working part time at the Texas State Capitol, I had some knowledge about how Texas politics worked, so I wrote the term paper as if I was a legal aid to a senator. I made up an entire scenario, explaining I (the legal aid) had been asked to research the topic because of an upcoming vote on a bill. In a class of 150, the professor handed out the top ten papers. Mine was one of them. My writing wasn't any better than anyone else's, but the way I presented it was. It was interesting, it was different, and the professor appreciated the creativity. So, fast forward to many years later, I'm finally writing like I was meant to and enjoying creating fictional situations that interest me.

ABOUT THE AUTHOR

Chris Pike grew up in the woodlands of Central Texas and along the Texas Gulf Coast, fishing, hiking, camping, and dodging hurricanes and tropical storms. Chris has learned that the power of Mother Nature is daunting from sizzling temperatures or icy conditions; from drought to category five hurricanes. Living without electricity for two weeks in the sweltering heat after Hurricane Ike proved to be challenging. It paid to be prepared.

Currently living in Houston, Texas, Chris is married, has two grown daughters, one son-in-law, one dog, and three overweight, demanding cats.

Chris has held a Texas concealed carry permit since 1998, with the Glock being the current gun of choice. Chris is a graduate of the University of Texas and has a BBA in Marketing. By day Chris works as a database manager for a large international company, while by night an Indie author.

Got a question or a comment? Email Chris at Chris.Pike123@aol.com. Your email will be answered promptly and your address will never be shared with anyone.

Available Books in the EMP Survivor Series:
Unexpected World – Book 1
Uncertain World – Book 2
Unknown World - Book 3
Unwanted World – Book 4
Undefeated World – Book 5 (coming early 2018)

Book 3, Unknown World, is a standalone book and continues the EMP survivor series as Amanda and Chandler face new struggles in their quest to survive. Just go to Amazon, and type in keywords: Chris Pike EMP Survivor Series. Or type in the book title. Book 4 is the story of Kate Chandler and Nico Bell. The series will be wrapped up in Book 5 – Undefeated World scheduled for early 2018.

UNDEFEATED WORLD BOOK 5

Undefeated World (Book 5) will be the last book in the EMP Survivor series and will wrap up all the storylines into one epic story. We'll be heading back to East Texas where we'll catch up with Holly and Dillon, and Ryan and Cassie. The cause of the EMP will be revealed, so stay tuned! An early 2018 publication date is projected.

WHAT'S NEXT?

A three book series in the post-apocalyptic genre is in the initial stages of outlining and plotting. I'm hoping to release two of the books in 2018 while the third one will follow soon after. There will be no EMP, still there's gonna be a lot of mayhem. I guarantee it!

BEFORE YOU GO...

One last thing. Thank you, thank you, thank you for downloading this book. Without the support of readers like yourself, Indie publishing would not be possible.

I've received a lot of emails from my readers, and for those who have written to me, you know I always answer your emails, and I don't spam either.

An easy way to show your support of an Indie author is to write an honest review on Amazon. It does several things: It helps other readers make a decision to download the book. It also allows the author to understand what the reader wants. For example, my readers asked for no F-bombs and no adult situations. I listened and followed through with the requests. I've learned good writing and editing is extremely appreciated and I will always strive for that.

So please consider writing a review. I will be forever grateful. A few words or one sentence is all it takes.

Also, this book has been edited, proofed, and proofed again, but mistakes or typos are bound to happen. If you find a mistake, email me at Chris.Pike123@aol.com and it will be corrected.

Lastly, a big shout out goes to the people who helped with questions, editing, formatting, audio, cover art, proofing, legal advice, encouragement, and everything else that goes into making a book: Alan, Michelle, Courtney, Cody, Felicia, Kody, Kevin, Hristo, Anne, Mary, Abel, Mikki, Mick B., Ken D., Vlad, Marty, and Robert.

For my readers who have written me, y'all are the best! You've encouraged me and have allowed me a glimpse into your life. I am truly honored. Thank you. If you'd like to connect with me on Facebook, I can be found at: Author Chris Pike.

Until the next time, and as one of my readers wrote: Read, enjoy, learn, and save some more food.

And regarding the ongoing theme in the EMP Survivor Series, remember the three Fs: Faith, Family, and Firearms.

Forever!

All the best,
Chris

"Victory or Death" Letter

The world famous "Victory or Death" letter was penned by Lt. Col. William Barrett Travis while besieged within the Alamo by the Mexican army in San Antonio de Bexar. The Travis letter is universally regarded as one of the most heroic letters ever written. Facing certain death, Travis vowed never to surrender or retreat and to "die like a soldier who never forgets what is due to his own honor and that of his country – Victory or Death."

The Travis letter was dated February 24, 1836. Some have mistakenly referred to this as Travis' last letter from the Alamo, although he wrote at least four more letters. Travis wrote a letter to General Sam Houston dated February 24, 1836, which urgently requested aid for the Alamo. It was received by the Convention at Washington, Texas on March 5, 1836. The delegates to the Convention at Washington had declared the independence of Texas four days before on March 2, 1836.

Travis never did surrender or retreat. After a thirteen day siege by thousands of Mexican soldiers under the command of Mexican President Antonio Lopez de Santa Anna, the Alamo fell on March 6, 1836. All of the Alamo's 189 defenders, including William Barrett Travis, were killed. The country he and others died for, the Republic of Texas, was only four days old.

The original "Victory or Death" letter written by William Barrett Travis on February 24, 1836 is located in the Texas State Library and Archives in Austin, Texas.

66955587R00137

Made in the USA
Lexington, KY
28 August 2017